Scheherazade's Façade
Fantastical Tales of
Gender Bending, Cross-Dressing, and Transformation

edited by Michael M. Jones

Circlet Press, Inc.
Cambridge, MA

Published by Gressive Press
an in imprint of
Circlet Press, Inc.
39 Hurlbut Street
Cambridge, MA 02138
www.gressive.circlet.com
www.circlet.com

ISBN: 978-1-61390-058-1

Printed in the United States of America.

Contents

Introduction

Once upon a time, there was an anthology. It had many adventures on its path to publication, but after several years of delays and slight bumps in the road, it finally found its way onto bookshelves and e-readers and its treasures were revealed to the world. This is that anthology, and it has as many tales attached to its creation as it does stories in the table of contents.

The short version is thus: *Scheherazade's Façade*'s original publisher ran into some difficulties, and we reluctantly parted ways, promising to stay friends and all that other stuff one says when this sort of thing happens. I spent over a year seeking a new home for this collection, sidling up to nervous-looking publishers and going, "Psst, wanna buy an anthology? Real cheap, only read once by a little old lady on Sundays. Mind the pages." Almost all of them backed away and muttered politely as how they had perfectly good anthologies at home, and the baby was boiling and the coffee pot was being eaten by dingoes. A few outright ran for the hills, causing me to rethink my strategy of approaching them in the restroom and stealing their toilet paper. Luckily, Cecilia Tan at Circlet Press came to my rescue, giving me both hope and a publisher willing to take this all the way. One spectacular Kickstarter campaign, several hundred backers, and more than a few favors called in later, and here we are. You're reading these pages—physical or electronic—and probably wondering when this Jones guy is going to get done with the introduction and get to the stories. And to that I say patience! It's taken me three years to get here; I'm entitled to a few pages of my own. Allow me to revisit what I wrote for the Kickstarter campaign and original call for submissions, because it still sums things up perfectly.

History, literature, and mythology are replete with stories of those who, for one reason or another, disguise themselves as the opposite gender, or are transformed into that which they are not. Whether it's for love, ambition, or self-preservation, whether it's to challenge the status quo or simply to embrace their true nature, whether it's done willingly or thrust upon them, there will always be those who cross-dress and blur the lines between genders. Scheherazade's Facade takes its inspiration from those themes. From Bugs Bunny's dress-wearing shenanigans, to Mulan's impersonation of her father, from Tamora Pierce's Alanna of Trebond, to M*A*S*H's Klinger, this collection's antecedents are everywhere.

The premise of this anthology is simple. For centuries, readers have thrilled to the tale of Scheherazade, the vizier's daughter and renowned storyteller of *One Thousand and One Nights*, taken as a bride by a king notorious for executing each wife after the marriage's consummation. To avoid suffering the same fate, Scheherazade spins stories for the king, night after night. But what if there was more to the tale? What if someone was not as they seemed? Through tales of magical transformation, cross-dressing and gender bending, our storytelling heroine postpones her death even as she entertains and enlightens her audience.

For this collection, I looked for a wide variety of things. First, all stories had to be fantasy. "High, low, dark, historical, romantic, urban, mythical—just about anything goes as long as it has those fantastic elements to it." Second, I wanted "stories in which the protagonist or other major characters are disguised or transformed, or otherwise challenge traditional gender roles... heroes and villains, warriors and tricksters, drag queens and cross-dressers, cisgendered, transgendered, and everything in-between."

The authors who responded knocked the requirements right out of the park, delivering a dozen stories of amazing skill and variety. I fell in love over and over, with each new addition to the table of contents. They came from all over the world, from England and Ireland, France and Canada, the Philippines and America, bringing with them unique viewpoints and fantastic takes on the theme. In these pages you'll find shape shifting dragons, triumphant drag queens, tragic selkies, lost princes and would-be warriors. You'll find star-crossed lovers and mysterious travelers, and hopefully you'll enjoy them as much as I have.

Once upon a time, there was an anthology. And everyone lived happily ever after.

Michael M. Jones, June 2012

The Secret Name of the Prince
Alma Alexander

Khshayarsha had been given a royal name—but that was the only gift that he had of his family. He did not remember his father, only the story that armed men had burst into their home in the middle of the night when Khshayarsha was barely more than a baby and had taken his father away with them. The man who had been the head of the household, the man Khshayarsha might have called Father once he had learned to speak, had never returned. In the aftermath of this ruin, his mother had sat like a statue, blank-faced and silent; she had not eaten nor allowed a drop of water to pass her lips if she was not fed by another hand or forced to swallow water trickled into her mouth slowly from a chipped cup. She had clung to life even thus, stubbornly, perhaps waiting for her husband to come back against all odds—she had put forth what protection and power she had, leaving herself vulnerable and out in the open, the only target left for those who had taken her husband—but eventually she too was gone. Khshayarsha had still been too young, could not remember ever having heard the sound of his mother's voice.

It was Shahrazad who took care of him. Shahrazad, the elder sister, the only thing that stood between him and the place where both his parents had somehow vanished to and left him. Shahrazad, who had dressed him as the girl-child their mother's final glamour had made him seem like; Shahrazad, herself under the guise of a boy, who had smuggled him out of the place which had started to smell of death and abandonment... and taken him elsewhere, and hidden him in the dark, and told him that he must pretend—at least for a little while—to be somebody else, someone other than Khshayarsha.

"We should all take secret names," she told him. She had spoken in a soft voice which he would wonder, later, when he came to think about things, if she had used because she had wanted to soothe a fractious toddler or because she was so afraid of being overheard. "A new name for a new being, and then we have to change to fit the new skin. You can pick your own. And then you have to work at your transformation. Everything depends on how good you are at it."

"A name?"

"A creature, maybe," she had said. "What kind of creature do you think would be able to survive, hidden, quiet, waiting for the right moment to come back out into the sun?"

"A mouse?" he had offered, after a moment's thought.

"Mouse," she agreed. "We will call you Mouse."

"And what are you?" he had asked, rousing just a little.

She had thought about it, but not for long. "Desert fox," she said. "But it's a secret name. You must not tell anyone about it."

Even if there had been anyone to tell. They had been alone in the dark hiding place she had taken him to—the boy glamoured as girl, and the girl glamoured as boy, disguised to muddy their trail for those who still sought them—and often even she was gone, out somewhere alone, coming back with food wrapped in bazaar rags, or a skin of wine she would water down for him, or toys to amuse him in the dark.

And once, a book.

He had been too young to know his letters. He had no idea if his sister had ever been taught them or not, but she had brought the book and Mouse assumed that she knew how to read it—and so he had demanded that she read it to him, to while away the hours in which she was there with him.

She said yes, and she'd sit there with him in the crook of her arm and halfway across her lap, and he had thought she would read to him. It was only later, much later, that he thought about the fact that there was little light and that she could not possibly have seen enough to read from the book she held open before them as fluently as she told her stories. Much later, when she was long gone. It was much later, too, that he realized that she had been telling him only the truth—his favorite stories were those about Desert Fox, which was her own secret name between the two of them, and there could have been no stories written about the deeds of the Desert Fox in a book like the one she had brought back into their lair.

Know, then, O Mouse, that Desert Fox went out into the streets of the city in the daytime, dressed as a dirty street boy, the hair that had been her pride hacked untidily away just above her shoulders and swinging in matted tangles from underneath a sloppily tied head-cloth.

The streets were rough and dangerous, and there was a language to them all of their own—and maybe a language that changed subtly if you rounded a corner and turned into a new street. And it all had to be learned. And it was tough out there for one who was also learning to thieve cheese and day-old unleavened bread and olives for the Mouse she kept safe in the secret den where Fox lived… to which she must never, ever, not even accidentally draw anyone's eye for the Mouse was a Prince of his nation and would have to be kept safe from harm.

And the Fox would sometimes sit in the bazaar, cross-legged by the fountain where people wandered by, and would offer to sell stories for a coin if someone would give him—the ragged storyteller boy—a coin for his pains…and a beginning. And people often did not know that it was their own stories that they were telling to the boy, and that the boy was collecting them all, and hoarding them, and winnowing from them nuggets of precious knowledge which those who had told it would have died of mortification to know that they had let slip without realizing it. Or killed, to protect it. The boy had to be all things, he had to be bright and intelligent and spin a tale worth the coin—and he had to be carefully stupid, and pretend not to have heard the things that were left unsaid on the ground between them, those who bought stories and him who sold them…

In the beginning Mouse was young enough to endure his dark prison—the Desert Fox would take him out sometimes, at night, into streets empty of people, and wander with him on the cobbles still slimed by that day's market offal, and then away, into winding streets with high walls and secret gates and fragrant gardens whose scents spilled over the walls and into the street below.

"I remember," Mouse sometimes said, pausing underneath a particular archway hung with purple flowers or some kitchen gate into an alleyway where scents of sumptuous feasts warred with the odor of wasted and rotting food collecting in the gutters where bright-eyed night rats would sometimes gnaw and nibble at it before scuttling away into the shadows as Mouse and Fox approached with light step, themselves keeping out of sight. "I remember this. I remember, I was a boy back then."

"You are too young to remember it," Fox would murmur, smoothing back the hair that had been allowed to grow long, was braided down his back. "Not from before. And you are still a boy, underneath all this—and some day you will grow up to be a man. But not yet—not yet. And yet...you may not remember it from back then... but remember it now. This is what the real world smells like, the world to which you will return some day. Which belongs to you. Now, can you tell me how we came here? Can you take me back the secret ways to our home?"

And Mouse had learned them all, the tiny passageways between alleys where you would swear no space could possibly lurk, the hidden archways behind gates whose locks looked solid but were permanently broken or easily forced, the secret stairs which led into darkness from abandoned cellars piled with listing and leaking barrels and crates of soured wine and sprouting vegetables and spoiled flesh meant for the market but never quite having made it there. The windows which you could not see into, but could peer out of when you paused beside them, giving you advance warning of danger or uninvited company. The passages which unfolded behind what looked like dead-ends and catacombs blocked by iron bars... which were less of a barrier than they seemed to be at first sight.

He had learned to ignore the soft sounds of scurrying vermin feet or the occasional brush of fur against his ankle as something skittered out of his way—and not to see the bones which lay abandoned in the darkest corners, sometimes just scattered untidily and sometimes attached to dank walls by remnants of rusted iron rings around ankles or wrists.

"Is one of those my father?" he had asked Fox, once, on one of their forays.

"No," she had said. "Our father was never in this dark place."

The story book she read to him in their hiding place then gave him the answers to his questions. Answers he did not know that he could trust. They were Story, and Story was always Lie, even if it was breathed through silver. But with Fox, you never knew what was truth, and what she spun for him like gossamer, the threads of his life.

There was a man who was the younger son of a Padishah. His brother was the heir, the older son, but this man would be Padishah if his brother died before him... and then, after him, there would be others who would step up to the throne if he himself was not in the way.

And all was well while the older brother lived and waited to take his place on the Padishah's throne. But then the Padishah died, and his wives with him, and then his older son was poisoned. And the wife who carried his own son was found dead also, her babe stilled within her womb. And it was the younger son's chance to take the crown.

He had not wanted to do it—he had been happy with the life that he had had, Prince in his own right, a wife he loved and two children whom he adored. But there were those who insisted, told him that he must be responsible, be the King he was born to be. And so he said yes. And the very next day they came for him, the men of the people who would be King if he was not—and he was gone. Gone into a huge dark place where there was no light, and no warmth, and no hope. And his family was abandoned, to die alone.

His wife did nothing, or at least she did nothing that showed, nothing that could bring anybody down on her, or help them bring further destruction on her family. She sat and she waited, and others fed and dressed and bathed her, until the day she fell asleep and woke not again.

"But there were the children," Mouse had pointed out, when Fox had told the story.

"Yes," she agreed, "there were."

"But they did not take the children."

"They knew there was a son," Fox said. "But the only boy they could find was too old to be that son, and could not possibly have been the issue of the Prince and his bride. And they never found the babe, the true son, the heir, even though they turned the place inside out, and came back again and again to do it, trying to take those who had hidden the babe by surprise. But all they ever found was a dirty girl-babe which could not possibly have belonged to the Princess, and the only servant left to tend her, an urchin who cared for her as best he could until the time that she needed his care no more. And the babe was of no consequence—a dirty girl-child wailing in soiled diapers—and the urchin they had no interest in."

"And what was his name? The street boy who looked after the Princess?"

Fox's teeth flashed briefly in a grin. "Why, Desert Fox, of course," she said.

"The book is about you?"

"No," she said. "It's about you. The book is about what you are going to grow up to be."

"Where is my father?"

"You are going to find him someday. You are Mouse. You know how to go to the secret places in the city now."

He thought about that for a while, and then asked, "So I am the Prince's son?"

"No," his sister said gently. "You are the Prince now."

"And you are the Princess?"

"No," she said. "There is no Princess. I am the Desert Fox. Do you know what you must do if one day the Desert Fox does not find its way back to the den?"

"Yes," he said. "I know."

He was five, maybe, then.

Fox brought him clothes when he outgrew the ones he was wearing. The ragged storyteller from the bazaar had gained a following, a reputation, and Fox was away for longer now, working that patch, then stepping up to a better one, telling stories to more people, to people better dressed and better escorted, to women who dropped by to whisper things from behind their veils and then listen enthralled as Fox spun their lives into things rich and strange and heart-stopping, never knowing that they took away the storyteller's story as much as they offered him their own to change with spice and scent into something that was like and yet unlike themselves.

"Why do you do it?" Mouse had asked, when he was seven, or maybe eight. Fox had started allowing him to venture out by then, his hair allowed to grow long and worn braided on his shoulders, his long aristocratic feet toughened by callouses and darkened by ingrained dirt, darting here and there into quiet corners, taking things nobody would miss.

And Fox had sighed, and opened the book.

There was no light, and there was no hope. But there were stories—there were always stories. And even the darkest dungeon had gaps through which the stories would come—and bring hope with them. If the younger Prince had not been killed, if he had been kept alive for any reason, somewhere down deep where nobody would know his name—there would be a chance that some rat would bring him a fragment of tale, a snippet of story, a disembodied word about the storyteller in the marketplace—the one who was really telling only one tale, the tale of murder and of betrayal, and the tale of promise and prophecy, the story of how the old Padishah's blood was not all spilled and gone, that one survived, one lived, the boy whom they never found. That some day the right hand would raise the scepter of the land again, the right foot step onto the dais with the golden throne of the Padishah, the right lips utter the sentence that sent those who had drunk deep of royal blood in their thirst for power to their own fates in the empty dark—or into death itself.

That was the Fox's plan—that someday—however long it took—Fox the storyteller would come to the attention of the one who now ruled the land. That this ruler's wife and children might hear of the storyteller, and come and listen to his tale. That the tale might reach the ears that needed to hear it.

There were secret ways everywhere, even into the guarded halls of the Palace— and Fox had been into places it would have made the false rulers blanch to know that unsanctioned feet had walked—but there had been no trace of a prisoner held apart and alone in some more closely guarded fastness yet. But that didn't mean that one wasn't there. And it was that story, the story of a lost Prince held prisoner for so many years while his family, abandoned and lost, perished in his absence, that Fox put out into the world. Every day. With every other story that was told by the ragged little storyteller in the bazaar. Even those who did not know what they had heard had taken the story away with them—and had started repeating it, all unknowing.

There was a rising susurrus of whispers in the alleys, in the bazaars, in the tea-houses and the bath-houses and the hookah bars late at night, in whispers, when people thought nobody was really listening.

The story that the Padishah's throne was held by one drenched in blood and poison. That the true son of the last king lived, still.

That he was not the boy in the bazaar. But that boy knew who, and where. And there were still stories to tell. Stories which would take a killer down, and restore a bright young king in his place.

"Why not you?" Mouse had asked.

"They only believe I am a boy," Fox said. "The throne was made for you. Not me."

"But you are the one who would win it."

"I have no wish to be King. I am a teller of tales, a ghost in the shadows, the fairy tale told to the true Prince. I am my mother's last gift—I am enchantress, not Queen. She... held on... for a long time... because she knew he was alive. She knew, because it was her way to know such things. When they wed, they wed with their souls and not just their bodies. She would know if he died, as he would have known, when she finally passed. But until the very end all she would tell me—through the web of spells that held it all in place, held us safe—the only words, the last words I ever heard my mother speak to me, were *He lives still*. And then, at the very end, unspoken, in her eyes, looking into my heart and my soul, telling me to take care of you. That one day, you would find your way."

"But if they find out..."

"What would they find out? That you grew up a girl in the backstreets?"

"That you did not grow up a girl at all."

"Our mother's magic made that happen."

"Aren't there those who can track the trail of magic—by its scent, by the glittering hand prints it leaves behind on all it touches?"

"Who told you that?" Fox asked sharply.

"You did. It's in the book."

"The book is telling you more tales than I want it to," Fox said after a pause.

"But is it true?"

"There are such, yes. They hated our mother because her own magic was never a charlatan's trick. Some called her one of the Jinni, even—an immortal."

"Was she?"

"Mouse," Fox said gently, "She died."

"Because she was spent. She went away. Perhaps she never died the way you or I can die. Or my father can."

"There are those who hold her against him," Fox said. "You have to know that. There are those who supported what was done because the younger Prince had married a witch, and was tainted by magic."

"That means that I am the son of that magic," Mouse said. "Would they not seek to destroy me too?"

And Fox sighed, and took out the book.

Two were born to the Prince and his bride. Two, who split the legacy of their blood between them.

They had talked of this, before—they had agreed.

Any female issue was hers, the mother's because that magic ran to the female line, ran in that blood. A girl would be raised to be her mother's daughter, perhaps riding the edge of the uncanny before she could speak, because she had to be reined in, had to be trained, had to be molded so that the magic that would be in her would not spill over and touch the innocent and maybe harm where no harm was intended.

A boy child would be a baby Prince, raised to the royal line. A potential heir. Untouched and untainted by magic, unless his mother or his sister laid an enchantment on him—which he would know how to keep, being of their blood, but no more than that. The young prince would be all boy, all human, all royal, with no stain of magic upon him. And they could always prove that. He would be a great man and would do great things, but they would all be done by human hand and human power and human endeavor.

Know, O Mouse, that there is a secret place you have not been to yet. It holds your future safe. One day—you will know—there will be a key handed to you and you will open this last secret door. And you will cut the long hair that had protected you when you were a babe, and you will put on a coat of cloth-of-gold, and gird on your father's sword, and put on jeweled shoes and lay a golden circlet on your head, with a flaming ruby on your brow. And you will walk into the streets of your city and you will look enough like the younger Prince that they will know you—and the city will rise for you, and take you back on a wave of fury. The palace will run with the blood of the infidel and the impostor, and the throne of your ancestors will be yours again.

"I will kill?"

"If it comes to that, I will kill," Desert Fox said. "Your hands are clean of blood as well as of magic. You are your people's prince. They will remember that."

"Will you be with me...?" It was almost frantic, still a little boy's frightened voice, asking for protection, for help, for sanctuary.

"Long enough," Fox said.

"How long is that?"

"I will know. And so will you."

"But if you go—then who will stand beside me?"

"Someday... you will find a woman to do that for you. To stand beside you and be your right hand and the other half of your spirit."

"Like my father found my mother?"

Fox smiled. "If you are lucky."

Mouse was in the bazaar on the day that he saw the palace men come for Fox.

She had known he was there, his sister, and had looked calmly straight at him—through him—and then she had risen with composure when they had gestured for her to do so, with all the grace of a young man of her age, light on her feet, calm, serene. When they walked away towards the gate of the palace, it was she who led the way—as though she was the one in charge and they, the ones sent to get her, only an armed escort due to one of royal blood, men of no consequence other than that role, men who would give their lives to protect hers rather than possibly lifting a hand to her themselves. She did not look back.

Mouse went to the place where she had been sitting—the words had been ringing in his head ever since she had met his eyes so briefly—and tried to look around discreetly for something, anything, that might have resembled the story she had read to him from the book—*a key will be given to you*. But he could find nothing of the sort, nothing that looked anything like something he might recognize as a key to any door.

What he did find, buried under the cushions on which she had been sitting, was... the book itself. The thing she had been reading to him from for all these years.

Or so he had thought.

If there was writing in the book, it was in a hand too small for him to read—and the writing formed lines, which formed pictures, which *changed* before his eyes.

He gasped, closing the book, scurrying away with it before anyone noticed—but he was Mouse, he had been trained to be Mouse, and nobody was paying any attention at all to what an unimportant dirty girl-child of the streets was doing. Mouse slipped past people who could not seem to be able to see him at all, down increasingly less frequented roads and alleyways, through a half-open shutter propped ajar with a rock and through an archway behind it, and into a secret alcove beyond that, where the brickwork curved away from the street, hiding the cubbyhole from anyone peering inside, leaving just enough of a gap between the bricks for him to be able to see out.

The book... the book was the key. He stared at the lines of words, words of enchantment, which shaped themselves to his needs. The book was a map. And hidden between the pages... a dagger. Flat-bladed, flat-handled, barely enough to make the soft leather covers of the book bulge outwards in any incriminating way.

He heard the message she had left there. He took the dagger and he lifted up the heavy braid that had lain on his back for all the years of hiding, and sawed at the root of it until it parted; it fell through his opened hand, pooled darker than shadows on the dirty cobbled floor on his feet. He dropped the dagger beside it, and walked away, holding the book before him, somehow seeing things on its pages even in the darkness, following a road that his mother and then his sister had laid before him.

The walk was endless, and it seemed he walked deeper into darkness with every step he took. But finally he saw the faintest flicker of light somewhere before him, and rounded a corner and came unexpectedly into a place which, improbably, had a torch stuck into a sconce on the wall, guttering and flickering but seemingly not consuming the wood and the pitch which fed it.

A part of Mouse flinched at the implications of it. This torch had been burning here for a long time, waiting for him to come—burning bright without burning out. And what it showed, in the circle of its light, were the things that Desert Fox had told him that he would find here. A golden coat. A belt on which there hung a curved sword with a hilt inlaid in flaming gems. Shoes studded with jewels. A golden circlet with a crimson ruby set in it, glittering like blood in the torchlight.

Will I kill?

No, she had said. He would not do the killing.

There was a basin, and in it clean water. Mouse washed his hands in it, and then his dirty feet; he could do nothing about the thick skin and the callouses and the broken nails, he had not led a nobleman's life and his were not a nobleman's hands and feet. But they were clean enough, at last, and their shape and form told their own story in the end.

The coat fit him perfectly. The circlet slipped onto his head as though it had been made for him. The shoes wrapped his feet in soft comfort. The hilt of his father's sword slipped into his hand, easily, folded by a memory or a spell of enchantment—he did not know how to use that sword, had never been taught, and yet his hand lay on the hilt with a quiet confidence, as though he had done nothing but wield it all his life.

There was a door leading out of the chamber, and Mouse—and Khshayarsha, because he must claim his own name back in this hour—knew where it would lead. Out, into the street, into the city that was his own.

He heard their voices before he opened the door—a babble, a throng of whispers and shouts and incoherent fragments.

They found out that the Princess—

They say that the storyteller from the bazaar—the young man—that he—that she—that they are the same—

Her mother's child, they said—

They say she faced him—

Shahrazad—his daughter—the lost prince's child—she said—

"She said he lives," Shahrazad's brother, who had been Shahrazad's sister, said, stepping out into the streets. "I am Khshayarsha. The Prince."

He was not Shahrazad, or their mother, or a woman of the enchanted line, or a woman at all. Shahrazad had said that their mother would have known if their father was dead, that their bond was that close; he wondered why it was that the magic did not touch the men in his family, why was it that he had no sense of any of them, that the only reason he knew his mother had perished was that the boy he had known as Desert Fox had told him it was so. The boy called Desert Fox, who had been his sister, Shahrazad. But he did not know if his father truly lived yet... if Shahrazad herself had survived. Or, if she had not, if the youth called Desert Fox had done so instead.

But he let the crowd take him, carry him, deposit him at the gate of the palace. In the glare of lights and torches he remembered the dark way he had trodden to get here—the price he had paid for his passage—the thick dark braid of the girl he had never been, lying like a sacrifice in a light-less passage deep underneath the city.

Underneath his golden coat, tucked away against his skin, so close that he could feel the enchanted ink slipping off the parchment and tattooing into his skin, he had kept a single page from the book that Desert Fox had read to him from. On that page had been only a single word.

The secret. Their secret. The secret name of a Prince who had once taken on the soul of a girl to save the body of the boy who would be king.

Mouse.

The Daemons of Tairdean Town
C.S. MacCath

There are only so many things you can do with mutilated hands. Most objects are made to be managed by more fingers than you can spare; buttons are difficult, tools are a conundrum at best, and writing instruments are damn near impossible. If you're an attractive girl the hands get help; everybody loves a pretty cripple. But when the skin between your left eyebrow and the crown of your head is a thick mass of scar tissue that separates a mass of brown curls and burns too easily in the sun, you learn to button your own coat. The strange thing is, nobody will touch you, but everybody will talk to you, and they'll tell you things they won't even tell themselves. I guess they figure an ugly crippled girl is a safe repository for all the things they can't otherwise say.

And Tairdean Town was full of people who needed to talk. I could see it in their strained expressions as I wandered through the bus terminal. They looked as though they feared the muscles of their faces might disobey their brains and reveal the chronic sadness in their hearts. Made me wish I could draw them out right then and send them home to grieve, mend and fix their lives, but I knew better than that. It took a long time to build those barriers, and it would take a while to bring them down.

I was fumbling to put quarters in a soda machine when a sweet, blond-haired woman of about thirty-three offered to help. "Praise the Lord." She held open a palm full of coins. "Can I buy you a pop?"

I looked up at her and nodded. "Thank you! That would be great."

She put her coins in the machine, invited me to make a selection and backed away. I could see it in her well enough, the unrealized ambition hiding beneath her skirt, slipping sideways out of her rose-print turtleneck, extending outward from her perfect smile. She smelled like a diaper bag, all baby wipes and milk, and I was sure she had at least two children waiting in the car. But she wasn't straining against her life like the people around her were. She was simply choosing to focus elsewhere.

The bottle thudded down to the dispenser. She picked it up, twisted off the top and handed it to me. "Are you here to visit family?"

"No, just looking for work. How about you? Are you coming or going?"

She laughed. "Oh, neither. My husband is a bus mechanic. I was bringing his lunch. Do you have a place to stay?"

I took a sip and shook my head. "Not yet."

"Well, if all you need is a couple of weeks to get your feet under you, the church has a loft with a bed and a shower in the Ladies' room. That is, if you're not on drugs or anything."

It was my turn to laugh. "No, I'm not on drugs or anything, and I'm sure I won't need more than a couple of weeks."

"It's settled then." She thrust out her hand, and after a moment of surprise, I tucked the soda into the crook of my arm and took it. "My name's Jessica Parker, by the way."

"Good to meet you, Jessica. My name is Greta Baum, but my friends call me Piper."

So I rode to the outskirts of Tairdean in a blue mini-van with a "Come the Rapture, This Car Will Be Unmanned" bumper sticker plastered to the back window in the company of five shrieking preschoolers who were strapped into the seats. The far-too-perky teenage helper, who had just earned her babysitting license, shouted back at me over the din with helpful information about the fire department, the library and other landmarks as we passed them. At one point, the toe-headed toddler sitting next to me offered up the remains of his Zwieback toast for my inspection. I nodded and made happy baby noises at the bread, which made him smile. It seemed Jessica ran a daycare. I hoped she didn't run it in the church loft.

I began singing to the Full Gospel Tabernacle the minute she left me alone there; laying my palms on the dusty floorboards, coaxing the beams into wakefulness. After an hour or two I went down the stairs, hand on the polished railing, humming to myself and to the little Rosewood particles sleeping under the lacquer. The church secretary had recently left for the day; I could still smell her perfume and hairspray. So I sat down at her work station and brushed the few fingers I have over her African Violets and the plywood of her put-together desk. Plywood counts too; it's just a little harder to work with.

When I finished introducing myself to the pews, the pastor's conference table and the gargantuan Aloe Vera plant in the kitchen, I took my song to the grocery in town. There were children in back yards wringing a few final minutes of play out of the evening before their parents called them in for dinner and homework. There were men on porches wearing tattered rock-and-roll tee shirts with cigarettes hanging out of their mouths and beer bottles hanging from their fingers.

But most importantly, there were dreamers in most of the houses I passed. They were swathed in business clothes and hospital scrubs and mommy jeans, buried under 'how do we make the mortgage payment this month' and 'Daddy, look at me' and all the rest. If I could get away with it, I laid hands on the trees that leaned over family cars and hummed until the branches quivered above me. If I could not, I whistled my way across the edges of front lawns and nodded in the direction of oaks, birches and maples that nodded back, graceful gestures that might have been a response to the evening breeze, but weren't.

The grocery was the grocery, all side-long glances and plastic smiles. Nobody caught me singing to the bananas this time; that was good. And the liquor store was the liquor store; the proprietors of those places are almost always sympathetic in a creepy, 'poor handicapped lady needs a drink' sort of way. As if I could drink enough to forget that it takes both of my fists to hold a bottle. But whiskey helps me work, and not that crappy American stuff either. A little of the *uisque beatha* goes a long way when you want to loosen things up, if you know what I mean.

On my way back to the church, I took a few more liberties. It's all about the old folks after sundown. They don't get out much, so I have to get onto their balconies, under their flower-bedecked window boxes, and up against their apartment doors. The farther a thing is from life though, the harder it is to wake up. I've been caught more than once leaning back in some old lady's rocking chair, eyes half shut, lost in the way-down-deep conversation it takes to rouse a hunk of a once-living tree and get it to sing for me a while.

But getting caught is almost as fun as getting away with it. I play the simple card, bless the old lady or the cops or whoever in Jesus' name and simper off into the moonlight. A night or two later I come back and the old lady's daemon is taking shape right where I told the wood to put him. If he's solid enough, I curl up in the bushes and nap so my own daemon can talk to him.

"What did she miss out on?" he'll ask the old man. "Who did she love?" My other half, Jack, is a great communicator and a pretty good fuck, if the daemons who've had him are any indication. He's not broken like I am. He's not especially beautiful either, but he has a way about him that other daemons respond to. Good thing too, or I couldn't do this work. And it so needs to be done. Few people fully respond to the impulse to spread their legs, spread their arms and spread their ideas. Instead, they trade in securities; degrees in pragmatic disciplines for decent paychecks, husbands with good jobs for roofs over their heads, a couple of children to care for them when they can't wipe their own asses anymore.

It's not a bad life of its own accord, but it clips the feathers of their souls. Jack and me, we sew them back on where we can. It's not easy work, and it has cost me everything I wanted when my singer freed me and taught me the songs. His name was Jack too, and he was the first and last person who ever touched my body without revulsion. I buried him in Leipzig over a hundred years ago, long after he left the music and allowed his body to wither.

There were a number of cars parked in the church lot when I

got back, so I stuffed the bottle of Jameson deep into my bag and covered it up with a bag of oranges and a loaf of bread before going inside. The pastor's office light was on, and several men were sitting around his conference table. I crept by the door in the hope they wouldn't see me.

"I could have taken you to the store," the pastor said as I passed by.

"Oh, don't worry about it," I stuck my head into the room and smiled at its contents. "It's a gorgeous evening, and I needed the exercise."

"How long will you be staying with us?"

"Not long, I hope. And thank you for your hospitality."

"I didn't catch your name?"

"My friends call me Piper."

"I heard you were looking for work," another man said, his wrinkled face stretching into a solicitous smile. Crap. I hate it when they actually offer me employment. I've got plenty of money; grateful patrons and a long life are good for the purse. But I can't refuse either, or I risk wearing out my welcome.

"I had planned on picking up a paper in the morning. Do you have any leads?"

"As a matter of fact, I own the laundry in town, and we could use a girl in the evening." Crap, crap, crap. Well, at least there'd be less traffic and fewer people awake when I sang for the old folks on the way home.

"Thank you so much!" I told him. "When would you like for me to start?"

"Tomorrow would be good, if that's all right with you. 3:00 to 10:00? It's on the corner of Branch and Manchester."

"I'll be there."

Fortunately, I worked alone at the laundry. My predecessor had recently returned to college, and there was no need for more than one attendant at a time in so small a town. The day shift girl told me the old man's daughter was a florist (how convenient) while she taught me how to care for the laundry's many plants (thanks honey, I've got it). The picture windows were clustered with bright, blooming flowers, and there was a string of deep green ivy that stretched from a tiny pot in the window, up over the curtain rod, and across the room on insulated pipes that ran the length of the ceiling. The first thing I did was re-pot the poor thing, and then I whistled deep into its grateful roots.

A few nights after I started working, I came back to the church at around two in the morning and found a bewildered, middle-aged daemon with a thick, wavy mane of salt and pepper hair sitting at the secretary's desk. He couldn't see me; they never can, so I went up to bed and sent Jack down to talk to him.

"Are you all right?" Jack asked as he sat down opposite the desk in a metal, fold-out chair.

"What am I doing here?"

"This is where she dreams."

"She does, doesn't she?" The daemon reached into the bottom, right-hand corner of the desk and brought out a manila folder stuffed full of brochures and photos and held together with rubber bands. He unwrapped the rubber bands and opened the folder, smoothing its creases flat. "She wants to go to college, but Harold says she doesn't need it and won't pay her tuition."

"What's her name?"

"Helen."

"And what's yours?"

"Hele..." The man stopped, his mouth half open, and looked away. "I don't know. I don't think I have one."

"Does she think about you when she masturbates?"

The man looked back at Jack, startled. "I don't think that's an appropriate question."

Jack shrugged and leaned across the desk, folding his hands in front of him. "If she does, you have a little more power to help her."

"Oh."

"And you should have your own name. You're not Helen, at least not entirely."

"She likes 'Hank,'" he said, and then hesitated. "Why don't I remember being autonomous before?"

"Because you haven't been, Hank. And you won't be independent of her after I leave. Are you all right with that?"

"Yeah... so how do you... how does your woman do it?"

"Piper listens to me, and she's got a rare gift. She sings to living things, or to things that were recently alive, and those things sing about life to the people who touch them."

"Does she think about you when she masturbates?" A half-smile crossed Hank's face.

Jack returned the smile. "I see to it."

જી

I came into Helen's office the following morning to offer her a cup of coffee and found her rummaging through the manila folder Jack had been shown.

"Do you think I'm too old to get a degree in photography?" she asked me.

"Of course not! Do you think I'm too ugly to find a husband?" I replied and then laughed a little to soften the question. She grinned.

"Of course not!" she said, and then we had coffee while she showed me a stack of the loveliest landscape shots I had ever seen. They were hers, and as she slid them across the table for my inspection there was a gleam in her eyes and a breathless quality to her voice that made me wonder whether or not Hank's chest was covered in the same thick, salt and pepper hair his head was. I imagined I'd find out soon enough, and I was right.

That night, Hank learned what it was like to have a body. They all do, and most do it in exactly the same way; they eat too much, drink too much, smoke and fuck, pleasures their counterparts don't often allow themselves. Jack was happy to oblige him on all counts. That's my Jack.

Sometime in the early hours of the morning, long after they'd emptied themselves of desire, an elderly, female daemon began to appear in the front pew. She moved her fingers rhythmically, as if knitting or sewing, though her eyes were distant and unfocused. Once in a while her hands would stop and smooth a wrinkle out of her dress or adjust the tilt of her hat and then return to their imagined work.

"An older man in the church?" Hank asked Jack while they watched her from the opened, side-exit door.

"Probably, though people do sometimes have same-gender daemons. Is there someone who sits there every Sunday?"

Hank tilted his head and crossed his arms, a posture that reminded Jack of my memory of Helen. "Brother Bryce, the man who gave Piper a job. Lost his wife to Alzheimer's a few years ago. He'd never say so, but Helen thinks he's awfully lonely."

"Poor fellow. We'll see what we can do about that."

The following morning I got up early and went to Sunday morning services, where I discovered the Full Gospel Tabernacle took 'make a joyful noise' to enthusiastic new heights. It's as if God might have gone on a Saturday night bender and needed His followers to wake Him up for the worship and prayer-answering thing. At the front of the church, a graying stork of a woman with a fuzzy bun of hair pinned to her head banged out the four chords she knew on a piano and sang in a voice that could only be described as commanding; I could hear it from the coat room. The rest of the congregants waved their hands in the air, palms up when they weren't clapping and sang in a loud, lock-step unison.

Of course, Jack and Hank's love-making made my interaction with Helen a little clumsy. She was radiant though, and she hadn't yet made the connection between her improved mood and the reasons for it. So she was gracious with me, and I joined her in the pews when I had finished hanging the sweaters and jackets. Right about that time, a buxom, red-headed woman in her mid-twenties made her way to the pulpit. The music changed, an overhead projection of the next hymn was splashed onto the wall behind her, and she began to sing:

"You better go down in the name of Jesus—
When you go down!
You better go down in the name of Jesus—
When you go down!
I tell you right now, the Devil is a liar,
You better be full of that Holy Ghost fire,
When you go down in the name of Jesus—
When you go down!"

I grinned and thought about the night I'd just spent drenched in sweat and dreaming in the church loft, then opened my throat and sang while my palms rested on the bench in front of me. The music rose and thickened and stretched like bread dough. The worshipers raised their hands higher, clapped them harder, sang louder. A few feet began to stomp in time with the music, and Brother Bryce in the front row began to shout in the rolling cadences of glossolalia while another man interpreted for him.

I pushed, just a little, weaving my song around theirs. The people in front of me rose out of their lock-step unison and into a kind of chaotic higher order of worship, voices, hands and feet merging and diverging in multi-part harmony. And then, just before the rest of the church caught on, I retreated, and they fell back in line with the rest. Yes, yes. Things were going well.

Within a week, the Full Gospel Tabernacle became a gathering place, a musing hall, a fucking ground. It was never wild; the daemons who came together there at night approached each other like one might approach a wolf in a trap, weeping over the places that were broken and bleeding, cautious of mouths full of sharp, white teeth, determined to set the animal free. Jack kissed them, kneaded their shoulders, listened to their stories:

"...She can still sing, can't she? I mean, she's too old to be a country star, but she can still sing, and if she took a few guitar lessons..."

"...I wish he'd never had children. I know that's a horrible thing to say, and he loves his girls. But when he was young, he wanted to travel, to see the world, to grow old and tanned and leathery someplace warm after a lifetime on the road. But his mother told him to marry a 'neat babe', so he did. His girls were the only good thing he ever got out of that decision, and here I am wishing he'd never had them..."

"...Robert never used to hit her, but he would shake her from time to time. He'd tell her to 'snap out of it,' whatever 'it' was, and that scared me..."

"Is he hitting her now, Luke?" Jack asked, concerned.

"He just started about a week ago."

Jack dropped his head into his hands. "What's going on at home?"

"Well, she's sick of cooking all the meals and doing all the laundry and raising the kids all by herself because that's what Robert's religion tells him to tell her to do. She wants to close the daycare and get a job outside the house, learn a new skill, you know how it is. And I think we'd like to leave him when the boys are grown." He paused, ran his hands over his shaven head and across his beard and frowned. "Look, she didn't even start thinking about this stuff until you and Piper came along."

"We're not the reason Jessica's husband is beating her up, Luke."

"And it's not about what's going on at home," a female daemon leaned on the frame of the open door, her bloody arms crossed in a defensive posture. Moonlight illuminated a line of bruises on her face, and what remained of her hair was tied back in a messy knot at the nape of her neck. She wasn't completely solid, so she left no blood when she rose from her resting place, but her features were distinct enough. She looked like Jessica. "It's about what's going on in Robert's head."

"Oh, God." Luke reached out to her.

The daemon threaded her ghostly fingers through his corporeal ones, squeezed as if he might feel the pressure of her hand, and turned to Jack. "I'm sure you think you're doing a good thing. By and large, I think you're doing a good thing. But Robert's inner life isn't like most. I'm what he dreams about, and the only thing that keeps him from beating his wife to death is my skill at remaining buried in his unconscious mind. If you stay here much longer, I'll be too strong for him to ignore, and Jessica will die in bed with her husband's dick inside her and his hands around her throat."

I woke up gasping and jumped to my feet, Jack's horrified expression on my face, his fear in my mind, his tears in my eyes. I ran down the stairs, two flights, to see if I could catch a glimpse of the brutalized shadow who resembled my sweet friend. But when I skidded to a stop on the polished floor of the darkened sanctuary, she was gone. Luke was kneeling at the altar weeping, and a cluster of daemons was gathered around him. I went forward and sat down next to Brother Bryce's daemon, still indistinct, still moving her hands in the rhythms of some imagined craft, and prayed until morning.

Later that day, I asked Helen where Jessica lived, and that evening after work, I began a vigil behind the grape arbor in her back yard. The first three nights, nothing happened, and I returned to the church each morning in the early autumn pre-dawn damp and chilly. On the fourth night, I found her rocking back and forth on the front porch steps when I arrived. Her nose was broken but no longer bleeding, and one of her eyes was swollen and dark.

"Piper, what are you doing here?" she asked me as I sat down next to her and wrapped my sweater around her shoulders.

"Oh Jessica, oh honey, you need a doctor."

The woman's shoulders heaved, and she shook her head. "Please don't. He isn't usually like this, and I'll be all right in a few days."

I put my hand on her thigh to comfort her. She flinched. I gritted my teeth and thought about Robert's daemon's warning. "Is your husband asleep?"

She nodded.

"Good. I want you to go inside and wake the boys. Don't bother to dress them; their pajamas are fine. I'll come in behind you and call a cab." I stood and motioned for her to follow.

She reached up and put her hand on my arm.

"No, Piper. I don't have any money…"

"I have money."

"Not enough to…"

"Enough."

"Who are you?" Her question hung in the air between us like an iron pendulum at the pinnacle of its swing. I pushed, and the ball dropped.

"Jessica," I began, and sat down again. "Since you were about fourteen, you've dreamed of a tall, slender man with a shaven head and tightly clipped, black beard. His name is Luke, after a German Shepherd you had when you were a little girl."

She looked out at the street for a moment and then settled back against the porch pillar. "You're Jack." There was no trace of doubt in her voice.

"In a manner of speaking, yes."

"All this started when I brought you to the church."

"Yes. All this started when you brought me to the church."

"Why?"

I put my palms over the backs of her hands and met her gaze, forcing her to focus on my face. "Because I believe people are better off free, even if it hurts them to get that way, and because I can."

"Free to do what? Get beaten up? Wish for things they can never have? What's wrong with you?" her voice rose and trembled. She began to weep. "Are you… is Jack… some kind of demon?"

"Not in the way you mean it, no. Please, let's not talk about this right now. Let's just get the boys and go someplace safe."

Her nose began to trickle blood again. "Get off of my property." She raised her right hand, pointing at the street. "Get out of my church. Get out of my town. Don't come back." Then she lurched to her feet, ran into the house, and closed the door behind her.

On the way home, I stopped at a telephone booth to call the

police. My hand rested on the receiver for a long time. Sometimes I picked it up and began to dial '911' but could never bring myself to finish. Instead, I thought about the time, a hundred and forty-two years ago, when a singer named Jack told me I could choose my uncle, who had broken my body, or choose to be free. He gave me a choice. I owed one to Jessica, even if she made the wrong one. So when I was able to pry my hand from the phone, I went back to my bed in the loft. And when I was finally able to sleep, I didn't dream at all.

Helen came up to the loft and woke me in the morning. "We need to talk," she said, and I saw Hank in her face.

"Yes, Helen."

"Jessica called from the hospital this morning. She said Robert is in jail, and the children are with her brother."

"I see."

"She also said you came to see her last night, and she told me about Luke..." she paused, blushing, "and Jack."

"Do you believe her?"

"I know she's telling the truth. I know a lot of other things are true, too." She turned away, folded her hands in front of her, and twisted her wedding ring around her finger. Suddenly, she was a frumpy, middle-aged church secretary to me again, wearing department store perfume and a dress that fit too tightly around her thick middle. I motioned to the bedside chair.

"Sit down, Helen." She did, but she still couldn't look at me. "How much has Hank shown you?"

"I'm not handsome like he is." She ignored my question. "I...I was matron of honor at a wedding last year. Judy was getting married again, and we all thought it was great that she found somebody again after Frank passed." She gathered strength in the story and looked over at me. "Well anyway, we were all getting into our dresses in the Ladies' room, and I just couldn't...couldn't let them see me..." Helen's voice softened. "I got dressed in the stall."

"Look at my head, Helen. Look at my hands." I uncrossed my legs and scooted to the edge of the bed to be closer to her.

"Nobody wants me. And nobody has seen you naked."

Helen laughed out loud, a bark that broadened into a hearty sound and echoed in the church rafters. "Oh, yes you have! You might not have seen me undressed, but you sure have seen me naked!" She leaned forward, wrapped her hands around mine, and planted a firm kiss on both of my cheeks. "And I'm not sorry either! Harold hasn't been able to hold an erection in five years, and even when he could, he would plant his pointy chin in my shoulder blade and hump me like a dog. Lord Jesus, I hated having sex with that man."

My eyes widened, and though I tried my best for three or four seconds to contain it, a paroxysm of laughter forced its way out of me, and I crumpled to the floor. Helen laughed too, slapping her hand on her thigh, and for a solid two minutes we took turns trying to calm each other down without success. When we were finally able to speak again, Helen told me that she had feigned incredulity when Jessica spoke to her earlier but had encouraged her to leave Robert for good.

"If I give you some money, will you hang on to it for her?" I asked.

"You mean you're not poor, either?" Helen smiled.

"Not in the least. The people I help are good to me."

"And Jack is good to them." She leaned down and put a hand on my leg. "But I'm not the only person Jessica is going to talk to."

"That's all right. I'm almost done here."

"Hank will miss Jack when you go." She brushed my hair behind my ear with her other hand in a gesture that was almost motherly. I kissed her wrist as she withdrew it.

"And Jack will miss Hank."

That night Luke returned with a bottle of vodka and lost himself in a sea of fleeting daemon flesh. He didn't speak for several hours but buried himself in Jack's body and Hank's body and the bodies of several others, weeping onto their warm shoulders while they murmured into his ears and arched their backs and their bellies into the curve of his ribcage. When he was drunk and spent, Jack pulled him close and stammered an apology that Luke covered with his mouth, and the two of them rested a while in the center of a knot of daemons who held them together for fear of unraveling.

My dreams were of salt, stained glass moonlight and the persistent rhythms of Brother Bryce's daemon's hands. I woke in the morning with the taste of liquor and semen and vulva in my mouth. If the people of Tairdean didn't know what was happening to them now, they soon would.

As I was getting out of bed, Helen came upstairs wearing an uncharacteristic jeans and sweatshirt. "There's a moving party at Jessica's house; I'm closing up the church for the day to go and help. I thought you'd want to come along."

"I do," I told her and threw on a pair of sweats and a sweater. When we arrived, the house was full of people, not all of them from the church. More were arriving every few minutes, confused about the compulsion that brought them to an unfamiliar place in the middle of erranding, work, and other daily tasks in order to help a stranger leave her abusive husband. Some were aware, and though their daemons couldn't have shown them what I looked like, they gravitated toward me like magnets to a pole to offer thanks or recrimination or simply to see what their daemon's lover's woman looked like. Others were on the threshold of awareness, and their faces were masks of embarrassment and unfulfilled desire.

Late in the morning, I found a knot of women in the back of a walk-in closet while packing Jessica's bright, summer things into a box. They were naked from the waist down and devouring one other with sweet, sticky abandon. They took no notice of me, so I blessed their journey in my heart as I backed out and closed the door behind me.

When I went downstairs, the kitchen was buzzing with conversation. I poured a cup of coffee and settled into a chair.

"...When I talked to the bank, they said there were all kinds of small business loans for women, so I told them I thought Tairdean needed a coffee house, and they gave me a packet of information about how to write up a proposal..."

"...I know! And you can take a train from Halifax to Vancouver for just a couple of thousand dollars, everything included! I've decided to do it just as soon as I send the girls off to college; I don't care what my wife says..."

"I bought a guitar." The buxom redhead from last Sunday's service leaned down and whispered into my left ear. "I'm going to take lessons like Matthew told Jack, and I'm writing a song right now."

"That's wonderful!" I turned toward her and looked up into her shining and troubled face.

"But I don't know if I approve...I mean...I don't know if..." she stammered for a moment, seeking her courage. "I think gay sex is disgusting and immoral, and I can't believe any part of me would have anything to do with it!"

I suppressed a grin.

"Sometimes it takes a dose of the extreme to bring us back to the center of our lives. Besides, you made Matthew, so you can change him if you like." It wasn't entirely true, and I couldn't tell whether my answer made her feel better or worse. But she didn't say anything else, so I didn't press.

By the end of the day, everything that looked like it might belong to Jessica and the boys had been moved to her brother's barn for storage. It was only when he told Helen he hadn't asked for the help that I realized how significant the day had been.

"Oh yeah," a brown-eyed firecracker of a woman in her late forties shouted over to us as she unloaded a box from her arms. "I just figured possession was nine-tenths of the law, you know?"

"So you broke into her house?" Helen asked her.

"Oh no! We'd never do a thing like that! Sherry Phillips has Jessica's emergency key for when they go on vacation. We let ourselves in."

The following afternoon, I stopped into the church lounge to say hello to the ladies in the quilting club on my way into work. I found Brother Bryce sitting in the center of the room, a half-finished Bow-tie across his lap, surrounded by six or seven gray-haired women who were all talking at once.

"Brother Bryce! I didn't know you quilted!" I walked over to him and knelt by the fabric, examining the fine hand-stitching that held the patchwork pieces together. "This is expert work, too."

"Oh, those aren't my stitches, Piper. I can barely darn a sock! This is my wife Gertrude's work. She left three or four unfinished projects in her cedar chest when she went to be with the Lord, and I haven't been able to look at them since." There were tears in his eyes. "I just couldn't see letting them go to waste, so I thought I might learn to quilt and raffle them off for the Christmas fund."

"I'll bet she was quite the lady," I said, and thought about his prim little daemon, never quite solid.

"She was a corker," he replied, and returned his attention to the women around him.

I left the laundry that night under a mid-autumn moon, my breath a fog in front of me, my feet crunching on the first of the season's fallen leaves. There were dozens of daemons wandering about. Many were alone; watching clouds pass overhead, gathering leaves, petting stray cats who treated them like any other human. Others were clustered in groups of impromptu actors, musicians, comedians and their audiences. A few were gathered in knots of heated debate. Some played charades or chess. Some wrote or painted. I watched them all joyfully until the Sunday morning sun sent them home, and then I returned to the loft and dressed for church.

I had learned in my time at the Full Gospel Tabernacle that Pentecostal services were divided into three parts; singing, preaching and more singing. After I finished in the coat room and joined Helen in the pews, I spent the first third of the service pushing and restraining the congregants by turns. Their energy was getting away from me, and it was heady. They were awakened; most of them aware of their daemons, and many were openly watching me work. But after several minutes the wave crested without incident, and we all settled in for the message.

"Praise ye the Lord! Praise God in his sanctuary: praise him in the firmament of his power. Praise him with the sound of the trumpet: praise him with the psaltery and harp. Praise him with the timbrel and dance: praise him with stringed instruments and organs. Let every thing that hath breath praise the Lord. Praise ye the Lord! Psalm 150." The pastor laid a ribbon of bookmark between the pages of his bible and closed it. Then he raised his head, looked out at the congregation and grinned.

Here it comes, I thought.

"You know, God made us individuals for a reason," he said, and a scattering of 'amens' rose from the pews. "He gave us different gifts for a reason, and we enter into praising Him when we use those gifts to the best of our human ability."

"Hallelujah, hallelujah, hallelujah!" A portly, brown-haired woman in the back row raised her palm in the air.

"Jesus said, 'Let your light so shine before men, that they may see your good works, and glorify your Father which is in heaven'. He didn't tell you to hide what the Lord gave you. He didn't say to follow somebody else's lantern. No, the Son of God, the Prince of Peace, the Lamb commanded you, compelled you to shine!"

That was all it took. The church pianist, who had never left her station, spread her fingers and slammed them onto the keys, cutting the pastor off. The first two pews took her cue, surged to their feet and began to sing. The pastor's mouth fell open for a moment, then he laughed and nodded his encouragement at the rest of the flock, who rose to their feet as well.

I leaned back on one foot, put my ruined hands in my pockets and listened to the music swell. The hardwood floors, the golden, polished pews, the window panes and the ceiling beams pulsed with the voices of the congregation, the hammered repetition of piano chords and the remembered cries of daemons in the throes of a catharsis and release their beloved counterparts had never been able to have. Make a joyful noise indeed, I thought, and wept.

Then Helen ripped her blouse completely off her body and began to stamp her left foot in time with the music while she whirled the torn scrap of vermilion clothing around her head like a matador in a bull ring. A few seconds later the stork woman shot up out of her place behind the piano, lifted both of her hands into the air, and in her best church-woman voice began to shout in tongues. A bottle of wine emerged from a Bible bag, another from an already over-stuffed purse and before the pastor knew it, every person in his care was purple and fragrant and raving.

I lifted my voice along with the rest until Helen, red blouse a-waving, led the whole congregation out the emergency exit and straight into the jewelly autumn woods. I brought up the rear. The sanctuary behind me was almost quiet then except for a faint hum only I could hear, the voice of the church singing back to me. I turned and bowed to the waist, my hands settling on the door frame in farewell, and prayed the music would endure.

꩜

After I leave a place, most people return to their lives and never again question their circumstances. Others make changes, set down rules and clear space for themselves. A few are radically changed and never look back, never regret and die old, craggy, joyful. But when I depart, all of them have genuinely chosen, sometimes for the first and last time ever.

I chose to kiss Helen's mouth when she dropped me in the city on her way to college. It was a brave, fleeting gesture, and I was surprised at my own daring. "Good luck at university," I told her. "I know you'll do well."

She unzipped her handbag, pulled out a short stack of photos and handed them to me. Each one was a picture of the church in a different season. "Something to remember us by," she said and then put her hand on my arm as I opened the car door. "You're not too ugly to find a husband, Greta. But if you ever discover a husband isn't what you're looking for, I hope you'll come and find me."

Some dry well in my heart filled with water then, and for an instant I wondered if it was time to teach the songs to someone else. "I will," I said, and meant it. Somewhere in the recesses of my unconscious mind, Jack was cheering. He always does when I get it right. That's my Jack.

Kambal Kulam
Paolo V. Chikiamco

"Are you insane?"

Normally, these would not be the first words out of my mouth if a beautiful woman—dressed in a tight fitting tank top and cut-offs—met me at the door to her apartment and invited me in. However, when that woman is actually my very good, very *male* friend, I believe that a bit of freaking out is justified.

"Nope," Ericson said, as he stepped aside and let me enter his apartment. "Hell, I'm not even drunk. Petite it may be, but this body can really hold its liquor."

Ericson lived in a comfortable studio apartment in one of the more exclusive areas of Makati, close enough to the bustling financial district to be prime real estate. Of course, the location was wasted on Ericson; his line of work didn't involve much in the way of number crunching.

"Speaking of bodies, care to explain the new plumbing?" I cleared away a stack of magazines and plopped myself down on his sofa. "I can't imagine the change was pleasant."

"Hurt like a motherfucker," Ericson agreed pleasantly. It was strange to hear his usual foul language in such a sugar-sweet voice. "You don't really know what pain is until you can feel your pelvis crack as it—"

"Too much information." I suppressed a shudder. Ericson underwent drastic physical changes on a regular basis—that was an essential part of the job, and the transformations and attendant pain were about as dreadful to him as a corpse might be to a mortician. No matter how many times I've helped him on a job, the entire process made me uncomfortable. Still, even he must have balked at a change of this magnitude... there was a reason why few Kambal Kulam agreed to take on clients of the opposite sex.

"What are we looking at here? Five hundred, six hundred

grand? How much did this cutie have to pay to get you to agree?"

Ericson hopped on to one of the stools by the bar and grinned at me. I tried not to notice how cute it made him look. "Ah Joey, you need to learn to dream bigger. Try a million. And I'm giving you a higher cut—fifteen percent—so if I want to go into graphic detail, you'd best just shut up and listen."

I gave a low whistle. "That must be some curse she's trying to dodge. Did she tell you what you're up against? La-ga, Paktol, Sampal..."

The job of a Kambal Kulam was simple: protect clients from harmful curses by serving as living decoys. There were many types of curses available to a Philippine sorcerer, but the most deadly required the use of a sympathetic element, hair or skin or some bodily fluid of the intended victim. This made the curses very accurate, but left them with an exploitable flaw. Kambal Kulam made sure they were closer to the locus of the curse, then used sorcery to take on the form of the target, counting on their own aptitude with counter-curses to survive the hostile magic. A simple job, but a dangerous job, which was why Kambal Kulam were very well compensated—and why they usually kept a buddy around to make sure they didn't fall of a balcony while they were busy fighting off a magically-induced heart attack.

Of course, it would help me do my job if I knew what kind of curse Ericson would be facing.

"No clue," Ericson said, in the same too-cute voice. "I didn't ask Ms. Ricaforte too many questions once she floated a seven-digit figure."

"Wait, so you accepted this blind?" I was starting to worry that taking on this assignment had been about more than the money. "Tell me you at least know who's going after her."

"Oh, some mid-level *mangkukulam*. Has some cushy day job in a consulting firm. Lives nearby too, which is why I didn't bother moving to the client's house."

He reached behind the bar and took out a slim manila envelope. "Everything's in the file. You can look through it while I change."

I gave him another once over as he handed me the envelope. "Yeah, noticed the outfit. Did you go out and buy that just to shock me?"

"Oh no, these are Tessa's clothes." This time his smile was more malicious than mischievous. "Thought I'd play dress up a bit before she comes by on Friday to pick them up. I've got an entire box of them in my room—looks like you're getting a private fashion show tonight, you lucky dog you!"

"I should have known." I slapped the envelope down on my knee. "This isn't about the money at all. This is just you reacting to Tessa breaking up with you."

"What? Don't be ridiculous, Joey. A million bucks is a million bucks." Ericson wouldn't look at me as he spoke, instead heading back to the bar and the scotch he had waiting there.

"Right. So the fact that your client is just Tessa's size is entirely a coincidence."

"Entirely," he said, before downing his drink in one smooth motion.

"And I'm not going to find pictures of this Tessa-like body, in various compromising pictures, plastered all over the Internet tomorrow?"

"You know what? Mind your own business." Ericson slammed the glass onto the bar, before stomping into his room.

I sighed. Ericson and Tessa had been set to tie the knot in six months, but she'd broken it off abruptly three weeks ago, and neither of them had been willing to tell me why. Ericson had taken it hard, but when he told me he'd taken a new job I thought he'd decided to move on. Clearly, this was not the case.

I opened the envelope and was about to start reading the file when Ericson came back out.

"Ta-dah!"

I looked up to see Ericson striking a pose in front of me, one hand on a curvy hip while the other was raised to the ceiling. This time he was dressed in a tight pink number that ended in a short, ruffled skirt; I actually recognized the outfit—it had been one of

Tessa's favorites—which made me even more uncomfortable.

"You need help."

"And you need to lighten up." Ericson cocked his head to the side. "C'mon Joey, I'm stuck with this body until the curse hits anyway. What's the harm?"

"For one thing, it's going to kill any chance of you and Tessa getting back together."

"Hard to kill what's already dead." Bitterness and hurt laced his voice. Before I could say anything else, he held up a hand. "And no, I still don't want to talk about it."

I shook my head. "Hey look, if you want to cast yourself in the role of creepy boyfriend, knock yourself out. As for me, I'm going to make sure at least one of us has his mind on the job."

"Joseph Anthony Tuliao." Ericson walked slowly toward me, the sway of his hips carefully exaggerated. "If you actually manage to read a word of that dossier while this body is prancing around in next to nothing, I'm afraid I'm going to have to start questioning your sexuality."

"I hope you realize the irony of saying that while wearing a pink dress."

"Oh, you haven't seen anything yet," he said, but I'd already returned my attention to the file, and that's where I kept my eyes glued, even as Ericson's coaxing grew more and more insistent.

Despite his antics, the contents of the file made it clear that he'd at least made some attempt at research. While there wasn't much information on the client, Ms. Amanda Ricaforte—a short biodata, a photograph, and a lock of her hair for the transformation—there was a thick dossier on the *mangkukulam*, Arnold Segovia. Forty-three years old and married, but without children. There was a picture of him and his wife hobnobbing with the Mayor of Makati, so he was well connected. Still, nothing in the file shed any light on why he'd want to kill Ms. Ricaforte, or how he planned to do it. Most *mangkukulam* had an affinity for specific types of black magic—*mambabarang* used insects, for instance—but Segovia tripped none of the usual flags.

I heard the sound of bare feet padding across the floor.

"Unbelievable. You haven't even tried to sneak a peek."

"You're not my type." Not strictly true, not in *that* body, but my old friend didn't need to know that. I went back to the beginning of Segovia's dossier to check if I'd missed anything— but suddenly the file was plucked from my hand.

"Okay, I've had about enough of this."

"What the——" I began, then stopped, my mouth dry and my eyes wide.

Ericson tossed the envelope to the floor, then crossed his arms beneath his breasts, a part of his new body which I'd studiously been trying to ignore. That was proving to be much more difficult with Ericson clad in silky black lingerie, complete with garter belt and lacy stockings, looking for all the world like he'd just stepped out of a Victoria's Secret catalog.

"Ah... buh," I said eloquently.

That brought a smile to Ericson's face. "*There's* the reaction I was looking for." He tossed back his new head of hair, dark brown and curling down until the middle of his back. "I was beginning to believe that you didn't find me beautiful."

"Wait a second." I blinked. "Are you hearing yourself? You were upset because I didn't find you *beautiful?*"

"I..." Now it was Ericson's turn to be taken aback. "I... was. You were ignoring me and suddenly I felt... Oh God."

Ericson ran back to his room, and this time I followed, alarmed by the look of horror that had flashed across his face. I found him hunched by one of his bookshelves, holding an old, leather-bound book, and cursing softly in his now high-pitched voice.

"Shit, shit, shit..."

"Ericson, talk to me, what the hell?"

"It's not a curse, the stupid bitch, it's not a..." He took a breath. "It's a *gayuma*. Segovia cast a love spell on her. On *me*."

"Oh." Oh. "Is that why you've been acting so..." I waved my hands vaguely.

"Yeah, yeah. That's how this kind of spell works. It ratchets up the target's arousal and then…" Ericson ran his hands through his hair, then stopped and looked at me. He paled, then stood up suddenly and walked over to his bed. "Then it focuses that desire on the intended beneficiary."

"And you've got no way to fight this? Doesn't it matter that you're not even, ah, attracted to men?"

He sat down heavily on the mattress. "Joey, a love spell specializes in making people feel things they'd never normally feel." He shuddered. "Most people are bi anyway…"

Neither of us spoke for a minute. A million pesos or no, this had obviously become much more than we'd bargained for. "Should I call Tessa?"

"Absolutely not." His tone made it clear that this was not a decision that was going to change. "We can do this on our own. We just have to…wait it out, and make sure I don't go anywhere near Segovia in the meantime."

I straightened my shoulders. "Sounds simple enough. Is there anything you need me to do?"

"Yes," he said. "I need you to tie me to the bed."

I turned to him. "Oh come on, it can't be that bad."

Ericson's gaze locked with mine, and for the first time I could see the strain on his face; his cheeks were pale, his pupils dilated, like an addict in withdrawal.

"Joey, please. There are some…some old scarves of Tessa you can use." He gestured weakly toward an open box at the foot of his bed.

I quickly grabbed a bundle of scarves. Ericson lay down on the bed, spread-eagle; he kept his face turned away from mine as I tied his hands to the bed posts, but I could hear his breathing grow more rapid. I wasn't thinking all too clearly myself.

"Maybe we should use something sturdier to—"

"No time," he cut me off, his words clipped. "My feet. Then get out. Or I won't…" he trailed off as his voice cracked.

I tied off her… his feet as fast as I could, then moved to the door. "Joey…"

His eyes were closed tight. "If I call for you… don't come."

Ericson bit his lip hard; I could see blood welling up. "Don't come."

He lasted almost an hour before he shouted my name. Afterward, I had to turn up the volume of the television to drown out his screams. That was probably why I didn't hear him when he tore through his bonds and escaped out the bedroom window.

Even at ten in the evening, it usually takes at least an hour to get from Makati to Quiapo. I made the trip in under twenty minutes, earning three new scratches across the flank of my car, and the hatred of around two dozen drivers (and a rather persistent traffic enforcer). Quiapo is the dirty, vibrant, pulsing heart of Manila. It's also a haven for both people and artifacts of power. The city has the highest concentration of fortunetellers per square meter in the entire Philippines. That night, I was only looking for one.

"Come in, Joey. I've been expecting you."

When she first came to Quiapo, Tessa told fortunes at a corner booth at Café Istara for fifty pesos a session. Now, Tessa owns the Café, although she still divines the future from the same corner booth. When I arrived, she was behind the counter, emptying out the cash register before closing.

"You are? Did you have a vision or—"

"Doesn't take a *manghuhula* to guess you'd come down in person after our last conversation." The register rang once as she closed the drawer, a forlorn sound in the empty Café. "The answer is still no, but it's sweet of you to try so hard. I'm not taking him back, but if you sit down, I'll make you a drink."

"This isn't about that."

"You're not here because of Eric?" Tessa cocked her head to one side, one hand on her hip. It dawned on me how similar she was to Ericson—as he was now, at least. It wasn't just their body type, but their mannerisms as well. Except for the fact that Ericson was now a mestiza while Tessa's skin was the color of freshly ground coffee, they could be sisters.

I placed the envelope with the Ricaforte-Segovia dossiers on the counter. "I am, but it's not what you—"

"I don't want to hear it."

"Tessa, this is serious. He needs your help."

"Well, he's going to have to learn to get by without me, now isn't he?" She turned her back to me and began to walk toward the kitchen. I leaned over the counter and grabbed her arm.

"Tess—"

Something hit my chest, hard. I coughed and stumbled back; Tessa held out her hand, then leaned in and began to make soothing noises towards something I couldn't see.

"You'd better go," she said. "I know you're just being a good friend, but my *Aghoy* take their emotional cues from me, and you'll understand if they're easily upset."

"Dammit Tessa, he's running out of time! What could he possibly have done to make you this angry?"

"It's not what he's done. It's what he's going to do." Tessa swallowed hard. "I had a vision."

"Tessa, no offense, but your visions aren't always...precise." I approached the counter again, although I spared a wary glance for the upturned palm of her hand. "You once foretold I'd be invited to a threesome, remember? Not exactly your brightest moment."

She shook her head. "I've never had a clearer vision...I could literally feel the depth of Ericson's passion, his desire...I saw a face Joey. And it wasn't mine." Tessa dabbed at her eyes. "I didn't even think he liked mestizas..."

Alarm bells began to ring in my head. Quickly I opened the envelope and spilled its contents on to the counter. "Is this the woman you saw in your vision?"

I'd never before seen such a look of utter shock on a *manghuhula's* face. "Where did you...How did you...?"

"That's Ericson's new client—and as of right now, that's Ericson." I pushed the documents back into the envelope. "Come on, I'll explain on the way."

⁓

Tessa raised her upturned palm to her ear. "Ericson's in there all right...and Segovia's with him. Her. No one else is at home though.

Guess he didn't want any witnesses to this tryst."

We were inside my car, parked on the opposite side of the road from Segovia's home. I'd hoped that Tessa would be able to track Ericson down, but I'd also hoped that Segovia wouldn't be with him. I suppose one out of two wasn't bad.

"So what's the plan?" I asked.

"If we wait any longer the effect of the love spell might become permanent," she said. "I can break the spell, but I'll need to be close to Ericson to do it."

Of course. Why couldn't things be easy? "Next thing you're going to tell me is that you'll need to use True Love's Kiss," I said, then laughed at how ridiculous our situation would seem, if it wasn't so desperate. Then I saw her expression. "You're not serious."

"Nothing quite so dramatic," she said. "It's simply a matter of overcoming the artificial attraction with something real. If...if you're right and Ericson still loves me..."

"We've got nothing to worry about on that score. But how are you going to sneak past Segovia?"

"We'll need a distraction. You have a picture of him with his wife right?"

"Sure." I took the photograph out of the envelope and held it out to Tessa.

"No that's fine, just hold it there." She reached down the top of her blouse and took out an *anting-anting*, a triangular pendant of hammered bronze with an embossed eye in the middle. Tessa murmured a few words, and light spilled out from the *anting-anting*, bathing me in a warm glow for a second before disappearing.

"What was that?" I didn't feel any different.

"Check the mirror."

I pulled down the rear-view mirror—and saw Mrs. Segovia's face staring back at me. I stared at my strange reflection for a second before shaking my head.

"You couldn't have disguised me as the Mayor?"

"That'd be less of a distraction than his wife showing up while he's seducing his would be mistress." Tessa got out of the car and I followed suit. "The illusion will mimic your movements and facial expressions—just don't let him touch you. Don't say anything either."

"How am I supposed to keep him busy if I can't talk?"

"Just look angry," she said, as she began to circle around toward the back of the house. "Trust me, he'll do all the talking."

I waited until Tessa had vanished from view before walking to the gate and pressing the doorbell. I had to chime six times before an obviously irritated Arnold Segovia opened the front door.

"Do you have any idea what time...Lynn? Y-You're supposed to be in Cebu..."

I put my hands on my hips and scowled at him through the bars of the gate.

Segovia almost fell over, so quickly did he rush toward me. He fumbled the lock open with shaking fingers, but by the time he'd opened the gate, I had retreated halfway across the road.

"Darling, I don't know what people have told you but—"

He started toward me again, but I held out a hand imperiously, and he halted in his tracks.

"Lynn, I can explain."

I shook my head. He pushed forward again and this time he would not be deterred. I started back peddling, trying to keep my distance as he babbled on.

"Arnie!"

I don't know if it was Segovia or I who was more distressed when Ericson, wearing one of Tessa's little black dresses, came running out of the house in heels, tears in her eyes.

"Arnie, there's a witch in the house! She's come to take me away! Save me!"

"Ah, fuck."

I only realized that I'd spoken when Segovia whirled on me, his eyes widening. "You're not my wife!"

I did the only thing I could think of when faced with a furious *mangkukulam*: I punched him in the face.

Ericson screamed in rage, and I had a moment to realize I'd ignored the most dangerous threat before he pointed a finger in my direction and opened his mouth—

—only to have it covered the next second by Tessa's.

Ericson's eyes went wide, and he tried to pull away, but Tessa held him close, and soon enough Ericson began to return the kiss. With vigor.

I heard a groan, and found Segovia struggling back to his feet, one hand clutching his bloodied nose.

"You people have no idea who you've crossed."

"That's my line." Ericson came to stand to my right, his cheeks flushed with anger and humiliation. Tessa took a position to my left, and her smile could have carved diamond.

"Poor little *mangkukulam*," Tessa cooed. "Let us show you what real magic is like."

❧

"Nice dress."

"Shut up." Ericson pulled at the hem of the yellow sundress self-consciously. "Tessa had the notion that to make up for wearing her old clothes, she gets to decide my wardrobe until I change back."

"And when is that going to be exactly?" I took a sip of my coffee, then leaned back on the couch. Ericson's apartment seemed to have been left untouched since my hurried exit, two days ago. Not that big a surprise, since Ericson and Tessa had been staying at a hotel. "Ms. Ricaforte can't still be worried about Segovia."

"Oh no, he's...taken care of." Ericson and Tessa hadn't told me what they'd done to the mangkukulam, and I hadn't asked. When we'd left his house he'd been sitting on his doorstep, sobbing quietly. "In fact, she wired the money just this morning. I'll send you your cut tomorrow—I'm sorry, it's just things have been crazy, what with Tessa and everything..."

"You don't need to apologize. I take it you two are back together?"

"We're, ah, working out our differences." Ericson combed his hair down across his cheeks, fidgeting in his chair.

"You're fucking like rabbits aren't you."

"Oh yes," he said, his voice breathy. "Joey, I can't even begin to describe—"

"Then do me a favor and don't." I grinned. "You always were more adventurous than I was, Ericson."

"Ah." Ericson's voice lowered to a mumble. "Guess you wouldn't be interested then..."

"Interested in what?"

My friend looked up at me through long lashes, then took a deep breath. "Ah, to hell with it."

He placed one hand, palm down, on the table, and when he removed it there was a key card with the embossed logo of the Rinden Suites.

"Room 506," he said, as he stood up. "And if you're not there by nine, we're starting without you."

Ericson was out the door in a flash, while I sat in his couch in stunned silence for a good ten minutes.

I guess I owed Tessa an apology.

Driftwood
Tiffany Trent

My skin hangs on the wall, petrified, a warning to all of my transgression. The village elders would not have it any other way.

I sit in my sandpit prison, and the curled lattices of my own fins tempt me back out to sea. The pattern of my true face is in the driftwood. When I wore that face, I swam along the shore with my brothers and sisters. We leapt for the joy of sun and air and light. We herded the silver-sided mackerel and smashed through them with wide-open jaws. We took the bonito one at a time and bumped gannets squawking from the waves. We fought the toothed ones and danced with one another endlessly through the tunnels of waves and coral.

But then I saw him. And everything changed.

He came into the water, dark-haired, dark-eyed. The sheen of his skin drew me closer. I spy-hopped over the water. The notion of fingers, of feet, intrigued me. How do these fragile creatures stand against the waves? How do they not sink in the shifting sands? What language is his face speaking? What are these sounds I cannot understand? I wanted to see the webs between his fingers and toes, the hidden fins that held him buoyant in the surf.

Closer and yet closer.

His fingers scooped air and light out of water. There was nothing between them, no architecture to describe how they smoothed the waves into stillness, how the little fishes swam in shining circles around him. Yet it was all so.

And then, I stood before him. With feet and fingers. Long arms. And hair.

I understood then that we had the capacity for speech—he and I. I understood too that I could not speak my own language. My vocal chords, my lungs, my lips...everything was different. I looked over my new shoulder at my sisters. They rolled in the surf, sad, anxious, but nothing could be said. We would never speak again.

He reached for me, and without speech, without thought, I took his hand. His fingers laced through mine; my feet came down softly in the sand. My lungs breathed without pause. I stepped out of the waves—new-bodied, unbearably light and heavy all at once. My old skin shaped itself into my empty hand, a hide of living water.

He took me to his house on the outskirts of the village. He clothed and fed me and made love with me at dawn. I ate dead fish and was surprised when salt came from my eyes. I hated the smell of burning flesh most.

Slowly, I learned his language. I began to understand the things that made no sense—the endless attempts to control the marching of the dunes, the endless sweating over little furrows of sand. We took the dung of half-starved, big-eyed cows and mixed it with sand until it was black. We women grew things called sweet potatoes and peanuts and cotton. And when the cotton was ready, we hauled it in hot bales on our backs, bent double with the weight of it. It was like all the weight of water that I'd never felt pressing down on me, forcing me to the ground I'd never meant to walk.

My man was a good one. He told me his name—John—and he gave me mine. But I have never been one for such things. Names are poor attempts at the shapes they describe. A good one may hold you for a while, but not forever. We who are born of water know that all things are constantly shifting. Impermanence is the only thing that lasts.

He called me Maebelle because he said that I spoke with the voice of spring. He said my words were like little drops of silver rain. He especially loved it when I sang.

And he loved that somehow I could hear the songs of plant and field and river, such that I could hear the comfrey singing its healing song at the edge of the marshes or find a dark trickle of fresh water where no one else could.

But though John loved me, and though I had left the water to know him, something lived inside me that I could not give him. A small, soft, radiant thing. And it grieved me because I knew that while he wanted all of me, he would never have the best part— that shining, nameless thing.

When I could, I went to the shore, to the rocks near where he'd captured me with my own curiosity what seemed ages ago. My brothers and sisters crowded as close as they dared and though we tried words, it was deaf wood talking to blind stone—we could not speak. Dark, mineral tears fell from their eyes that they had lost me. I didn't need words to understand how they longed for me to step into my old skin and return to them again.

If I had been wise, I would have.

I contemplated it for many a year, but the simplicity of life with these people was a welcome trade. For, truly, it was not love and its pleasures that kept me with John. It was a resonance, like the soft throb of the tide that kept me by his side. I feared what might happen if one day that perfectly-pitched tide might ebb away; if some storm broke from the depths of our being, making our little life impossible.

All the while that radiant thing, the thing that I could not give him, drifted in the blue sea of our togetherness, waiting patiently for a time when something or someone might call it home.

When Adrianne came to our village, she was desperate, feverish, so malnourished that she was translucent as a worn shell. She had escaped the masters to the west, praying for a life on the island free from terror. She had crawled onto the shore after swimming the channel between the island and the mainland, and couldn't walk when I found her. I nursed her because I was the only one who could truly heal—even the old midwife deferred to me by then. We kept her in our hut because it was easier for me to tend her that way. She slept uncomfortably on a little grass mat in the corner, working through the fever that came of her festering scars.

Some people whispered. Perhaps John was taking a second wife in the old way. Perhaps this girl would give him a son. By then, everyone had very nearly forgotten my origins; it mattered very little to them anymore, except for my barrenness. I cleaned the wounds on Adrianne's back and shoulders and ignored the rumors. I heard them, and I knew it shamed my lover that my body bore no fruit. But there was nothing left in me save that shining, moving thing. And I could not give John that. It did not belong to him.

It belonged to her.

I gasped when I saw the hollow place in her, the neatly-shaped space in her soul. She had been waiting for this thing; she had been beaten because she, like me, was barren, and her master had hoped to get many children off her to work his fields. But there had been nothing, and she had been punished for it.

My fingers tightened on her shoulders as I stared down into that needing, child-shaped spot. No human man could fill this space; no human man understood the truth of it.

But I did.

She cried out in pain. She would need healing first.

Slowly, she recovered from her journey. When she could walk again, I took her down to the water's edge. My brothers and sisters greeted her, spy-hopping and smiling their great smiles. They knew the good thing that was to come. Most times, we leave the water for our own pleasure and curiosity, but there are rare times when we are able to aid someone. They could see this would be the case with me and Adrianne, and they were pleased.

But Adrianne took more convincing.

I knew, though I had never done this before, that humans have difficulty accepting impermanence. Surely, yes, they reap the benefits of the tides, but they force something to stay that should not. They love permanence of form. They don't know that they can slip their bodies if they wish and dive deep, like us. Somehow they've tricked themselves into believing they're changeless. They've forgotten what they can be. There are still some few who can transform—even we had heard rumors of a man who made wine from water once—but those with true memories are few and far between. They have all certainly forgotten how to change from a woman to a man, though it's very nearly as easy as changing water into wine.

Once, long ago, they came to us, taking on fins and tail and slick skin. And we welcomed them and loved them and filled the empty spaces where we could with our children. But that has happened less and less over the years, until now only we can make the journey from water onto sand.

Often enough, as I see now, they hate us for it.

So, I was careful with Adrianne. I made sure only to do things that delighted her, for there were many wounds to heal before the space inside her could be filled. I took her down to the sea. She came with me to the fields when she could. I brought her flowers and herbs; we lay together on the sand and counted the clouds. Nights when John was on the other side of the island hunting or working the master's rice fields, we sang together—slow, old songs that her people sang to remind them of what they'd lost.

And then one night like that, when my man had gone out fishing, and the wind whistled low and mournful between the stars, I heard her crying.

I went to her and I stroked her tangled braids from her face. The scars on her shoulders were soft and silver in the fitful moonlight.

"What is it?" I said. But I thought I already knew.

She ducked her head in shame and sobbed harder.

I slid in under the rough blanket beside her and took her in my arms.

"What is it?" I asked again.

Holding her was like holding a collection of bird bones; she was still wasted and frail. She ate very little, despite the fact that we could eat as much as we liked. I often had to coax her to eat at all.

She was afraid that she took too much.

"I just...I've never known..."

I knew what she was going to say. "So much happiness?" I asked.

She nodded into my shoulder.

How sad it is that a being so capable of so much sweetness should be afraid of joy, for joy is the birthright of all creatures, whether born of sea or land.

"You fear it because it might be taken away," I said.

She nodded again.

I cupped her chin and made her look into my face. Her eyes were dark and deep. Little flashes of moonlight danced in them. But the wounds within her, left from her old master, were poisonous and deep. They would cause her ending, as surely as my ending would come without my immortal skin, unless I could heal her.

And she could be healed if I filled that child-shaped space in her body. She would have a future in her descendants. Her grace and innocence would be as eternal as the waves.

"What if I said I could give you something now that would keep you here forever? Something born out of love?"

There was fear in her eyes, but there was also hope. "I want to stay," she said.

I kissed her gently—first her forehead, then her eyelids, her cheeks. She shivered when I kissed her lips.

My fingers feathered her silver scars, traced old designs from lost kingdoms down her breasts and belly. She laid still, transfixed, knowing that we were engaged in an even deeper healing than when I had worked on the wounds of her back. Only love could heal these wounds in her soul.

I moved down her body, taking the poison from her with my mouth and replacing it with light. When I came to the place in front of her spine, that sad, hollow, hurt place, she stopped me.

"What we do," she asked, "is this wrong?"

I looked up at her. I could not lie. It wasn't in my nature. "Some would say so. But they'd say you leaving your master was wrong, too. And yet you did."

She sighed, looking up through the flickering moonlight, her jaw working with unspoken words.

"Adrianne," I whispered her name across her skin. "What does your soul say is right?"

She reached for my fingers and placed one of my hands on her breast.

"This," she said.

She pushed my head between her thighs. "And this."

I smiled and dove into her warm, dark sea. And when her waves were breaking long and hard, the glimmering thing inside me blazed. My body grew a man-shaped stalk. And when I rose and entered her, I saw her eyes go wide in surprise. But there was also unspeakable delight. And that brilliant light in me that I could give to no one else surged between us, filling the sad, aching place in her. The gift was given, the deed done.

For this is the thing we water-children understand about love: it is a gift that comes in all forms and no one form is better than any other. We are each of us male and female within. It is only humans who have forgotten how to change with the dictates of the tides, and whenever they have discovered this capacity within us—to become what love demands—they have hated us for it.

For that reason, it is a secret we generally keep. But I was foolish and careless in my need, entranced by our beauty together. Little stars glimmered in her hair, and her body was like the skin of my long-forsaken people against my own. So I lingered just a little longer, a little too long.

And that is how John found us—our bodies joined, our hearts singing softly to one another. He ripped me from her body in horror. To his credit, he did not beat me or otherwise abuse me as I could see he very much wanted to do. He merely took me by the arm, dug my skin out of its oiled case in a trunk by the wall, and took me to the elders. They nailed my skin up for all to see and threw me in a hole dug in the sand in plain view of my skin, as a warning to everyone and a punishment to me.

And that is why I sit now, looking at my skin slowly petrifying on the wall, watching my own face disappear into the curves and lines of driftwood.

When they come for me, I see that Adrianne's belly is ripe with the child; she will deliver him in a few weeks. The light that was once inside me shines in her face. John will not let her approach me, and I hear her softly weeping. At first, I worried that he would harm her or the child, but I am relieved to see that his arm circles her protectively. He will raise the child as his own, though I know he will be hard-pressed to ignore my strange, sea-colored eyes looking out at him from the boy's face.

I hope Adrianne will stay with him. I believe that he will be as good to her as he once was to me. He will convince himself that I enspelled them both, that they are both victims. And he will be merciful to her for that reason.

But for me, there is no mercy.

I do not know what the village elders will do with me. I have long thought about it. I have long wondered what I wished. Anything seemed better than sitting down in that hole in my own filth, drinking what little water they saw fit to give me, chewing on scraps of fish hide or bone. I cannot remember how my body felt on the waves when I was with my brothers and sisters; I cannot imagine that water ever glided against my silk-smooth skin. I cannot remember what it was like not to boil with the heat of midday and shiver in the damp-fogged night.

They drag me out roughly and push me along across the sand. I glance at my skin hanging high on the chief's hut. If only I could run and leap; if only I could somehow call it down to me. But it is useless, hanging in the weather and away from me for so long; all the magic has leaked out of it. It could not take me home even if I could remove it from the nails on the wall.

They drive me over the dunes and my heart leaps when the ocean greets me with her long, green waves and cresting foam. I am comforted for the first time in many months. My brothers and sisters hide among the waves. I hear their songs but no longer understand their words.

Then, I see the stakes.

They shove me down and tie me spread-eagled on the sand.

John has the grace not to join them. He stands apart with Adrianne, refusing to meet my eyes or hear the pleas which leave my cracked lips against my will.

I do not want to beg for my life. If I am to die for giving love, then I would prefer to go with dignity. But there is no pride to be had in senseless murder. Killing a thing you do not understand does not truly extinguish it. The memory will still be there—in the waves, in the sand, on the faces of the children that come ever after.

There will be no more water and no more food. I will linger here, burned by sun, scourged by sand, lashed by wind and waves until at last I die. It will be long and painful, longer than it would be for a pure human. So close to the sea, the tides of my body strain to join it. So close to the sea, I am most alive.

It is night when something touches me, though I have lost track of how many nights it has been. My limbs hang like driftwood against the sand. The ropes break free. Or is it that my body is finally light enough to slip its earthly bonds and drift at last to sea? I drown in hands, fins, and sliding skin.

Pride
Melissa Mead

Just outside the village, Kayin paused to smear soot on his face and eat another handful of dried jana berries. The berries seemed to be working; his face had remained as smooth as a girl's through all his weeks on the savannah. A generous supply hung from the belt of his short skirt. Judging from the tenderness he felt higher up, the bitter fruits were on their way to giving him breasts, too.

"Well, it could be worse. They could be giving me moon cycles."

Kayin balanced the bundle of his aunt Zalika's clothes more securely on his head and strode into the village. He spotted the two-story council house right away, standing out among the grain fields and thatched huts. The men idling outside eyed him appreciatively, and he grinned. He hoped this village's landchiefs would be as easy to trick.

To Kayin's surprise, all five Chiefs were inside. The old woman with the gold pectoral on her chest had to be the wise Elephant Chief, and Kayin guessed that the short, plump woman and lanky young man in vigorous debate with her were the Talking Chiefs from the Baboon and Snake houses. The Baboon Chief was illustrating her point with conjured images of men and birds. Kayin, who shared his family's suspicion of both sorceresses and medicine men, edged away from them.

The remaining two Chiefs clashed fighting-sticks in more physical challenge. At first glance the muscular, massive Rhinoceros Chief looked like an unfair match for the slender woman opposite him.

That impression lasted about five seconds. The Rhinoceros could have overpowered the Lioness easily in a contest of brute strength, but her role was huntress, not warrior. She fended off her opponent with quick blows from her sticks, as though striking with cat's paws, then danced just out of range and darted back in to disarm him.

"Well done, Nyashia!" said her larger opponent with a rumbling laugh.

Kayin agreed. This Lioness was as impressive as any of his aunts, and nearly a match for his mother.

"I keep warning you about that last move, Abrafo, and you keep leaving yourself open. But who's this?" The Lioness turned, and Kayin abruptly found himself the subject of her full attention. He fought the impulse to step backward.

"My name is Kayin, Great Chief," he said, silently thankful that his name could suit either a boy or a girl. "I've come to join your village's Lioness Pride."

The woman stalked around him, examining him from all angles. Kayin hoped she saw a lithe, flat-chested girl and not a skinny, undersized boy.

"Why should I accept some smut-faced outsider? Weren't you good enough for your own village's pride?"

Kayin made a resigned gesture with a soot-smeared hand. "We were an insignificant village even before the bush fire. Now..." Kayin bowed his head, and saw the Lioness' fighting stance ease a bit. He looked up with hope in his eyes. "They say I carry a little of Lioness Zainabu's line in me"

Actually, as Zainabu's son and only child, Kayin had more than a little tie to that celebrated lineage, but a distant link was less likely to be investigated. Still, it was enough to widen Lioness Nyashia's eyes. The other Chiefs had gathered to examine him as well.

"You don't say. I hadn't heard that the great Zainabu had daughters to carry on her line. I'll consider giving you a trial, provided none of the other Chiefs object. But if I find out that you've lied to me about your lineage, you'll spend the rest of your life mending the other girls' spears and cleaning their kills."

Kayin nodded. After all, the Rhinos he'd met had already declared him beneath their notice, so if this didn't work he'd spend his life cleaning kills for his mother and aunts. At least here he'd do it without his mother's disappointment hanging over him.

"Her ambition speaks well for her," said the Snake Chief.

"You know I won't object to having another pretty girl around," said the Rhinoceros Chief, grinning.

The Baboon Chief was grinning too. The twinkle in the sorceress' eyes made Kayin nervous. "A lone survivor with a trace of famous heritage... You know how I love a good story, Nya. By all means, keep her."

The Elephant Chief took Kayin's chin in her hand and studied his face for a long while.

"That's a hard lineage to live up to, isn't it?" she said. "But I think you can do it."

Kayin bowed.

"This way, girl," said the Lioness Chief. It took Kayin a moment to realize that she'd addressed him, and the Lioness Chief scowled. When Kayin passed her, she hooked a foot around his leg to trip him.

Kayin saw the foot coming and reacted as he'd seen his aunts do; falling forward, rolling, and then bounding back up and turning to confront his attacker.

The Lioness Chief looked surprised. "Not bad! Maybe you do have the lineage. We'll see."

Over the next week the Lioness Chief took Kayin to the training grounds. Hour after hour he leapt over logs, stalked imaginary zebra, and threw spears at a grass target. Lioness Nyashia went on training the others just as though he weren't there. Kayin wasn't even sure the Chief even noticed his efforts until one day, without warning, she summoned him to stand in front of the pride and painted a yellow stripe down his nose. The other young Lionesses cheered. Kayin felt a smile spread across his face.

He'd done it. He was a cub in Nyashia's Lioness Pride.

Over the following weeks Kayin learned how little he'd mastered of the hunting skills his mother so cherished. He learned to stalk everything from lizards to eland, to make his own spears and traps, and to kill swiftly and cleanly. Most importantly, he learned to work with a team. Learning to hunt wasn't nearly as hard as living in a compound full of girls... young women, really... without giving himself away. Kayin soon got a reputation as a shy, hardworking youngster who always bathed alone and never let her hair grow long enough for the others to braid. He knew the activity helped the young huntresses relax after a day of drills and hunts, but it had the opposite effect on him.

"You really should let your hair grow, Kayin," said Ebele, the oldest of the Pride's girls still in training. "Otherwise the Rhinos will mistake you for a boy!" She rubbed his scalp-short curls and pulled him into a rough hug.

The Pride had laughed at his look of alarm. Kayin mumbled something about the heat, grabbed a water gourd and headed for the river. He dumped the first gourdful he drew over his head. It didn't help.

"Hot today, isn't it?"

Kayin dashed the water from his eyes. The young man addressing him topped him by at least a head, and his build would have marked him as a Rhino even he hadn't had a warrior's red stripe painted down the center of his face.

"I'm Buru, Lioness," he said.

"Kayin."

He'd hoped the brief answer would discourage the Rhino, but the young man lingered, watching while Kayin filled the water container.

"They say you're of Lioness Zainabu's lineage. That's impressive. Our Chief says that if you weren't a girl you'd make a good Rhino. Er, no offense meant, Lioness."

Kayin shook his head. "Lionesses feed the tribe. Rhinos kill other men. I wouldn't make a good one."

"Only because you're a girl."

"No, not that." Sour old hurts twisted in Kayin's gut. "You have to be tall to be a Rhino. Muscular. Solid. I'm too puny."

"Hey, don't listen to that kind of talk. Just because you hear it from some nobody..."

"From Lioness Zainabu."

"Oh. Well, still, she's a Lioness. What do women know about these things?"

Kayin just looked at him.

"Oh. Right. Sorry, Lioness. Um, I should get back to training."

"You do that."

Kayin hoped that the young man would respond to his coldness by avoiding him, but Buru seemed determined to make amends for his slip by following Kayin everywhere and praising every kill he made, even the rabbits. The Lioness Pride watched Buru's attentions with glee.

"Kayin's found herself a husband already! Did Buru really give you a set of bracelets, Kayin?"

"I hear he carries water for her."

"I hear he missed training to watch Kayin sprint."

"A Rhino, miss training? What did you do, Kayin? Get a love potion from the Baboons?"

Kayin refused the bracelets and ignored the stares. He sighed with relief when Buru and the other Rhinos went out on patrol.

They came back just a few days later, with a crowd of excited children running ahead of them. The village buzzed with gossip, especially when Chief Nyashia assembled all the Lionesses on the training field.

"What's going on?" Kayin whispered to Ebele.

"The Rhinos caught a spy. I believe your Buru is claiming credit."

"He's not my—"

Kayin stopped in mid-protest as Lioness Nyashia, with Rhino Chief Abrafo on one side and Buru on the other, followed the stranger onto the training ground.

Even dusty and bleeding from a split lip, Lioness Zainabu radiated confidence. Kayin wondered how many Rhinos it had taken to detain her. He suspected that his mother's split lip had much to do with the swelling bruise around Buru's left eye. She didn't walk like a prisoner, either. Buru and the Rhino Chief looked more like her honor guard than her captors. When Zainabu took

her place next to Lioness Chief Nyashia, the Chief looked honored,
not affronted.

Kayin cringed inside, even while holding himself at strict
attention. Lioness Zainabu had won them all over, as she always
did. They'd drag him out and humiliate him in front of the Pride...

"I'm Lioness Zainabu," said Kayin's mother to the Pride.
"Naturally, some of your Rhinos aren't about to just take my word
for that. I've had reports of a rogue lion, a man-eater, in this area.
I intend to prove my identity by bringing it back."

Lioness Nyashia stepped forward. "Lioness Zainabu has
graciously offered to choose one of the younger girls to carry her
spear. I'm sure you all understand both the honor and the danger
involved. If you wish to decline, step backward."

No one did. Some even stepped forward. Kayin held still and
tried to look inconspicuous. Lioness Zainabu scanned the line of
girls, back and forth, as though she were considering each one,
but inevitably her gaze fixed on Kayin.

"You. Come here, girl."

He strode forward, ignoring the disgruntled murmurs of
"She's just a cub!" and stood in front of both Lioness Chiefs. Buru
grinned at him. Kayin stared straight ahead. Even though he was
about to be revealed and shamed, at least his mother would have
to acknowledge that he'd taken the humiliation like a Lioness. He
took a deep breath.

"Well, what are you waiting for?" said Lioness Zainabu. "Pick
up my spear and let's get moving."

She strode off. Baffled, Kayin grabbed the spear and hurried to
catch up. To his horror, Buru followed.

"What are you doing?"

Buru didn't bother to whisper. "Is that really Lioness Zainabu?"

"Yes."

"Really? I thought she was lying. But even if she is Lioness
Zainabu, she's still a trespasser. The Rhinos are keeping an eye on
her until she brings back that rogue lion."

"Not just the Rhinos!" A girl bounded up to them. Unlike the sleek Lionesses, she was short and plump, with a quick impertinent smile. Painted blue bars shone on her cheekbones like uncanny second eyes.

"We don't need Baboons!" said Kayin and Buru at the same time. Even Zainabu stopped in mid-stride and scowled.

"Well, you've got me anyway. And one of the Snakes, Chinwendu, will be coming soon. By order of the Elephant Chief. I'm Imani, by the way."

Lioness Zainabu glared at the tail of students following her and stormed into the council house. The Elephant Chief smiled at her.

"Oh good. You found your Lioness."

"And a handful of hangers-on! I told you: I wanted to take one person with me, not every Chief's prize pupil!"

"I would have expected you to choose Ebele. Kayin's shown great promise, but Ebele's closest to joining the adult Pride."

"I chose Kayin. What I did not choose is this menagerie of other youngsters you've foisted onto me."

"Now, Lioness, surely you understand that Chiefs can't just let armed strangers wander into their villages. And since no one here can vouch for your identity..."

The old woman broke off, coughing, but Kayin had an uncomfortable feeling she glanced at him first. He kept silent. Buru shot him pointed looks, waiting for him to speak up, but kept his mouth resolutely closed.

The Elephant Chief sighed. "...you're in the Rhinos' custody until you bring back that rogue lion. I never send my warriors out without a healer along, and the young Lionesses are ready to begin learning to work with the Baboons."

"They don't need magical monkey tricks. I've never needed a sorceress to do my tracking for me!"

"But you had to learn to work with them during your training, yes? Kayin is no different."

Zainabu cursed, argued and finally, to Kayin's shock, pled with the Elephant Chief, but for once she didn't get her way, and the five of them headed out.

Lioness Zainabu stalked through the knee-high grasslands for hours without speaking. Kayin felt like he was five years old again, dragging his mother's hunting spear and hoping that she'd turn and notice him.

He wished Buru would stop noticing him. The young Rhino strode next to him with his chest stuck out, trying to look imposing. Lioness Zainabu and the apprentice Snake, Chinwendu, paid him no attention, but Kayin caught Imani trying to smother giggles behind her hand.

At last they reached the edge of the teakwood forest. Out of the blazing sun, Zainabu stopped, took a drink from a waterskin and offered at to the others. Kayin used his mouthful to wash down his daily handful of jana berries.

"Aren't you going to share with the rest of us, Lioness Kayin?"

He froze. "Um, you wouldn't want these, Great Chief. They're not really ripe. They're..."

She caught his wrist and looked. "Jana berries. So that's what you did." She released her grip. "Oh, Kayin."

"Don't be angry at her, Chief!" said Buru. "I don't mind that she didn't share."

Zainabu gave him a strange look. She caught Kayin by the arm and dragged him deeper into the privacy of the trees.

※

"Why, Kayin?"

"I didn't think you recognized me."

"My own son? My only child? Of course I knew you, Kayin! Even in that ragged old skirt. Even despite the jana berries."

"What are you doing here anyway? Who's governing the home Pride?" said Kayin.

"Your Aunt Zalika."

Kayin felt like he'd been gored. He looked down at his borrowed skirt. Aunt Zalika had been so eager to lend him her clothes, so enthusiastic about his plan. He'd thought she sympathized with his need to become the young Lioness his mother had so wanted.

"She wanted you to leave. She knew you'd come looking for me."

"Of course I came looking for you, Kayin! For all I knew you'd been kidnapped or killed." She paused, looking at his smooth face, his small but definite breasts. "I have to admit, this was one thing I didn't expect. What were you thinking?"

"That it would be better for everyone if you had a daughter instead of a son." Kayin returned her glance. For once Lioness Zainabu looked uncertain, and that brought Kayin's frustrations to a boil.

"It's all you talk about! Hunting, and the Pride, and how wonderful it is to be a Lioness. And now I'm one."

Lioness Zainabu shook her head. "No. A Lioness would never deceive her pridemates this way. Being part of a pride is about trust, Kayin!"

"I thought you'd be proud of me," said Kayin, looking at his feet.

"Kayin, I was always proud of you. If I wished for something that you couldn't be, well, that was my fault, not yours. From what I heard from Nyashia, you've become a skilled hunter, but you're not a Lioness. Perhaps you could become a Rhino."

"You know I wouldn't survive my first battle. And you always call them "second-rate butchers," anyway."

"Kayin, you can't go on deceiving Nyashia's Pride!"

"You recognized me. You deceived the Pride too. You knew, and you didn't..." Kayin stopped short. "There is no man-eater, is there? You were hunting for me. The only Lion around here is... me."

"Lion?" said a strangled voice. The voice rose to a scream. "Lion?" Buru surged forward and punched Kayin, knocking him to the ground.

"Did you think you were being funny?" The young Rhino kicked Kayin in the side. "Did you like making me look stupid?"

Buru bent his leg to kick again. Kayin grabbed his other ankle and hauled him off balance. Zainabu pinned him to the ground.

"Never asked you," Kayin grunted, trying to sit up without

feeling like he'd been stabbed in the lung. Hands pressed down on his shoulders and arms.

"Kayin's right, you know, Buru," said Imani. She and Chinwendu came to Kayin's side and gently made him lie down again. You've been mooning over her...I mean him... like a lost buffalo calf for weeks, even though Kayin did nothing to encourage you."

The reminder did nothing for Buru's temper. He bellowed and thrashed. Zainabu adjusted her grip, and he yelped and went silent.

To Kayin's humiliation, Imani and Chinwendu stripped off his shirt. Imani's eyes widened, but neither commented. She transformed a sheaf of leaves into clean cloth bandages and wrapped them around his ribs.

"Sh...He has to be able to breathe," Chinwendu protested. "And I don't think anything's broken."

"I'm not binding his ribs. You handle the healing. I'll stick to magic." Imani touched the bandage, and Kayin gasped in relief as a band of cold soothed his bruised sides.

Imani grinned. "Better?"

"Baboons are such show-offs," Chinwendu grumbled. He tended to the rest of Kayin's injuries in a more mundane fashion. Kayin lay still, chastened. The Talking Tribes were clearly more useful than he'd thought.

He limped back to the village, refusing offers of help from Imani and Chinwendu. At first he rebuffed their attempts to chat and joke with him, but when his mother marched along, staring straight ahead with a fixed expression, and Buru glared at him in red fury, hour after hour, he started replying just for the distraction. By the time they reached the village he had both Imani and Chinwendu laughing at the story of his first attempts at walking in a skirt.

His laughter died when they reached the council house. Small children had already run ahead with the news of Kayin's deception. A crowd had gathered to gawk at the returning party, and Kayin could hear Rhino Chief Abrafo and Lioness Nyashia shouting inside. Even Lioness Zainabu hesitated before entering, though she did enter, and the others followed.

Lioness Nyashia looked too angry to speak. The Rhino Chief had no such inhibitions.

"That...that undersized trickster has made a laughingstock of the whole village!"

Zainabu turned on the Elephant Chief. "I would have taken my son away, and no one would have been the wiser. Was it worth disgracing your village just to humiliate me?"

"Humiliate you, Lioness? I wasn't thinking about you at all. I was thinking about Kayin, who deserves better than to be smuggled away like a thief in the dark. I was thinking of this village, which could use someone of Kayin's skill. Kayin, come here."

Kayin came forward. The Elephant Chief frowned. "Those are some ugly bruises."

"I had a run-in with a maddened beast. Great Chief," said Kayin. He was careful not to look at Buru, but the young Rhino must have done something to hint at his guilt, because Chief Abrafo's furious expression took on a note of consternation.

"So; you're closer kin to Lioness Zainabu than any of us suspected."

"Well, some of us suspected," said the Baboon Chief, with that irrepressible twinkle in her eyes. "But Lionesses are so prideful about associating with the Talking Tribes that there was no way to be sure."

"Kayin's not bad, for a Fighting Triber," said Imani.

"Kayin is male," said Lioness Chief Nyashia, her voice chill. "I don't care whose line he's from; I will not be made a fool of in front my girls."

"But doesn't every pride need a Lion, as well as Lionesses, Great Chief?" Kayin begged.

"Not mine. By the Huntress, I'll run you into the dirt. I'll—"

"He's not under your authority any more, Nyashia," said the Elephant Chief.

"Let's go home, Kayin," said Lioness Zainabu.

"What?" Lioness Nyashia went rigid with rage. "This boy's just stained the honor of our Pride, of our village, and you're just going to let his Mama take him home?"

"No." Kayin bowed to Nyashia, the Elephant Chief, and the others in turn. "I have no skill at magic or healing, and no stomach for warfare. And my greatest debt is to Lioness Nyashia." He took a deep breath. "Not because of what my mother wants, not as a test of some disguise, but because I owe it to the Pride, I would earn her forgiveness."

"Impossible," said Lioness Nyashia.

Breaking all protocol, Kayin whispered in The Baboon Chief's ear. She frowned.

"If you're looking for a potentially excruciating way to die, that's an interesting method."

"I know. But do it, Great Chief. Please."

Eventually, the Chiefs consented. The Baboon Troop kept Kayin with them for a week, and Chinwendu and the Snake Chief came and went. News of Kayin's punishment raced through the camp. The Lioness Pride argued for days before sending Ebele to Chief Nyashia.

"We've decided, Lioness. The Pride wants Kayin back."

"You've decided? Aren't I your Chief?"

Ebele smiled. "But aren't we your Pride?"

Lioness Chief Nyashia snorted. "If Kayin survives, and can still hunt when the Baboons and Snakes are done with him, I'll consider it."

"Thank you, Great Chief. Oh, and we all think we're ready to start working with the Baboons."

Nyashia allowed herself a sour smile. "I think you're all looking for a source of gossip. Ask me when they're no longer holding Kayin."

All the Lionesses, Baboons and Snakes were watching when Kayin limped out of the Baboon's camp to stand before the Chiefs. Even some Rhinos came, although Buru wasn't among them.

"Great Chiefs, I've wronged this village," said Kayin in a voice an octave higher than it had been. "Pray allow me to make amends by hunting for you."

"Are you certain you're ready, Kayin? You seem in discomfort," said the Elephant Chief.

Kayin blushed and looked down at her feet. "It's nothing, Great Chief. Just a little...uh...."

From her place alongside the Pride, Lioness Zainabu laughed in realization. "Moon cycles! My son is now my daughter, and my daughter is a woman!"

Kayin gritted her teeth. "Mother..."

But now Lioness Nyashia was laughing too. "You didn't think you'd get all the benefits of being a Lioness and none of the pain, did you?" She shook her head. "I never thought you'd go through with this, but you truly are dedicated. Welcome to womanhood, Kayin. Welcome to the Pride."

Keeping The World On Course
Tanith Lee

Bianca: Why
Did you not tell me you were so strong?

Simone: Why
Did you not tell me you were beautiful?

A Florentine Tragedy
Oscar Wilde

They hated each other. It would be true to say, they had fallen
passionately in *loathe* from the first moment of meeting. Nor was
it only the other's appearance each one was so allergic to; their
individual manners, their voices and mode of talking, their very
accents—one of the country and one of the town—were in each
case unbearable to the other one. Each hated too the other's *clothing*.
They hated each other's hairdressing. They hated each other's personal possessions, (a small lunch-basket, a pair of scissors.) They
hated even the air the other inhaled and exhaled. At the rustle of
her dress, *his* spine would clench and his guts lurch, as if he had
just seen a particularly rare and dangerously venomous insect dive
through the room on a murder mission. At the tick of his watch
her heart would stamp its foot with nausea and rage.

Which was a little unfortunate not only for themselves, but
also somewhat for anyone else at all sensitive who occupied the
same large office in that building.

It was the Sunsea Building, by the way. Here many and various
aspects of sun and sea were presented, assessed, processed and
marketed to and for the surrounding areas. A very pleasant
environment this, normally, with living windows that showed
visions of rolling sapphire summer surf, walls decorated by

facsimilous shells, seaweeds, and deep ocean creatures, a solar roof
which dispensed the safest, purest, and most healthy sunrays from
dawn to dusk. Nor was the work ill-paid. Nor was it dull. Mtr
Molter had himself been quite contented there for two years. Until
she arrived: Mz Kyte, his demon. While she had been delighted on
arriving. Until she encountered Mtr Molter: *hers*.

Although polite and not unreasonable to anyone else about
them, both Molter and Kyte were rather aloof. Not exactly *guarded*,
more self-contained and seemingly self-sufficient. One realized *he*
possessed a large cat (or several cats perhaps) by the quantities of
fresh and cartoned deluxe cat food he occasionally returned with
from his lunch breaks. *She* apparently fed a lot of birds, judging by
the bags of bird nuts, seed, dried avian-alluring this and that which
sometimes accompanied *her*. Both were fastidious and wholesome,
though neither noticeably interesting in either appearance or
demeanor. For example, they were not 'closet' actors, writers,
musicians or aviators—like two thirds of the rest of the staff. They
did not throw or attend wild parties that lasted all the four days
every staff member took weekly for his or her leisure. Nor did they
ever pull up at the building's gates in exquisite vehicles, or have
themselves collected by fascinating persons. That they had families
seemed unlikely.

She was about thirty-five or six, pale, fairly tall. He was
apparently twenty-nine, swarthy, clean-shaven and shaven-headed.
That was all one could say as to their physical distinctions.

However, when Mtr Molter had to go by Mz Kyte's station, or
to endure her passing his own, such a burning volatile horror and
annoyance radiated from him it was difficult for anybody to ignore
it. But he at least was silent. Should *she* closely encounter *him*, her
smoldering repulsion tended to erupt from her with a tiny yet
unnerving sizzling sound. As if she were actually on the boil.

Once and once only, they had been forced by circumstances to
find themselves, along with ten staff colleagues, inside one of the
spacious, reliable, and well-designed elevators.

Afterward the rest of the people present had not known what

to do: whether to laugh, shriek, or flee the premises in a panic attack. For throughout the single brief flight—lasting only one story since both Molter and Kyte had instantly pressed the panel for the very next floor, and rushed out in opposite directions the moment the car landed—the two haters had reached a crescendo of hostility. During this they both made weird noises, she sizzling and hissing, even he rumbling and roaring under his breath. While an invisible twin electric charge of complete detestation had swelled like a psychic plague bubo, threatening momentarily to explode and kill everyone else in the lift.

୭

The town stood on a plateau among hills. From its brink it was possible, on clear days, to see as far as a great city miles off below. In modern times the old carriage ways down to the valley had been expanded into roads, and a selection of steps and mechanical devices put in to carry people up or down. Aside from these, a railway was cut through the hillside over a century before, and this too, fairly effortlessly, brought visitors to and from the town.

Even so, the town never seemed quite used to strangers. It often thought it still saw them in persons who had already lived there some while. Or, conversely, mistook someone or other on a day trip for a long-established resident.

Lalilda was quite aware she fell alternately into both these categories., She was sometimes greeted as a familiar. On different occasions remarked as a newcomer.

That she was often *noted* was as a rule less the product of any mistake, than because she was very beautiful. Darkly red hair hung shining halfway down her back. Her skin was creamy and seemed quite flawless. Always dressed most immaculately and in the foremost of artistic contemporary fashion, her clothing yet remained decorous. Her skirts inclined to length; her necklines did not plunge. Her hands, feet, nails, make-up, were all perfect. Between darkened lids and long black lashes, the pale intense blue of her turquoise eyes was piercing almost as a double moonrise.

On this particular night, some two and one third years since she had first come to live in the town, Lalilda was going for her evening stroll. She did not, admittedly, stroll out on every evening. (One might assume she was either too tired then, or busy elsewhere.) After the stroll, which involved a park and three or four tree-lined avenues, and ended in the town square with its softly lighted dolphin fountain, she intended to have supper, in solitary splendor, at a glamorous café named The Bay Tree. For these events she wore a long dress of flame red silk, tied at the waist with a scarf of black lace stitched with crimson brilliants. Her high-heeled crimson shoes struck nimble little bell notes from the paving; her walk was graceful, and displayed her wonderful figure, slender yet full-breasted, to great advantage.

It was on the third of the avenues that she became alert to someone who seemed more than usually intrigued by her. A single glance over her shoulder next revealed that she was being followed.

This had, now and then, happened before. Generally nothing came of it, or nothing more than a courteous or mildly enthusiastic advance from some man or other, whom, to his often evident distress, she would always gently and firmly answer with No.

In this instance though, Lalilda experienced a most unusual stab of alarm.

The one who tonight was following her she had previously herself *noticed* in the park. Normally Lalilda did not pay much attention to any other human thing on her strolls, or adjacent to her solo suppers. It seemed rather as if she might have had enough of other people during her working hours. But this fellow had caught her eye. A youth, or very young man, he had been sitting idly on a tree-hung bench, and beneath an ornamental lamp, apparently engrossed in a book. She had glanced at him, than away. *Then* surreptitiously back again. He had jet-black hair tied back from his face in a long tail. It was a cruel face too, fine-boned and heartless, with long black brows, a long chiseled nose and long, narrow, sensual mouth. She had not thought he was aware of her swift scrutiny. His eyes remained downcast on his book. But for someone who did not want to look about, he seemed intent on being the focus of all eyes. His clothes were flamboyant, cut in a current male fashion called *Arrogance*: a black-green satin coat with embroidered sleeves, a shirt whose snow-white lace and ruffles might have been copied from the princely wear of the 1600's, black trousers so form-fitting they would leave less than nothing to the imagination, and black leather boots with a score each of buckles in green quartz.

Of course, he was handsome. Lalilda, being no fool, had to admit this. But no doubt, his eyes would be the weak feature. Probably too small, lackluster, unintelligent, full of appetites or only stupidities, lacking all fire. And for *that* reason the book was his excuse to keep them hidden.

Alas. The single brief glimpse she had now gained of him, as he patrolled with lion-like, casual *determination* behind her, revealed his eyes to be, of all his excellent facial attributes, possibly the best. Long-lashed as her own, and of the coolest grey, unblinkingly, thinkingly, they were fixed only on herself.

After this she was conscious of him at every step. Conscious of how her walk must look to him, the lithe sway of her hips and dancer's waist, the backs of the red stems of her heels. Her wave of hair.

Lalilda, to her deep dismay, realized she had, even under close restraint, become aroused. Which now made her every step into an aggravation, between extreme excitement and, frankly, fright.

He isn't, Lalilda sternly told herself, *looking at me. He is simply going in the same direction. And why should he take any special note of me? He's YEARS younger—oh ten at least. Nor is he unworldly or naïve. That's quite obvious from his face! He seems to have undertaken all sorts of adventures and crimes and is old beyond his years—only his extreme youth—oh the wretch is probably only SIXTEEN—prevents him from being raddled. Just wait a year or two, my boy. Then how handsome will you be?* But that thought, even more alarmingly, filled Lalilda with an awful sadness and pity. Oh God, she wanted to protect him from himself. This was hopeless.

And—he was spoiling her lovely evening, to which always she looked forward so much.

Lalilda thought, *If I slow down, halt, pretend occupation with, say, my shoe—he'll simply go past me.*

Sensible and furious, she consequently stopped, and did (*without thinking?*) the most lascivious thing she could then have done. She bent flexibly down the whole length of one leg, and drew off her right shoe to examine it. By which gesture, giving the young man a most entrancing view of her small yet rounded bottom, gleaming like soft fire in its stretched silky sheath of dress.

Now she was straight again, fiddling with the shoe. One foot was, because of this, three inches higher than the other. Inevitably she wobbled. At that instant there came a firm, warm hand beneath her elbow, to steady her. Or to unsteady.

Appalled, if thrilled, she found herself looking directly into the face of her pursuer, at last a mere foot or so from her own.

"May I assist you, madam?" he asked in a light tenor voice the color, (to Lalilda's ears) of refined carob chocolate mixed with ice.

"No, thank you. You may not."

"But I already have, you see."

"I do *not* see."

"If you don't see, and a tragedy," said the gorgeous young man, "that eyes of such blue beauty should be blind, then I feel even *more* obliged to assist."

"You are obliged to do nothing!" snapped Lalilda, enraged at his word-play. "Unhand me, sir."

He grinned—his teeth were white as stars—and let her go.

She nearly toppled. So he caught her back again, now by both shoulders, and smiled delightedly into her "blue beauty" of eyes. Perched on tiptoe on one side, and the other on the three inches provided by a shoe, she found he was now her exact height.

"Madam," he said, "I am, by name, Zaivenn. That will answer your unspoken question. Therefore I shall ask mine, as follows: Do you believe in love at first sight?"

Zaivenn had in fact been in the town for less than five months.

Like Lalilda, although at that juncture he did not of course know it, he too spent a lot of his evenings in his new apartment. He studied literature and read a great deal. Coming out into the town on those nights when in the mood for it, he still tended to sit in the park or the square, to read a book or make notes. When he went to dine, frequently at an elegant restaurant named The Serpent's Egg, (which possessed a genius chef) he also continued his studies. They were used to him there, couthly eating his meal and sipping his (sometimes eccentric) choice of drink, (black burgundy with a raspberry torte, vodka with roast beef) and all the while a book before him. He did however study too the other customers. Under cover of reading or deep thought, a deal of spying might be disguised. Especially women were the objects of Zaivenn's pensive, decadent and hungry gaze.

Until tonight, even so, allure had never blossomed into desire. Indeed, he had once or twice misled a young woman, by some frivolous flirting look or aside, to believe he was engaged by her. Only to put her off with a rather sadistically apologetic regret.

Lalilda though had, he reckoned, bloody well got the better of him.

Confound her, he thought, in an entirely hidden whirlpool of reluctance and rampant lust, *what is she? Some wretched witch? She has* *ensorcelled me—I'd like to have her on this very spot, I'd like to kiss and lick her to* *death, I want to ride her and make her faint. God above, this is utter madness. I've* *always managed to escape this torment in the past! Why now? Oh, she's beautiful* *beyond bearing, I'll give her that. Those* EYES—*that* BODY—*and the scent of her—* *cedar and night-blooming jasmine—God, God, I'd like to dive into her skin and* *swim about in her and drown. I'm lost. I'm done for. I deserve every unspeakable* *punishment which is now going to fall on me, witless oaf that I am.*

"Do you," he had asked her, "believe in love at first sight?"

The woman with red hair like the sheen on mahogany, like burgundy, like the planet of war—met his eyes with two turquoise daggers and said, "Perhaps. But this, sir, isn't *that.*"

"How do you know?" he said, with a flawless playful lightness, while his heart galloped about in his breast like an insane horse, and threatened to kick him unconscious.

"You're drunk," snarled Blue Eyes.

"Drunk on *you*."

"Let go," she said."

"Then," he said, "put on your shoe. If I let go of you now, you'll tumble on the street."

"Very well." (Even her scowl was delicious.)

And alas again. *Because* he held her, she could not don the shoe without leaning against him.

Both of them drew a simultaneous gasp of shock and ecstatic agony. Currents of hot electricity ran through either equally. For half an instant, she became limp. He found the strength then to support her. He saw tears gleam in her fiery eyes, only increasing their incandescence.

He was both drunkenly pleased, and ashamedly sorry. He wished to protect her from himself.

Then he found she had kicked off the other shoe. Now three inches shorter than he, the unknown sorceress took his face in her hands, and pressed her delirium of a mouth to his.

Never in his life had Zaivenn enjoyed a kiss of such profundity. Their two tongues met like snakes and married like swans. Their bodies grew together and sailed up into the sky and hung there, burning bright, she at his mercy, he at hers.

"My name is Lalilda," she whispered, as she drew away and they discovered themselves still on the street. He reached for her but she moved aside. "Say my name."

"Lalilda," he murmured. "Lalilda, I love you. And if I don't make love *to* you, it will kill me."

And he thought *Fool, fool, shut up. It can never happen and you damn well know it can't, you damnable blockhead.*

And "No. No, no," she muttered.

But she was trembling. As was he.

He said to her, "Promise me this. Think about me. Take time. Make a decision on me—joy or death sentence—whatever it must be. Then meet me tomorrow where first I saw you—and you me, I believe. The park bench by the tree under the lamp."

"I—" she faltered. How husky her voice, but so low and sweet. She would sing contralto, he thought. He thought, *I have gone mad.*

"Promise me. You can't deny me that, Lalilda."

She said, now so very low and softly he barely heard her, "I promise, Zaivenn. I will meet you tomorrow, and at the same time. But only to bid you goodbye."

Then she turned, and barefoot, she strode away from him, such long strides, graceful still, but as if to eat the paving up and put as much distance as she could between them.

I'd do better to shoot myself tonight, he thought.

No, I'll wait. Just to see her once more.

ॐ

Lalilda entered her apartment building by the back way, and ran upstairs. Locked inside, she noted her cat, a huge black and white female also of nocturnal habits, was still out. As well; Lalilda was beside herself with anguish and despair.

Standing in the bedroom before the long mirror she tore off her dress, her underclothes and essential accessories. She tore the lustrous wig from her shaven head, so the adhesive strips that held it secure scorched her scalp. With harsh hateful blurring strokes she smeared the make-up from her face and neck, hands, legs and feet, and posed there, glaring in at her ruin. For now she was Lalilda no longer. Now she was truly (though *never* in truth) a short, thin young man of twenty-nine, who knew that even before nine the next morning, his first unwanted stubble would be faintly bristling jaw, arms and legs.

You fool! Screamed Lalilda in his head. *What have you done?*

But never until now had temptation of this sort come to him. Neither woman nor man had ever inflamed him to longing and sexual desire. Or worse, far worse. To *love.*

Zaivenn—that handsome and glorious man, that youthful god.

Again, "You fool," he said, but not in his thoughts, instead aloud in his bitter broken masculine voice with its accent of the town. The voice that lacked all the honey and the crystal of *Lalilda,* the woman he became when dressed. The woman he truly was.

"You godforsaken fool," said Mtr Molter. And wept.

Zaivenn entered his own apartment by a back way, and quite slowly and with the usual lack of eagerness. Not, that was, because his home was unpleasant, quite the reverse, nor even because his crow, a huge black male bird with a single white circle round the left eye, was as ever nocturnally absent. Zaivenn wished very much the crow had tonight decided to stay in. But then, he wished the same about himself.

Sluggishly, he stripped off outer garments, underclothes and bindings, and out rolled the necessary appendage with which, the trousers being so fashionably tight, it was always wise to equip himself. There he stood then, in front of the mirror, a very slim, full-breasted woman of rather above average female height, and stared at a face that now, Zaivenn believed, was a thickly-browed, pop-eyed travesty, having raw bones and an ugly nose and chin. With squeamish vitriol he—now she—rinsed the dark powder off her brows, lashes and hair, and twisted the latter up into the nasty knot she effected when at work.

Tears ran down that lessened face, and seemed to drain the grey eyes of all their depth and color.

"Fish eyes," brutally she said aloud. "You love her? Well. If she could see you now, that lovely, sensational, stunning woman—If she knew—oh, how she'd laugh. Or probably she'd scream for the police."

"I wish I was dead!" shouted Mz Kyte, in her country accent and her shrill voice which, when a male, she never had. She shouted at her reflection, and therefore the reflection shouted it right back at her.

Never mind. Looks *could* kill. Tomorrow she would meet her only love, under the tree. And, on hearing the truth, Lalilda would cut her fatally through with scimitars of turquoise.

The next day was the last day of the working week for half the staff at the Sunsea Building. Among these were Mtr Molter and Mz Kyte.

Everyone else seemed rather happy. Molter and Kyte, however, did not seem happy at all. Each of them was sunk in an almost psychopathic gloom, in the course of which they spilled water and tea, broke pens in two or four in their fingers, shouted in wild rampages at their work, and misheard everything that was said to them, causing an outcry of absurd proportions. "I asked you about the contract for Rose Fun Bookings—I did not tell you you had put your nose on crooked!" exclaimed a colleague, cowering behind paperwork as Mz Kyte stooped towards him like a bird of prey. "I didn't! I didn't!" squealed another colleague, running away from Mtr Molter, who seemed to have swollen up like a short balloon, "I didn't say to him he ought to wear stilts. I only mentioned my brother's kilt—"

This pandemonium reached a climax less than fifteen minutes before everyone was due to go home. Very unluckily, both Kyte and Molter had needed to go on some minor errand, and both had sprung up and come marching from their stations, evidently barely seeing anything else in the world. They met almost in collision at the center of the office floor.

A hush of hypnotized dread enveloped the scene. Out of it Kyte and Molter raised their heads, she white as bleach, and he purple as a burst aubergine.

"Out of my way, you pathetic scum!" yowled Mz Kyte.

Mtr Molter growled like a feral cat. "Don't talk to me, you filthy bitch," he added.

"How such rubbish as you dares to work at this place is beyond me," elaborated Mz Kyte.

"How does *anybody*, with you here? One look at you should empty the building!" extemporized Mtr Molter.

Some of the other employees were meanwhile sidling away around the desks, aiming to get out by the exit before this confrontation should escalate into full-scale war. Others only hung there, stone still, petrified as if by a gorgon.

But precisely then both Molter and Kyte spun around, and

bounded headlong, (as before, after the elevator) in opposite directions, scattering books, papers, discs, unsecured electrical equipment and chairs as they did so. Both Kyte and Molter were also later reported to have been mumbling the same phrases, which had to do with last straws breaking their backs, or last nails being knocked in their coffins, or ropes for hanging being too good, etc.

Then the jolly celebratory music came on that indicated the workday had ended.

All and sundry fled the building. Which, fortunately indifferent, spread wide its solar beams and cleaned itself with golden light.

"It stayed with me, the scent of her," Zaivenn said to the crow, who sometimes remained in the apartment while they both got ready for the evening. "How can that be? That perfume of cedar—jasmine—her *skin*—even when that *bastard* got in my way at the office. Oh, I'll kill him one day, I swear it. But no, I shan't live to kill him, the bastard. I'll be dead myself. *She'll* kill *me* tonight." (His marvelous garments were all purest white for his meeting with Lalilda. When she pierced him through the heart, he wanted the blood to show.)

The crow, having spruced himself up with a good preen, took a drink from his beaker and ate a nut, then glanced meaningfully at the high window, always left ajar for his convenience.

"Too much to hope you'll come back early to comfort me," said Zaivenn. "Don't trouble, old friend. I know you can make your own living. And I know you're faithless, too. That swine who feeds you roast chicken in the next apartment house. You won't miss me."

The crow shrugged, (as they do) and flew up and out into the sunset.

Zaivenn took one last brooding look at his handsome image in the glass. As if he bade himself also farewell.

"How I detest her, that monster," Lalilda said to the cat, who sometimes remained in the apartment while they both got ready for the evening. "I'd kill her if I could. I'd poison her, or strangle—no, never that, how could I bear to touch her. And to have the impertinence to have *grey* eyes—I never before noticed she had them. But almost the same color, that... *silvery* color—but not like, how could they be—not like *his*. Oh God, what am I going to do? I'm going to my execution." (She had dressed for it, too, all in deepest black, with little black ankle boots only one inch high so *he*, her beloved nemesis, should be taller by two inches. As he watched her die from his fatal blow.)

The cat, having spruced herself up with a good lick and polish, took a drink of milk and ate a small sardine, then squinted purposefully towards the high window that, via the roof, gave access to a handy cat-supporting creeper going down to the street.

"Too much to hope you'll miss me," said Lalilda. "Even if I live, I'll only be a shell. Never mind. That's all I ever was. And I know you're faithless, half the block feeds you. Good luck, sweetheart."

The cat smiled, (as they do), and sprang up to the window and out into the dusk.

Lalilda took one last startled look at her lovely image in the glass. As if seeing herself for the very first time.

❧

Life being life, the Place of Execution was dressed for a festival, ribbons and multicolored paper lanterns tied to the lamp standards, vendors of food, drink, dolls and various trinkets spread along the walks and under the trees, people everywhere, a band and dancing on the central lawn.

The agitated hearts of both Lalilda and Zaivenn stuttered in affront. In their darkest and most desperate hour there was to be no privacy. In fact, they were to have an audience.

She, approaching like a slender black wolf in fear of traps, found him pacing like a caged starved white puma beneath the familiar tree. Its leaves shove like a fierce lime-green beacon from the doubled lamplight. And off to one side the band played danced tunes and love songs.

"This is madness!" she exclaimed.

"Madness, he agreed, with a snap of his white teeth.

But he came to her at once, and towering over her by the full two inches, took her icy hand in his icier one.

"Where can we go?" she moaned.

"Anywhere but this bloody circus."

"Only to say goodbye," she said.

"Wait. Wait -" he begged her. "Not yet—"

"Not yet then ... no, not yet—"

A drum-roll cracked the air, which was already endlessly fracturing with raucous laughter, the clink of glasses, the lumbering of gladsome if unskilled dancers, the sputter of snacks frying and coffee bubbling and cheap if quite tasty champagne being relieved of its corks, not to mention jingle bells, and the squeak and twitter of disturbed birds, who thought dawn had returned too soon. The drum-roll portended the start of a lush waltz. On the bandstand a portly popular singer with a fine voice stepped forward to great applause.

The clapping broke inside the ears of Zaivenn and Lalilda like a million glass pipettes crunched under the feet of an invading army.

And now, Oh God, (if very charmingly) the singer ladled on the air romantic helpings of love.

Lalilda closed her eyes. "Leave this to me," said Zaivenn. He threw his arm about her and steered her through the writhing press. Past red lips and sparkled eyes and children covered in ice-cream and flower-sellers and strawberry-colored lanterns. And all the time the song sang on: *l'amour, l'amour, l'amour...qui fait le monde... la ronde*—

The lovers had reached, (mostly due to Zaivenn's determination, and merciless boots and elbows) the farthest edge of the park. The noise, the music, were fainter. Outside the gate a long avenue, lit only by ordinary street lamps, and many of these half-smothered in the foliage of trees, beckoned like a cloister.

They hurried into it, and beneath the wall, dashed themselves into each other's arms. "How I've missed you—so much—your touch, your scent, your hair, your voice—" "How have I lived without you all this misery, this century of time—"

At last, panting and wrung out as if after a long frantic swim to shore from a sinking ship, they drew apart and stared into each other's souls.

"And do you now mean to say goodbye to me for ever?" he asked.

"I must," she said. "Oh no," she said. "How can I? But what else...."

"This."

Back into the sea they went, and swam again in the deluge of the storm. *L'amour l'amour... le monde... la ronde...*

Exhausted a moment, when next they drew apart, standing hand in hand as, since history's earliest human sunrise, lovers have stood, they made a temporary plan.

Zaivenn: "There is a hotel. No, I've never been to it, but it lies behind a restaurant I know, in quite a decent street. Not to do anything but talk. We'll sit all across the room from each other, and drink iced coffee."

"To talk," she echoed. "Oh, if I say a word—"

"We must," he said.

Lalilda: "You have no idea what my honesty will cost me."

"Nor you," said he, "what the cost will be to me."

"It's better we should end this now," she said.

"Then," he said, "walk away from me. I swear I won't follow you, though my life will go out at once, like a candle flame."

"How can I leave you when you say such things?"

Hand in hand they walked quietly down the avenue, entered a boulevard, crossed it, moved in among a selection of gardened buildings, and over narrow roads where vehicles sometimes edged along, or other walkers sometimes went by. Most of these last turned their heads in wonder, seeing two people of such great beauty, and so well matched, moving so steadily, but as if to the strains of a funeral march and never a song of love.

The private sitting room in The Sweet Apple Hotel had furnishings of pink and green, and they were served their coffee and little emerald liqueurs on a silver tray.

No prettier stage-set could have been devised for the tragic, and potentially violent, melodrama that had now to be begun.

Both heroes of it were finally blank white with terror, shaking and half dead.

It therefore seemed to them only the smallest step to take, to plunge right over the precipice.

"I love you," Lalilda said. "But any liaison with you is impossible. There is a single reason."

Zaivenn nodded. "I might say the very same to you. I love you. My chance with you is non-existent. There is a single reason."

"I'm not what I seem," she said.

He was, despite himself, surprised. "You are not?"

"Perhaps," she said, "we should say no more—"

"I am not," said Zaivenn, "a *man*."

Lalilda gave a faint shriek.

"You see," he said. "There. There's no more to say. It's done," he went on, ignoring his own statement. "Never in my life— *never*—no one—none but you. I couldn't resist. You're all I want. I *knew* you the instant I saw you, as if I *remembered* you. But it's useless. You're a woman and I am—not a man. I—am—I am a—a *woman* too. Save I'm not. Not the true self of me. But physically, in the body I was cursed with, I'm a woman. A woman. A woman." Then he bowed his head and added, in a low raw voice, still masculine, but all broken again, like a strong sword defaced by a hammer, "Do you want to see? I can show you. I'd rather die at once. But if you want, or need—"

"I," interrupted Lalilda in a high thin wail, "am *not* a woman. I'm a *man*. I'm ugly and thin and stupid. But really I'm none of that. I'm what you saw and loved, and she—*she* saw and loved *you*. And you *are* a *man*. To me, a man. But now I must go away." She got up and valiantly lifted her head. "Show me and tell me nothing else. Nor will I. If we must strip our psyches to the *bones*, as we have, why do we need to do to ourselves anything worse?"

Zaivenn leapt to his feet. He stood glaring at her, while she glared back. They glared as if they hated each other. As if their predestined love, created somewhere other than on Earth, had ended with their first earthly meeting in a sunny room full of shells and sea-horses and octopuses, on finding, each of them, that the other was *not* as expected—as *promised*: and posed there wrongly a woman and there wrongly a man. And so they had loathed each other on sight, and wished to kill each other, for coming into the world in such a ridiculous disguise, Lalilda a *male*, Zaivenn a *female*. As if to hide, each of them, not only from the other, but from their betrothal already made, millennia ago, in heaven.

Zaivenn said, as he had not, before, "*What is your name?*"

Lalilda told him. "Molter. I work at—"

"I know where you work. Oh *God!*" shouted Zaivenn, so the drinks on the silver tray shivered almost as much as he did. "And who in hell do you think *I* am, then?"

Lalilda turned her face. "No."

"Yes. *Kyte!*" Zaivenn roared. And then, in a whisper, "I am Kyte. The Sunsea Building. I could tear you in piece—" he said. "I could break you in shreds of silk and alabaster—I could eat you alive—"

"And I," she screamed, "could dismember you and sew you inside my heart—"

Zaivenn crossed the intervening space and caught Lalilda to him. He held her fast against his body. And as she felt the flowering of his desire press through every pore of his skin, and so through hers, so he in turn felt her—that *other* part of *her*, that still *male* part—flower hard as iron against his center, her center, his.

"Do it then," said Zaivenn, "rip me in shreds, sew me inside you. Just don't tear the binding where it holds my—how shall I say—upper story in."

"And you," said Lalilda, gripping him close, rubbing against him, "eviscerate *me*. But mind *my* breasts, if you would. They're very comfortable, you see."

"They feel quite real...."

"And so do *you*. Is this my erection or yours?"

"Both."

Hysterically they laughed, and laughing went into the other room, in which a sumptuous emperor of a bed stood smilingly waiting, covered in sheets the shade of sunrise.

Nightlong the bell of the hotel named for an apple rang to the immense and stifled cries of love. They were loud less in volume, than through their intensity and ravishment.

All over the town, the plateau, against the pelted sides of hills, through the train tunnel (in a sweetly louche appropriateness) up into the star-strung harp of the sky, the double hymn of rapture flew. Across the little streets and noble avenues, a black and white cat paused, raising one semi-translucent ear; a crow dozing in a tree opened his white-eyeliner eye.

They rose breast to breast, man and woman, woman and man, locked together, two perfect severed halves, rejoined and mended.

Kissing and sighing, singing and calling, mastering, mastered, re-mastered, moving like a beautiful mad mechanism from the dark into the light into the dark into the light—

Ah, who invented this paean of the flesh? Some great composer of symphonies. Some god or God or Humanity itself, in a very talented moment, some genius too powerful to remember, too mysterious to forget.

The joy, The unspoken words made into a song. And this peerless music added. Since there it was; *l'amour qui fait le monde... la ronde:* Love which moves the sun and the other stars—love which makes the world go round.

"Kiss me." "I'll never stop." "Who are you?" "Your self." "And I am you."

"I never wanted a surgeon's knife," both of them later confessed, "to pare me into another shape. I hadn't the money anyway, or the faith. And too, some strand within me, perhaps, was woven in the prefigurement of that other thing *you* also are.

"This outer image we put on, the *real* one," they said. "The truth of me. Wearing my heart on my sleeve. Wearing my *soul* on my sleeve."

Love. What is love? Nothing, of course. Although it moves the sun and the other stars, and keeps the spinning world on course.

స్త్రీ

Perhaps predictably, the office in the Sunsea Building regarded the new state of affairs as both silly and amusing. No one was rude enough actually to laugh out loud at the couple in their presence. Few were perceptive enough not to, everywhere else. Oh the hilarity. *Kyte* and *Molter*, in a union! Gazing or winking at each other, sometimes all across the desks, going to meal-breaks arm in arm, he in his broad-soled shoes and she in her flat ones, and she still an inch or so the taller. And she a good six or seven years older than he was, too. But such adoring looks they cast at each other. 'Love's Young Dream' all right. As if they had no idea at all what they, and *this*, must seem like to everyone else in the building— even the town. (Or as if, frankly, they did not care?)

Mind you, it was a relief, was it not, to have these tender smirks and hand-brushings if they had to pass each other in the room, as opposed to the tumult before. In fact, (no one admitted at all to this) their lovingness fell all about on everybody, like a soothing and much needed summer rain. Laugh at them as the rest might, the rest yet experienced some strange periphery pleasure that, for the most part, they were all far too limited to grasp. Even that handful of colleagues, traveling one day ten floors up in the elevator that also bore Mz Kyte and Mtr Molter, and came staggering out, merry as if at a wedding, slightly nicely drunk and oddly aroused, giving each *other* hugs and meaningful looks, as if the wing of the love-god had tickled them. When it had only been the proximity of the ridiculous K and M, kissing each other the lightest kiss upon the lips.

They loved each other. They loved everything about each other.

The other's dull work clothes, the other's eccentric, pedantic ways. Their different accents—which now each could put on, or leave off. They even loved each other's personal possessions—the little lunch-basket, the pair of scissors. And seemingly they each loved also the other's pet, he often arriving now with a bag of avian treats, she with a bag of feline ones.

But too, their love was, plainly, like a secret, from which everyone else was always inevitably excluded, left out as quite irrelevant. The outsiders might only, with a pastel, unconscious envy, peer in passing through the curtain—which was the *visible* aspect of the love of Kyte and Molter. And the curtain, really, was unpeerable through. Unreadable shadows merely vaguely appeared on it, (for example, the kiss in the lift) perhaps thrown their by the radiant inner (hidden) lamp that had been lit by lovelight. But the shadows were never enough to reveal such a thing. No proper clue; no slightest hint. What could one do then but scoff and laugh at them? As so often people find they must, at miracles.

And after work, as Kyte and Molter wandered away into their private lives, in a sort of daze and dream, shining in the rays of the late afternoon, they seemed to melt into the golden light. Out of which, now and then, that other couple occasionally reappeared., the red-haired beauty with her handsome black-haired companion. For certain, nobody mocked the slight just visible difference in *their* ages—she just a touch the elder. (Nor did anyone realize that in this case, a man passing superbly as female may well look a little older than his age, while a woman passing with similar finesse as a male will, generally, seem just a little younger than her years.)

In the town, this beautiful pair of lovers were, undeniably, sometimes speculated upon. Yet a certain surreal royalness about them prevented any definite intrusion. Gossip restricted itself to the normal manner of the town. That was, sometimes they were recognized as life-long residents; sometimes taken for utter strangers, alien and intoxicating as if only recently landed from the planet Venus.

And was there a home for any of these wonders to go to? Indeed there was. What must that then be like? It was relaxed and happy and humorous. A match of partners lived there, Mtr Molter and Mz Kyte. But then did the *Venusian* partners also live there? Of course they did, on those *other* days and nights. The days and nights when, dressed to kill with all the finest erotic weaponry, not Kyte and Molter but Zaivenn and Lalilda came together, two arrows each seeking the other's heart, and finding it. Then the 'home' flamed like a volcano, and shook and bellowed with ecstasy, so not a brick or stone of the town did not sense it. And the rain of diamond fire that fell then everywhere—a wonder a single street lamp was ever needed, or a single star.

As for the cat and the crow, they fought like cat and crow, since for a while they hated each other. In a later while they came to scent upon each other the personal perfume of their original friends, Kyte and Zaivenn, Lalilda and Molter, these endearing aromas now always mingling with their own of Crow and Cat. In the end, the cat, fed and stroked often by Zaivenn, and the crow, fed and smoothed equally by Lalilda, (and witnesses besides to every pheremonally tasty transport), grew resigned.

Not a year after their initial introduction, by which time all four (or six) flat-mates were sharing a single spacious apartment, the crow and the cat would occasionally go out together at night, return together at dawn—more or less—the bird flappily flying down or up, the cat slithering and clawing through another handy creeper. They would sleep against each other when the fancy took them, fur to feather. It had been known for the crow to groom the cat, or the cat to permit the crow to ride on her back. Once in a while, one would bring the other a small gift from the outside environ. The types of which (the nature of animality being what it presently is) are better left undescribed.

But the bliss of their human companions must, ultimately, prove also beyond description. Even those who regularly visit heaven and return, can seldom recollectively retain enough of its splendors to tell anyone—as the light of the sun blinds, so making it invisible. But, seen or unseen, the sun still lights the sky. *l'amour qui fait le monde la ronde.* Mz Kyte and Mtr Molter are doing their duty by the world.

A Bitter Taste
Aliette de Bodard

Naryati numbers her days like the days in a dream, knowing them to be more numerous than the grains of rice in a harvest: every hour slowly bleeding into the next, every evening as grey and featureless as the skies overhead.

Once, she knows, things were different. She remembers living in a palace of white marble; remembers the clatter of chariots across the battlefields, and the rattle of dice over the banyan-wood board as her husbands wagered their kingdom.

But she has come here, to this city called London, where the monsoon never comes, where the river exhales smoke and the cars jammed in the streets make a noise to rival the Thunder-God's lightning bolts.

She does not remember why, or how, or even how long ago.

❧

Naryati is standing in line at the Tesco's supermarket when she first notices the woman staring at her. She has seen madmen before, so at first she does not react; merely waits for her purchases to be done: chicken legs and rice that will taste bland no matter how many different spices she adds.

But the woman does not move, or gesticulate, or do any other thing Naryati has seen madmen do. She merely stands, smiling as if amused—an amusement that does not reach her dark, hollow eyes.

When Naryati bypasses her, the woman's arm shoots out, and grasps Naryati's wrist. "I've looked for you, sister."

The last word she uses is not English. It's in a language far older and far more powerful, and it means "you who have shared my husband".

"I don't understand," Naryati says, and the woman smiles again.

"I am Medhavin."

The name, although unfamiliar, is dark and fearful, and Naryati, staring at Medhavin, sees the woman's brown face melt like heated gold. Bloodshot eyes watch her amidst grey fur, and Medhavin's mouth has filled with yellow fangs.

Rakshasa. Demon.

Naryati tries to withdraw, but Medhavin is holding her fast. "Do you think you can run away that easily, sister? Come, let us walk." Effortlessly, she drags Naryati out of the supermarket, and onto the busy thoroughfare of West Cromwell Road. People turn, briefly, to stare at the commotion; and then go back to their shopping carts, pretending not to see.

"Leave me alone," Naryati says, truly frightened now. Her dream-life has shattered, leaving only the cutting present. She looks at the faces of the crowd, hoping to see one of her husbands. But she has done this for so many years, and still they remain hidden, forever out of her reach. Even Kushala, the master bowman, has not found a way to walk the paths of time.

Medhavin waits until they reach a quieter place, on the edge of a square. Then she turns, and says, "Did you think you could run away forever?"

"I didn't run away. I—I lost myself." And she knows it is the truth, but not the whole truth. To hide her fear, she says, "And why do you call me 'sister'? You have no right."

Medhavin smiles again. It never seems to reach her eyes. "We both slept with Panka, son of the Sun. But only to me did he give a son."

"No," Naryati says. "No. You lie."

"Open your eyes," Medhavin says. "How long do you think you can hide, Naryati? War has come, and you must play your part. You must join the fight."

"I have already fought," Naryati says, struggling to remember her last days with her husbands. "There was a battle—and—" It comes too close to the dark place in her soul, the wound she knows cannot heal.

"And my son died." Medhavin's voice is quiet now, almost thoughtful.

"I'm sorry," Naryati says, knowing she has told this to many mothers, that she will have to do it again, and again, while men on both sides slaughter one another, giving the earth a harvest of blood.

Medhavin laughs, bitterly. "You? You haven't lost anything, Naryati. Your three husbands are still alive."

"I—I don't remember."

"You have to." There's a fervour in Medhavin's voice that makes Naryati back away; in the *rakshasa's* eyes she sees the blood-thirst, rising and rising until Medhavin's human form collapses inwards, leaving only the demon, a monstrous shape with four arms and clawed hands, reaching for her heart.

No.

She pulls and pulls at her wrist until it comes free. Pain tears through her, but she doesn't care, she's running as fast as she can, down Warwick Road and back towards her own small flat.

Running, but not safe. Not any more.

⋙

That night Naryati dreams of the warriors arraying themselves on the battlefield, their chariot drivers readying their spears and their bows.

She sees Kushala among them: Kushala, third of the three brothers who are her husbands, and the one who won her hand at the archery contest. It is wrong of her, but she has always liked Kushala better than the others.

Kushala's chariot driver has his back to her. For a moment she cannot remember who he is, and then he turns, and she is staring into Supta's face, seeing universes born and destroyed within his dark gaze. A god's face—for it is the Preserver who took flesh in Supta.

You must come back, child, Supta says, but she cannot remember the way. *There can be no fighting if you do not come back.*

You don't need me, she whispers. *I am a woman. Women don't wage war.*

Supta's face is stern. *There will be no war unless you give back what you stole from him.*

He means Kushala. But she has never stolen anything from him, she has never—

She remembers her fear of the coming war, her knowledge that she would be mourning the warriors dead in battle. And then everything blurs, until the years become like so many grains of sand.

Kushala is facing her, but he does not see her. She longs to run to him, to lose herself in his embrace, but she cannot, she is held fast.

Kushala...

They are not looking at her any more. She struggles against the bonds that anchor her to this place and time, but they hold fast.

And then everything fades, passing into oblivion, until it is as if neither of them had ever existed.

Naryati wakes up sweating, with a bitter aftertaste flooding her mouth. Outside, it is dark, although her alarm clock says it is eight o'clock.

She rises from her bed, and moves to the small kitchen, turning on the gas to heat herself some milk and water. As she puts the tea bag—some Chai Masala—into the boiling liquid, she wonders why she started drinking tea. Back when she was a princess, and the wife of the three Bhisvana brothers, there were herbal teas, but not this strong, acrid brew that she makes every morning.

Her mind is sharp this morning, and the day is not like any other. Her dream-life is gone, irretrievable.

Supta's face will not leave her mind, nor his words.

You must give back what you stole from him.

She is no thief. She is no coward. She stole nothing.

But Supta is God, and why should he lie to her?

She stares at her hands, which have grown pale from lack of sun. How long has she subsisted in this dream trance, seeing one day follow and merge into another? How has she lived?

She does not remember.

What she remembers is this: it is the thirteenth day of the battle, and she stands on a rise, staring at the field strewn with corpses. Carrion birds caw above her, and the stench of the dying wafts up to her, so strong it makes her gag.

Kushala's chariot is wheeling its slow way back towards his encampment. Supta, holding the reins, stands tall and dark, brooding.

Slowly, Naryati descends, walks among the dead, seeing every face turned towards her. Hands reach for her sari; moaning voices beg her for comfort. She can offer none.

She walks, unbending. But inwardly she sees the dead: her husbands' teacher Dambha; Utsava, her husbands' uncle, falling with a dozen arrows embedded in his chest; Jamanbadhu, the youngest among them, slaughtered like a deer at the hunt.

There is no honor on the battlefield. No glorious battle—just a massacre on both sides.

And she thinks of the dead to come, of the many widows that will mourn come battle's end. No one is safe from a stray arrow or from a wound that festers—not even Kushala, or Hastipaka, eldest among her husbands.

The thought of their lying at the mercy of the crows and jackals sends a shard of ice through her heart.

It cannot go on.

Afterwards, it is a simple matter to sneak into Kushala's tent while they are having a council of war. It is a simple matter to spread her moon's blood on the arrows, until they lie soiled at her feet, their divine potency extinguished.

She walks to their war council, and stands on the threshold of the pavilion, staring at her husbands: at Hastipaka, born to rule over the wide reach of the world; at Panka, whose strength is that of the Sun his father.

At Kushala, who has risen, surprised. "Naryati? This is no place for you—"

She walks to him, in the growing silence, and kisses him, presses herself against him. And in that moment, dancing on the rhythm of his heart, she reaches out into his mind, and she steals his supreme, god-given weapon: *Pahadeva*, the one that will never miss its mark, or fail to kill.

It tastes bitter on her tongue.

And then she walks away, leaving them frozen behind her like so many children's broken toys.

In the present, in her small flat off Earl's Court, Naryati stares at her hands, remembering the bitter, exhilarating feel of *Pahadeva* within her. The same taste she woke up with this morning.

She is a thief. She is a coward.

And yet she is right. She cannot let kin slaughter kin until no one is left.

She can feel *Pahadeva*, nested close to her heart—the weapon ready to be called with a word, save that she would never be able to wield it. Only one who has the Destroyer's divine favour—such as Kushala—can wield *Pahadeva*.

But it can be stolen. She stole it. And then she ran away. Knowing the prophecy: *Pahadeva* means victory. Without that weapon, her husbands cannot win the war.

Naryati stares at the white walls of her kitchen, remembering that last kiss, remembering that betrayal.

She has—to see them again.

To be forgiven, a small, treacherous voice whispers within her, but she is not listening.

Naryati works as a cook at a restaurant, not far from Old Brompton. Every day she makes flatbreads and spiced rice dishes that smell like home—save that it is wrong, it never tastes or looks as it should.

She walks home after her shift, alone—she has made no friends, has not confided in anyone—and suddenly she realizes someone is following her.

She turns, cold fear in her belly. It is Medhavin, wearing a black trench coat and an iridescent scarf, neither of which can disguise her true appearance to Naryati's eyes.

"Go away," Naryati says.

But Medhavin only smiles. "You remember. When are you going to fight, Naryati?"

"I took *Pahadeva* so that there would be no more fights," she says, her voice shaking. "No more needless deaths like your son's."

Medhavin's eyes flash. "My son was a true warrior, and they will forever sing of him. To kill him, the Duptas had to use the Thunder-God's weapon—the weapon of the king of the gods himself."

The Duptas. Her husbands' cousins, more numerous than the stars in the sky. Her husbands' rivals, arrayed against them in battle—knowing that the winner shall reign over all the cities of the fertile world. "Your son died for nothing," Naryati says. "As did all the others."

"My son died to make Hastipaka king in Avuyavaman. To make you a queen." Medhavin spits on the pavement as they walk on Old Brompton Road, past the vast houses of the rich and powerful, past the towers of the hotels for businessmen, and the numerous pubs that disgorge light and warmth and the acrid smell of alcohol onto the street.

"I don't want to be a queen," Naryati says, realizing, frightened, that it is the truth.

Medhavin's face has grown thoughtful. "You are a princess, born in a palace of white marble. Born to rule the world at your husbands' side."

"Yes, I know," Naryati says, and the thought tastes bitter on her tongue, as bitter as *Pahadeva* after she stole it from Kushala.

"And yet you'd deny all of that?"

"And you?" Naryati asks. "Why should you want them to win?"

Medhavin stops, stares at her. Her fake human face has turned as black as tar. "Make no mistake. I am *rakshasa*. I revel in blood, no matter who sheds it. But for Panka's sake, I support your husband. I'll see Panka come into his rightful inheritance. I'll see him purified by the sacred waters, and sit on the throne by his brothers' side."

Naryati laughs bitterly. "That's reassuring."

"Believe me, you don't want me for an enemy." Medhavin's face is slipping away again, revealing her true, savage self, its fangs stained with blood. "For years I've had to live in the shadows, hiding and starving. For years I've been waiting for you to walk through the paths of time and come to this place."

"Why did they send *you*?"

Medhavin smiles. "I am not the only one. But the men are unwilling to stray far from the battlefield. They wait, Naryati. They wait for you there."

"My husbands—" And this time she cannot keep the anguish from her voice—the knowledge that when she stole *Pahadeva* she forever set herself apart from them.

Medhavin's face changes, becomes predatory once again. "As you left them," she says. "Do you want to see them?"

"I see them in my dreams." A half-lie, for she has had only one dream—but that alone was frightening enough.

"Dreams lie," Medhavin says.

Not those ones, Naryati thinks, remembering Supta's face. She knows Medhavin's offer is going to be one more hollow trick, one more snake that will bite instead of protecting. And yet she cannot refuse.

Medhavin takes her to the Tube, into a train that rocks and whines as it passes station after station. At last they stop at Leicester Square, and take the escalators upwards, back into the fresh air of the night.

They walk out of Leicester Square's bustle, and into the darkened streets of Soho. Medhavin never stops, or looks behind.

No one approaches her—something in her stance promises blood and pain to the foolhardy.

Medhavin enters a small, unprepossessing nightclub where even the bouncer seems bored. Looking upwards, briefly, Naryati catches the name "City of Heaven" written in English. But underneath is another word, in a language since long forgotten: "Avuyavaman". One of the cities Hastipaka should have been ruling.

Inside, a few fevered customers move to the rhythm pouring out of the loudspeakers. Medhavin walks past all of them, until she reaches a small alcove lit by purple neon lights.

A man sits there, his face half in shadow.

"Medhavin?" His voice is like the purr of a feline.

"Look who's come," Medhavin says.

The man shifts in his chair, and the shadows on his face rearrange themselves into some other pattern: Naryati sees a woman's face staring back at her with thoughtful eyes, hears a woman's voice.

"Well, well," the woman says. "I'm impressed, I must admit. What do you want?" This to Medhavin, who has moved to one side, her eyes straying to the dancers on the floor.

"You know," Medhavin says.

"You know what I want as well."

"Tell her about it. Maybe she'll see what is at stake."

The woman smiles, and abruptly it's a man's smile again. "Welcome," she says. "I am—"

But Naryati, staring at the man's face, remembers. "Vivarji," she says. "And you weren't born a man."

Vivarji smiles, and again her gender seems to shift. "No. Welcome back, sister." This time it is the English word, the one that means they shared a father—and no other meaning lies hidden within. "The years have treated you well, I see."

Naryati feels old, as out of her time and place as a land-bound swan. She and Vivarji, even when young, shared little, and they both know it. "Spare me the courtesies. I've come here—"

"I know why she brought you here," Vivarji says. "She has need of strong magic, and her kind has little left in this world."

"And you?"

Vivarji smiles—again, that disturbing expression, halfway between a seductive simper and a boy's mischievous grin. "I am man and woman, as the fancy takes me. I have the Destroyer's favour—and He is a god to be reckoned with. There is power in all that." She stares at Naryati's face, and shakes her head. "Don't worry. There are only the three of us there."

Naryati swallows. "I'm not worrying. I want—" And again she stops, because she does not know. "Why are you here?"

Vivarji shrugs. "Battle has its uses—and its limits. I took a man's shape to have my revenge on the killing fields, and now I'm done." Her eyes shine, a fey, opalescent light that moves beneath her skin. "I don't care who wins."

"Medhavin told me you could show me the battlefield."

Vivarji's ambiguous smile widens. "Of course," she says. Naryati expects her to set a price, something unreasonable, but Vivarji merely rises with a toss of her head. "Come."

Naryati follows her into the basement. Here, it's dark and cool, and the walls muffle the disco music upstairs. It's feels empty, too: she can see a few battered chairs strewn about, and a table standing crookedly on three legs.

Vivarji is looking at her as if expecting something, so Naryati says, "I'm ready."

Vivarji chants, slowly at first, and then the words become audible:

"By the River Kuni that birthed us all
By the Moon that holds our fates
And by the Crown that lies unclaimed
I beg of You, Lord Destroyer,
Let the Third Eye open."

Over and over, until Naryati feels the power gathering in the room, raising goose bumps on her arms.

A man's face—the Destroyer's face—appears before Vivarji,

with wild, savage eyes: nothing like Supta's dark, comforting gaze. Light converges to His forehead, where the tilak, the sacred mark, shines red in the dim light.

But it's not a tilak. It's widening, splitting in two halves; oozing light, and the raw power rises in Naryati too, until every breath she takes burns with the bitterness of *Pahadeva*, with the desire to release the weapon and watch the nightclub, the city, crumble into feathery dust.

Vivarji stands tall, wreathed in light. Power hangs over her like a shroud, and for the first time Naryati sees that she is not man, or woman, but both at the same time, and yet neither.

And then the eye, the Third Eye on the Destroyer's forehead, opens itself completely, and swallows Naryati in blinding light.

She stands on a rise, staring at the battlefield. Save that it has changed, grown alien to her. The colorful silk tents have become drab, grey-green, and the chariots are gone, replaced by metal machines.

On the battlefield, men with assault rifles are rushing forward. Her husband Panka leads his men, hurling grenade after grenade into the fray. Shara, the low-caste warrior who commands the opposite army, is in the forefront, screaming some order that gets lost over the explosions and the thunder of bullets.

She turns, briefly, and glimpses a slit of blinding light, already fading. Behind, she knows, lies London and the safety of the nightclub basement.

She feels Vivarji's presence in her mind, like a vague ache, and instinctively knows that the way is not closed yet. *Bring me back*, she thinks, but Vivarji whispers, *You wanted to see. There's no other way.*

A man sits not a few paces from her, oblivious to her presence. He wears camouflage clothes, and the helmet resting on his knees is of the same drab color as the tents. An assault rifle hangs on his shoulder.

Coming closer, she sees two things: the first is that he is

Kushala, but a greyer Kushala, wan and diminished enough to be her grandfather.

The second thing is that although he appears to be sitting, his eyes are closed—he is sleeping.

Still fighting her feeling of dislocation, she kneels, and touches his shoulder. He starts, both hands going to his face to shield himself—and it surprises her, because she half-expected him to go for her throat. Then he recognizes her, and sits bolt upright. "Naryati? Have you come back?"

There's such yearning in his voice that she wants to kiss him. But she knows things have changed. "I came to see—"

"How we were doing?" his voice is bitter. "Well, as you can see. Without *Pahadeva*, neither side has the advantage, and so the battle goes on. It never ends. Every day the dead rise again and fight anew." His gaze holds her for a while, and she sees all the horrors he's witnessed, all the blood and the gore and the companions dying at his side, and the wounds that fester and will not heal.

"I'm sorry," she says. "I thought—I thought I could make a difference."

Two people are walking towards them, wearing the same camouflage uniform as Kushala's: Supta, as dark and youthful as he was centuries ago, and Hastipaka, eldest among her husbands, walking as if bent under the weight of the assault rifle on his shoulder.

Kushala is not looking at her. "You did make a difference."

He tears her heart—Kushala was always the perfect warrior, never afraid to go into the fray, never cynical nor sounding so weary.

Hastipaka is upon them now, smiling. "Naryati. At last."

There is something—too intense in his smile. *Bring me back*, she almost says to Vivarji, but she cannot leave Kushala without a word.

Supta is more guarded. "I see you still have it."

"Well?" Hastipaka says, shaking his head impatiently. "Give it back, so we can get on."

"No," she says. "It's not yours."

His face darkens. "Nor is it yours."

"Then it's for Kushala to say, isn't it?"

But Kushala is not looking at either of them. His eyes rest on the vast expanse of the battlefield—she can hear gunshot, and the screams of those who fall—, and he whispers to himself words she cannot hear.

"He can't fight now," Hastipaka says impatiently. "Give it back."

"You presume," Supta says, sternly, to Hastipaka. "It belongs to Kushala. You may not wield it."

Hastipaka shakes his head angrily. "Then give it to Kushala."

Naryati steals a look at Supta. He stands by Hastipaka's side, his gaze remote. He does not judge. He lets her choose.

She stares at Kushala, at what he has become. Through her fault. She thought she could spare them from the massacre. Instead they are dying this slow death—traveling forward through time, fighting a battle they cannot win.

Slowly, she kneels before Kushala. "It's time. Time to end this." She tilts his face towards hers, until their lips brush as if for a kiss: the last kiss, the one that will make everything right, now and on all the paths of time.

༄

Within Naryati, *Pahadeva* is rising, a bitterness that floods her mouth, ready to be passed on. But Kushala's lips are cold and unresponsive, like the touch of a dead snake, and she jerks away.

As she does so, she sees Hastipaka's face, and his gaze resting on her with an unhealthy hunger. His eyes are cruel.

And she knows; she knows why Supta rebukes him. She knows that no goodness can endure untarnished for so many years. She has a vision of him, come into his power, and of his hunger that will never cease, that must be appeased by streams of blood.

All this, in a heartbeat; and then she is up, and running back towards the top of the rise, screaming to Vivarji to bring her back, screaming for the door to open until the breath burns in her lungs.

The Destroyer's face hovers over the ground, and slowly the tilak on his face splits open, widening as the Third Eye opens, slowly.

Too slowly.

Yet, turning back, she sees Hastipaka has one hand going for his rifle—but has not reached it. Kushala is slowly rising, but he will be too late.

The door widens, until she can taste the smoky air of the nightclub in London. Almost there—

But through the frame tumbles Vivarji, dishevelled and leeched of colors by the light. Medhavin stands over her, her demon shape made manifest, her mouth split in a fanged grin.

"Going somewhere? You won't pass."

Vivarji is lying at Naryati's feet, blood pooling on her forehead. Her head lolls back; as it does so, the door vanishes, and Naryati is standing alone, between Medhavin and the men down the rise.

Hastipaka's rifle is trained on her, even as he walks closer to her—not that makes any difference, since a bullet can kill from ten paces as well as from three. "If you move, I'll shoot you."

Naryati, breathing hard, watches Medhavin. Who has not moved, but is smiling broadly. "You think I'd leave you come back? The war has to end."

"It has no end," Naryati whispers, but none of them are listening to her.

"I thought you'd come to reason without a threat," Hastipaka says. "But since you insist, you leave me no choice. Give *Pahadeva* back now."

"Or?" Naryati raises an eyebrow, displaying calm she does not feel. "You'll shoot me? Your wife?"

Hastipaka's gaze is somber. "I'm ready to pay the price."

Kushala, behind him, looks sick, but he does not move. He has shrunk to this shadow that cannot speak, that looks away, haunted by all the horrors of the battlefield. Supta is standing, one hand on Kushala's shoulder, but it's at her that he's looking.

I tried, Naryati whispers. *But he is no longer the man you thought would hold the throne.*

Perhaps Supta sees this; whatever the reason, he's not moving. There's only Hastipaka, his gun trained on her; Medhavin, inching ever closer, all four of her arms twitching like snakes, eager to seize her and drag her back to Kushala's feet.

She cannot surrender. And yet she sees no way out. *Pahadeva's* bitterness floods her mouth, but it's as useless to her as Hastipaka's rifle would be—she is a woman and her place is not on the battlefield, not on the killing grounds. *Pahadeva* is Kushala's.

No, not Kushala's.

Unbidden, words she heard centuries ago come back to her. *Only the Destroyer's chosen may wield Pahadeva.*

But the Destroyer's favor does not stop at Kushala.

She thinks of Vivarji and the unearthly light flowing towards the other woman, the divine power that filled her. And then she is on her knees, holding Vivarji in her arms, shaking her, begging her to come back to life.

Medhavin glides closer, taking her time. "She won't help you," she snickers. "You've lost, Naryati. It's too late."

Please, Vivarji. Please. Wake up. Wake up.

She prays to all the gods she thought she had forgotten; to the Destroyer who opened the door for her; to the Preserver who has taken flesh in Supta; and to the Creator since long removed from the world he made.

Wake up. Please let her wake up.

Medhavin's hands fall on her shoulder, the claws digging in deep. Pain fills Naryati's whole body as the demon lifts her and Vivarji, as easily as two broken dolls. Pain, pain radiating from her transfixed flesh, until she has shrunk to nothing but this, but deep, deep down, part of her is still whispering its endless prayers.

Please please please.

Vivarji's body jolts back and forth under her, like a horse with shattered legs. Her eyes snap open, abruptly, and confusion floods her face.

"Naryati?"

Medhavin is carrying them both to Kushala. Hastipaka's face is a mask of smugness.

There is no time. Naryati twists and writhes until Vivarji's face lies under her. A fresh wave of pain travels from her pinned shoulder, but she pays it no heed.

Her lips brush against Vivarji's, and then she's kissing her, kissing a woman, kissing a man, kissing something beyond her. Bitterness wells up in her, fills her breath and her mouth.

Pahadeva.

She feels it like a thread, slowly spinning itself together in the space between her lips and Vivarji's lips. Everything around them freezes into insignificance.

Pahadeva.

And then it slips away from her, as easily as an exhaled breath. No more bitterness in her mouth; no more sense of coiled power.

Vivarji's eyes close for a second, and when they open again they are filled with light, the same blinding light as the Third Eye. The light spreads, until it covers her, blurring every feature of her face until Naryati can no longer decide which gender Vivarji is now.

It spreads, surrounds Naryati, insinuating itself in every one of her wounded shoulder's throbs. And then she lands heavily on the ground. She picks herself up with difficulty, and looks just in time to see Medhavin burning.

The light is eating at the demon like acid, taking out whole chunks of its body at a time. Medhavin does not cry out. Her eyes are on Naryati, dark and vengeful. But it is too late.

Vivarji is standing, riding the crest of the power. Her outstretched hands are twin suns. On her chest, two breasts flicker in and out of existence.

Hastipaka stands frozen, the rifle dangling from his fingers. Vivarji turns, stares at it for a while, and it crumbles into dust. She stares at Hastipaka, too, until he starts swaying, but Supta's voice stops her.

"You may not kill him," he says. "He can only die at the battlefield, at the hands of his enemy. Like all of us." His voice is tinged with resignation.

Vivarji's face shifts towards Supta, and they exchange a long look before she turns away.

"Naryati," she says, and her voice is stronger than the gunshots or the explosions.

Naryati, whose shoulder is still aching, shivers. "Thank you. We're leaving," she says.

Supta and Kushala are only a hand span away. Supta's face is blank, carefully not disclosing any emotion.

"It will go on," he says.

"It has to," Naryati says. "Do you want a king like him?" She jerks her head towards Hastipaka, who is still shaking.

"Perhaps not," Supta says. "But you know the war cannot end."

"Because you're too stubborn to give up."

Supta shrugs. "We tried peace-talks a long time ago, before the war started, but it didn't work. Now no side will back down, of course. Had you not stolen *Pahadeva*—"

She shakes her head, repressing the twinge of guilt. "What's done is done. We can't go back."

"You could stay," Kushala says, and she hears the pain in his voice.

"I can't. I've changed too much," she says, and she knows it's the truth. Knows that everything that happens is her fault, and that the guilt will gnaw at her heart every day and every night. But you cannot call back innocence once it is lost; and the paths of time cannot be walked backwards. "I'm sorry."

He looks at her, and for a moment she sees a shadow of the old, carefree Kushala. "Don't be," he says.

The ache in her heart strikes deeper than the pain in her shoulder. "Come with me. We can both be free."

But he shakes his head, very gently, and in his dark eyes she sees the memories of war. "My place is here. Outside of the battlefield I have no role, and no peace of mind."

"Goodbye, then," she says, and she does not know why her eyes sting.

She bends, quickly, before she can think, and kisses him on the mouth, deeply. His breath mingles with hers, and for a brief moment she is young again, a princess in a palace of white marble, born to rule, to be queen.

Too late.

She pulls away from him. Vivarji is waiting for her, the power of *Pahadeva* coiled around her like a cobra. The gateway has opened again, towards London and her other life, her empty days and nights that will never blur into each other again. Her trance has shattered, and she is alive once more.

Vivarji, perhaps sensing her thoughts, says, "You can stay in the nightclub for a while, sister. You'll see. It's not so bad."

And she has only Vivarji's word for that as she walks forward, leaving the battlefield behind her, leaving Kushala behind her. As she steps through the gate and back into the smoke-filled nightclub. Something aches, in her heart.

And the taste in her mouth is no longer bitter, but all the same it reminds her of ashes.

Going Dark
Lyn C.A. Gardner

When he died, I lost not only Grandpa, but his world. Grandma sealed the darkroom. Mother told me my tears were selfish, but I heard my parents discussing it in low tones late at night. Their bedroom door spilled a copper square while Dad rumbled, "There's nothing to worry about. Your mother won't let anyone in the darkroom."

Mother's taut, high voice carried across the hall. "Imogene's going to look someday. It's human nature. And she won't understand."

Dad said, "Gene can handle it. He's ours." His fierceness made me shiver. "It's not Gene we have to worry about."

Mother said, "Sooner or later, that darkroom's going to open."

As she spoke, I could almost feel the white-painted door beneath my hand, so snug where Grandpa had fitted it when he'd converted half the laundry room. He'd drilled in a tiny lock at the level of my eye. When the lock was thrown, a red circle filled the hole above it to let us know he was going dark. He'd installed a doorbell buzzer, with a second push button upstairs in the dining room in case Grandma needed him; they glowed faint orange through their cloudy plastic covers.

When Grandpa was alive, I loved to press that buzzer. If I waited patiently, the door would open, and Grandpa would welcome me into that safelight glow. Under the orange lamp, black-and-white scenes stood out sharp and clear, the white spaces glowing as prints floated in the wash or dripped slowly from the line. Grandpa showed me how to focus the enlarger on a tray lined up beneath it, then switch off the lamp and insert the paper—a catcher's mitt extended blind, an act of measurement and faith. He walked me through the stages of the chemical process, dressing me in rubber gloves that stretched up my arms, a rubber apron that covered me neck to knees, and a surgeon's mask and hood. With steady hands and quiet patience, he showed me how to hold the tongs, warning me to take care: even a single drop could hurt me.

When we went to his house before the funeral, I stood in front of that locked white door for a long time. I thought that if I pressed the buzzer.... Several times, my hand reached up, finger pointed as I screwed up my courage. Surely it would not be a terrible wait. Surely he would come.

Mother came. She took me to the church, where they spoke of a proud, headstrong man I didn't recognize. I thought of the darkroom. While I sat here, was he opening the door at last, poking his head through the crack, wondering where I was?

After the service, Mother sobbed in the parlor lined with Grandma's blue glass vases and Grandpa's photographs. Dad stroked her hair and held her close, murmuring, "It's all right now. No one will ever know."

The next two years passed in a haze as I sought to fill the hole that Grandpa left. By sixteen, enough girls and boys found me attractive that I seldom lacked for dates. I could slip into one gender or the other so fully that once a shift was complete, I'd get ribbed by other guys for looking pretty enough to be a girl, without them suspecting I sometimes was one. It took a lot of effort, and multiple observers complicated things. With a given name like Imogene, teachers called me "she" by default, but I lined up with the boys until that incident in gym when Jonas ripped my shorts. I had no warning—no time to decide, to sprout the appropriate attributes. My baby-doll blankness shocked everyone—while they remembered. It's hard to keep your eyes on me if I don't want you to. And once you forget me, it's easy to turn a thin shoulder, get thinner, and slip entirely out of sight.

They told me I was striking, when they did notice—perfect proportions, natural grace, a complexion that neither tanned nor burned. My hair was jet, my skin pale white—an alabaster some admired. Mother described it differently: "There's something cold about her, Ronald." And Dad replied, "Well, Sally, he warmed up to your father like a flower to the sun."

In Dad's eyes, I was unique—above gender, and thus destined for great things. I knew his love was speaking, but when I thought of Dad, I felt confident despite my strangeness. Being a boy and my father's son felt right. Being a girl was mostly an expectation I fulfilled to please female relatives like Mother and Grandma. I saw how irritated Mother got with me when I had a boy's flat toughness, as if I had somehow rejected her.

As I grew older, my face sharpened to reveal Grandma's high cheeks and definite nose. That made things worse. When Mother said, "You take after your grandmother," it wasn't a compliment. Grandma and I had always shared a strong bond, but as much as I loved her, I knew that things had not been easy for my mother as a child. I tried to forgive the strained way Mother handled me, as if I were a raging fire and all that shielded her was a pair of gloves.

Even Dad was careful, his hugs definite but quick. Only Grandpa hadn't kept his distance. I'd lived with my grandparents from time to time when I was too ill and weak to go to school. When I turned twelve, I felt as though I was cracking out of my skin. I lay on the red, tasseled studio couch in the darkroom while Grandpa cheered me up with funny stories. I helped him with color experiments, painting black-and-white prints and glass slides with watercolors. That was the only year he tried a color drum. I can still hear his nonsense curse-words whispered like jokes in the total darkness as he struggled to dial the colors right. But when he succeeded, the results were breathtaking—rainbow-beautiful, glossy life whose magic he projected onto me in the darkness till I felt I wasn't missing anything at all.

Without Grandpa, the emptiness ached so much I filled my life with as many people as I could. Dad got me an old blue Buick with wide, plush seats. I loved coasting down the night streets, my left hand easy on the wheel, my right entwined with my current conquest. I was all girl or all boy. Life's sweetness swelled me. I drove home afterward with the windows down, letting the night air brush me clean. Their adoration filled me with a vibrancy I hadn't felt since Grandpa's slideshows. My whole being burned bright with passion as I focused on each love, imbibing the perfume of that presence—a lust of the heart and soul. But when my hunger for someone got too intense, strange things happened.

Susannah and I went to concerts. While I drove, she winked beside me like a star in the passing lights as she played songs on the stereo that made me wish I were that beautiful inside. We'd sing along with favorites, our voices lifting heavenward together. Because I loved her, I left when all I wanted to do was hold her through the night. But Susannah's heart wound down one night while she lay in bed. She'd been warm in my arms, her breathing relaxed as she fell asleep, her lips curving sweetly as I kissed her into dreams. Judging from the time of death, she must have slipped away as I climbed out her window.

Rachel and I haunted the botanical gardens, climbing into the tree house observatory to watch the eagles build their nest. We soared, seeing those giant birds hovering with immense grace, the two of us breathless on that deserted platform. One day Rachel flew from her locked bedroom, where she'd been grounded for seeing me. They said she'd threatened to run away. But the window had been locked on the inside, and she'd left all her things. The clothes she'd worn lay in a rumpled heap inside the door.

Tony taught me to shoot pool, leaning in so close I could smell boy-sweat and the aftershave he didn't need. Stretched over the table, his blond hair fell into his eyes and his metallic blue shirt showed off his hairless chest. His impish grin and bold suggestions dissolved into little-boy tenderness in his room above the garage. He told me that after he got home from our dates, he liked to sit in his car listening to the radio with his eyes closed, imagining I was still with him. But he'd been so tired lately. The last night I'd seen him, he'd laughed breathlessly over how lightheaded he felt, as giddy as a kid. His parents called to say he'd fallen asleep with his convertible running in the garage.

I cried all night. I hated the sun that rose into a beautiful day—

and the boundless life and energy that filled me. When I came down for breakfast, I heard Mother and Dad fighting in the kitchen. Dad raised his voice to be heard: "It's not his fault."

"That doesn't matter. Without Father—"

"Sally, the time would have come, regardless," Dad insisted. I recognized the strained patience in his voice. "Even with your father's help, you know that Gene would have had to find his own way. Everyone deserves a life of his own."

Mother said tartly, "That doesn't give her the right to steal other people's."

I huddled against the wall. The kitchen door swung wide. Mother drew back when she saw me.

Dad led me to the table, his hand gentle on my shoulder as he encouraged me to sit down. "I know what it's like to lose your first love," he said quietly.

After a moment, Mother added, as if in apology, "Tony was a good-looking kid."

Her unexpected kindness took me off guard. "Susannah," I whispered. "Rachel—"

Her voice hardened. "Other girls. They couldn't have been more than friends."

"Sally," Dad said.

"Well, you're not going to tell her," Mother retorted. I had never seen her cheeks so pink. "There are some things she needs to know!"

"Not now, Sally!"

"The point is, Imogene, you've got to learn to keep your hands to yourself!"

But that was advice I knew I couldn't keep. Dad's sad eyes said he knew it too. Still, he tried. "I know it's difficult, Gene. I don't want to infringe on your autonomy. You'll be a grown man soon, and the choices you make now will shape your future. I think the time has come for us to sit down together and make some decisions."

The first one we made was to let me home-school myself for

the remainder of the year. I enrolled in photography classes at the Fine Arts Center while my parents worked ever-longer hours. Soon, instead of meeting people, I was observing them in fine detail through my lens.

When school let out, we drove across the flatlands and up the foothills to Boulder, Colorado. As much as I wanted to see Grandma, I knew it wasn't a vacation, but a retreat. I felt enervated at the end of that long drive. Grief and loneliness had depleted me.

For our arrival, Grandma had arranged a family reunion. We wove through relatives and friends who filled the patio and the shade beneath both grape arbors. Cousins played croquet up and down the terraced back lawn. I stumbled over a painted ball and sat down hard. No one noticed me. They frowned a little, stepping over my leg as if it were a misplaced wicket. Painfully, I got to my feet and hobbled away, feeling faded and sun-sick.

For dinner, we sat around the picnic table on the screened-in patio, while Grandma reclined on a scarlet chaise lounge. Cousins passed dishes up and down the table, knocking elbows, joking as they jostled each other. All of us spoke at once, so I didn't realize at first that no one seemed to hear me. Those passing dishes hardly glanced my way. Of them all, only Grandma noticed me, with a bird-sharp twinkle in her kindly eyes. As the conversation lulled between dinner and dessert, she patted the cushion beside her. On the tray next to her, photographs rested in uneven, precarious piles. As I sat beside her, she picked apart old photos that had curled together, introducing me to family I'd never met. One shot showed her as a toddling infant, bald and smiling, holding the hand of a beautiful boy in velvet and lace. "That's my brother," she told me. I'd never known she had one.

We spent the rest of the evening sorting photographs, chatting, happy. I loved Grandma's stories, and each picture brought up so many memories. Her guests stopped to say goodbye one by one. When they had gone, she gazed at me with watery blue eyes, wrinkles draping the beautiful shape of her face. "Would you like to stay here, Imogene?" she asked.

"Of course!"

"You'll need a darkroom, dear." She reached for the long chain around her neck where she kept her keys, unclipped one, and pressed it into my hand. "The darkroom was Grandpa's *sancta sanctorum*. He wouldn't even let me in to clean."

"I'll be careful, Grandma. You don't know how much this means to me."

"Oh, I think I do."

Grandma lay back and napped. In the soft wrinkles of her worn face, a secret smile nestled, as if she still watched from behind the crumpled petals of her lids. I sat and held her hand, then curled up beside her. Wizened and dear, she'd shrunk to a full foot shorter than my five-six. The breeze blew in through the screens, cooler as it edged toward evening.

I woke to Mother's voice. She had her hand on Grandma's shoulder, calling her gently. Blackness had changed the vista below to a stream of sparkling lights—the constellation of Denver in the distance. I stared at those earthly stars while my mother called repeatedly. Grandma's hand was cold and stiff.

Mother screamed and pounded me with her fists: "How could you!"

Dad came running. He pulled her back. She wept wildly in his arms. Over her shoulder, he said, "It wasn't your fault, Gene. Your mother doesn't mean that. Grandma was an old woman. She died happy, with her family around her. I'm sure she was glad you were holding her hand. She loved you very much." His mouth trembled, and tears slid down his cheeks.

I felt numb. None of it made sense. I had to get away. I ran inside and stood before the darkroom door. I stared at that white paint, scuffed with years. Mother's angry sobs scraped at me. I inserted the key and shoved at the stiff door to my sanctuary. It gave with a groan, swinging fast to thump the wall.

Grandpa had blocked the window glass with aluminum foil. The overhead bulb glowed a tired yellow. I was surprised it burned at all. The dry, dusty air felt cool with disuse. I closed the door, sealing out Mother's howls. I held my breath, listening. "I'm here now, Grandpa," I whispered.

Dust coated the equipment covers and cabinets. Grandpa's hand was visible everywhere, his presence palpable in the neatly ordered shelves. I moved down the counters, touching enlargers, trays, tongs, filters. Grandpa had labeled everything, his printing painstaking—and pained. With his nerves on fire at the end, it must have cost him a lot to pen these careful notes. They hadn't been here the last time I'd visited.

I wept, my hand across my mouth, as I stared at the racks of powdered chemicals and paper, the file cabinets full of stencils and negatives, the cracked sink in the corner where the finished prints had floated, free. "I'm sorry," I sobbed. And then, startling myself, I shouted into the yellow light: "I'll bring you back!"

After the funeral, there was no talk of going home. Dad landed a job at the University of Colorado at Boulder. With his new classes and departmental duties, we seldom saw him except at dinner. I worried about him. The harsh dining room light didn't do us any favors, but even with Mother's home cooking, Dad looked like he was putting on years, not pounds.

Dad and I talked about the things we had in common: sports, music, detective stories. Mother bustled back and forth to the kitchen. She seldom sat down with us. Now and then she'd interject a sharp question about school, or a complaint about her more difficult clients at the florist's. We didn't talk about the future. Worry etched Dad's face, and Mother's shoulders slumped. They went to bed so early now, before dark settled into the crevices of the city down the hill, as if merely being with me was wearing them out.

I felt unreal—except in the darkroom. School existed so I could hook up with new friends; the darkroom was my education. I burned brightly; I wanted to burn out. Maybe if I spread myself thin, sipping from the lips of many rather than drinking deep of a few, no one would come to harm. Any frustrated passion I put into photography, fitting myself into that instant's flash before the shutter sealed in the dark once more. I worked late into the night. At first, these hours felt brittle, thin, as though I might crash through the shell of my life into something else. But soon all those captured images filled me with such zest, I didn't even want to sleep.

Grandpa had loved to rise at dawn and explore the sloping streets beside the mountains, searching for the perfect angle, the perfect slant of light. I felt freest when, like him, I would walk among the foothills in the early morning. Then it didn't matter so much that Dad and I had awkward silences, that Mother avoided my eyes. Sometimes she'd reach out to touch me, then draw back. Her expression reminded me of how crushed I felt when I looked at Grandpa's pictures and realized just how far away he was.

I unearthed his slideshows and tinkered with the projector and reel-to-reel. With the blinds closed and Grandpa's soothing voice quoting poetry above the music, and Grandma smiling back at me from so many pictures, I could almost believe they were still alive. As the colors shone through the air to paint the blank screen, I slipped into that stream of light, standing before the projector to glory in the feel of all those other days flickering through me.

Grandpa spoke to me in the darkroom. Souvenirs of his travels lined the walls—handwoven blankets, sculptures of clay and stone, straw dolls. The closet shelves held antique cameras. His careful notes filled the margins of photography books. I learned from the mistakes he'd saved, prints that didn't meet his exacting standards. On the backs, he'd written descriptions of what went wrong. I felt as if he were watching me, gently guiding my hand. And gradually, I began to see it, around the edges—the clues, a master plan.

I had all the ingredients I needed, but it was hard to find a photo of Grandpa alone. Mostly he'd included himself in family portraits, using a delayed shutter. I found a few later self-portraits in which he was pensive, his gray hair thin, his face freckled with age. I selected a full-length pose in which his eyes were lighter and he looked as though he were about to smile. He stood before a barbed-wire fence that guarded a barren meadow, his shadow stretching up the hill.

I waited until my parents went to bed. Then I focused the enlarger, watching his features resolve in reverse—hair, eyes, and teeth blackened in a gray face. The shadow was an amorphous burst of light behind him. The technique was intricate. I created a positive on film, using different filters and multiple exposures to play with contrast. Once I'd developed the image, I moved to the bigger enlarger and projected it onto a larger sheet of film. Negative to positive to negative, I moved closer to life-size. I cut huge swaths from my oversize roll of printing paper. There must have been some of Grandpa's wizardry left in his equipment: the image got sharper as I progressed, instead of blocking up into stark, high-contrast masses like a linoleum-block print.

The baths were tricky. I had to block off the downstairs hall and use the laundry. Punchy with lack of sleep, I chuckled to myself as I thought I was lucky he hadn't been a larger man. I stirred the final wash by hand, counting time. With such a large basin, I was glad for the rubber gauntlets and apron Grandpa taught me to wear. The sharp, acrid odor of the chemicals leaked through the paper mask. By the safelight I'd plugged into the hall socket, I could see the dark stain spreading as the giant image came to life.

Solarization was the final step. With a series of partial prints, I pieced him together in a glowing, silvery 3-D whose ghostly edges leapt off the page. In the fixing bath, the images were so clear I thought I saw him floating there. I lifted him carefully, avoiding the hypoclear, and dropped him in the wash.

After many hours of soaking, I was able to tease the image free from its backing.

A hand clamped my shoulder.

I turned with a cry of joy. He held me tight. I hadn't been hugged that way for years.

He whispered, "You've turned out well, child." The orange safelight made him strangely dark, as though the high-altitude sun had finally tanned his Irish pallor. He smelled of chemicals, the way he often had. His patient eyes looked darker than the sky-blue I remembered, but his false teeth were brighter than ever.

"Mother will be so happy to see you!" I turned on the overhead light and flung aside my gauntlets, apron, and mask. I was dazzled by the thought of Mother's face finally lighting up. I felt light-headed with chemicals and lack of sleep.

He sighed, his face tight with distress. Our shadows pooled over the gunmetal file cabinet, making jagged teeth out of Grandpa's figurines. "I should have warned you. The cost—"

"Whatever it is, it's worth it, to have you back!"

His face softened. He took my hand. We slipped through a darkness slick as water off resin-coated paper. Grandpa glided up the stairs in his moccasins. At the landing, he paused. Cautiously, his face pinched, Grandpa took my arm. "Don't go up there, child."

I heard them shouting. Glass shattered upstairs—Grandma's beautiful blue glass!

I broke away.

In the living room, Mother paced, clutching the phone in a stranglehold while the cord snagged on shag. Cold poured through the hole in the picture window. On the broad windowsill, I saw the curved handle and fluted lip of the blue glass basket that Grandpa gave Grandma at their wedding. Shards of blue glass littered the floor.

Mother turned to me. "Wouldn't you know, it's Gene," she said bitterly.

A chill touched me as she used the masculine form for the first time.

Mother said, "You didn't even think it was important enough to tell us. After all, it's happened so many times before."

I looked around for Grandpa, but he stood out of sight in the kitchen. I supposed he didn't want to shock her. "Can it wait? This is important—"

"Important?" she said sharply. "More important than murder? But why should I be surprised? Just look what you did to Mother!"

Dad put a restraining hand on her arm, his face etched with worry. "Honey, give him a chance—"

She shrugged him off and hurled the phone at me. "We just got a call. Your girlfriend Jasmine—"

"What happened to Jasmine?" I cried. I had no girlfriend, but I didn't bother to correct her. Jasmine was a friend, and that was bad enough. I had called her several times during the long process with Grandpa, needing companionship badly as I burned the candle at both ends.

"Don't you understand? There's nothing left of them, these kids you love! Just their clothes on the floor! They don't even pack!"

Dad tried to hug her. "It's not Gene's fault. It was never his choice—"

She stiffened in his arms. "Then whose was it? Ours?"

"What happened to Jasmine?" I demanded.

Mother grabbed her coat. "Let's go see!"

"Honey—"

"Ronald, for once, Gene's going to confront what he's done!"

Dad sighed and handed me a coat. We piled into the car. I would have slid into the back, but Mother wedged me up front between them. Dad glided gently away from the curb while Mother raved. I saw Grandpa watching, pale as a ghost, through the broken window.

We rolled down the dark road, our headlamps creating murky puddles in the long stretches between lights. I shivered under a wave of weakness and dread.

Jasmine's house blazed a block away, doors and windows thrown open, police cars flashing. Dad slowed to a stop on the other side of the street. We stared at what lay on the sidewalk. Shoes. Clothes. Her red faux-leather purse. An open cell phone, next to a huge mass of dark stuff that looked like the remains of a campfire doused by water.

"Where is she?" I asked dumbly. This couldn't be happening. I'd been so careful.

Mother slapped me. "That was Jasmine! Don't you understand yet, you freak?" She shoved me. I clutched the dashboard to keep from pushing Dad. He edged the car away from the curb. Mother said, "I don't want him touching me!" She punched me in the arm.

People ran out, shouting at us—Jasmine's parents, her brother.

I felt sick. Dad drove off as Jasmine's father pounded the trunk.

Mother shouted, "Pull over! Pull to the side of the road! Throw him out!" She yanked at me.

"I didn't do anything! I don't know what happened!"

Dad swerved as Mother grabbed the wheel. I was crying, yelling, "Mother, no!" I pulled her arms back, struggling with her. "You're going to make us crash!"

Dad said, "Calm down, both of you!"

"I want Gene out of this car now! It's him or me!" Mother cried.

I saw a red light whizz past overhead.

We struck—

Weight crushed me. The impact stopped me like an electric jolt. My heart stuttered, then beat so fast I couldn't catch my breath. The world went patchy. Mother was moaning, "Oh no, oh no." I felt hollow, used up. I cleared my throat and called to Dad. He grunted. I reached out through the haze for his large hand. He squeezed mine back, moving his thumb reassuringly against my palm the way he did when we prayed together at dinner. His hand was warm. Wet.

His fingers stilled. Grew cold.

They dragged us out. I didn't want to let go of him. In the hospital, Mother screamed at me, "You killed him! I hate you! Murderer! You're not my child—you never were! Ever since you were five years old, you've done nothing but drain everybody dry!"

By the time they took Dad away from me, she'd already gone.

࿐

I couldn't believe that Dad was dead. Or that Mother had left me here to face his death alone. As soon as I could, I escaped the hospital and fled back to the darkroom. I pushed the door shut so tight no crack remained. I could feel the darkness welling up and pressing with the weight of the dead on the other side.

I wanted to hurl all the darkroom instruments against the wall, to tear through the aluminum foil to break glass. I held myself back, not wanting to hurt Grandpa by destroying his things. He watched while I roamed restlessly. As I stomped near the bench, the magnifying lens sent a spasm of light across the floor. I took out bottled chemicals and started sloshing them in their tubs, heedless of gloves, heedless of anything, least of all how they seared as they splashed my arms.

"Is she really my mother?"

"Yes."

"Not anymore. She said that, in the hospital. Not anymore."

"She's in pain."

I needed to do something. I knelt by the long bench and started pulling out boxes from the shelves underneath. I broke through seals of dried yellow tape and paged through prints in cardboard frames, stiff postcards with scalloped edges, thumbnail Brownies. I found negatives for Grandma and Grandpa's wedding and photos whose doubles lived in our family albums. Baby portraits followed, one after another, till I couldn't tell the generations apart. I found experiments: strange combination prints that married baby hands, dresses, noses, eyes, as if Grandpa had been on an abstract quest for beauty. In others, the shape of a child had been blocked out by dodging, and nothing new inserted in its place.

And there it was. "Imogene, age five." Two pictures, side by side. We might have been identical twins, down to the ruffles on our shirts and the dimple in each chin. But Grandma sat in a Victorian chair, her brother standing tall beside her, while I was cradled on Mother's lap, Dad gazing down lovingly behind.

Grandpa spoke softly, with that faint lilt from his father. "There's something I have to tell you."

"Was Mother right? Am I a monster?"

"No, honey."

"That year when I was twelve." My voice broke. "I almost died, didn't I? When I got home, Dad was so gentle with me. So kind. His eyes welled up a lot. Then he'd give me the most heartbreaking smile. But Mother— Sometimes I think she would've been relieved if I hadn't survived."

"Don't say that, sweetheart. You know she loved you."

"Loved," I repeated bitterly.

Steadily, he met my gaze. "Yes. Before you died and I reprinted you kids."

"Kids?"

"You had a twin brother. You two loved each other so much, and kids burn so much energy. You hugged each other, and suddenly there was only one."

My eyes filled with tears. No wonder Mother hated me. Now I understood why, when she claimed to love me, Mother only described what a sweet little girl I'd been at three and four.

"So my brother is dead, too."

"But you're not," Grandpa said quietly. "You're someone new."

"And Grandma?"

"She grieved over you babies. And you're not the only one who lost a brother. When I first brought you two back, I didn't know how to sustain you safely, and I needed depth. I didn't have enough pictures, especially for any point past the time you'd died. You two had always looked a lot like your grandma and her older brother. You loved to play with Uncle Fred, but he was already seventy-five, and his constitution wasn't strong. His wife said he died in his sleep."

Grandpa took my arms and I saw that where the chemicals had struck me, my flesh stood in gray bubbles and corrosive boils dark with blood. Crisped skin fell in black flakes. The slick skin beneath had a yellow cast. The stench of fixer made me dizzy and sick.

Grandpa washed my arms, singing quietly. The notes lifted a faint memory to the surface, fragile, washed out: lying in a crib beside my brother, listening to Grandpa sing lullabies. "I remember," I murmured as I felt the edges of that old grief, the shape of my brother inside me. He'd been so close, nestled against my heart, that I'd mistaken him for myself. The cool running water in its circular bath soothed my burned arms. I slumped against the porcelain lip of the sink, closing my eyes so I wouldn't have to see the delicate leaves of black peeling off like mica to reveal the chemical stain beneath.

Grandpa patted my arms dry. Even wrapped in towels, they

seemed thinner than before. There was urgency in his thin, taut body as he said, "You know what we have to do."

"No! You just got back!"

He said gently, "You know I don't belong here."

"And I do?"

Grandpa collected the scattered versions of the print I'd used to bring him back, all the different sizes and stages, while the wind howled against the blacked-out windows. He looked at me intently, as if calculating the angle for the perfect image. At last, he said, "Somewhere in your makeup, we all survive. Your parents who gave you life, your brother, Grandma and me—"

"Dad and Grandma are dead, and Mother hates me! You're the only one who cares—"

"Enough of that," he said. His face was stern, his tone gentle. He hugged me. "Just live for me, child. For all of us. Live, and remember."

I remembered that sadness in Dad's eyes sometimes, when he looked at me. It wasn't blame. I knew he treasured me. He'd always taught me to relish life, to store up happy memories against the bite of loss—a means of keeping those we loved alive. But I wanted more than that.

Grandpa picked up his stack of paper and film and glass, a ragged mix of shapes. He slid them into the fix. I yelled and grabbed for them, then snatched my burning fingers from the pan. Gingerly, I fished with tongs.

Behind me, a match scratched with the stench of sulfur.

He smelled like film burning. I turned in time to see his outline glow red as his insides crumpled, shriveled, blackened— I grabbed a clean tray and ran for the sink. Flames burst out from his edges. His eyes glowed like coals, and yet he looked so calm—resolved—

I hurled the water. Steam whined. I staggered forward into a cloud of smoke. The fire went out and Grandpa's ashes tumbled to the floor.

"Oh, God," I moaned, teeth chattering. "God help me!"

Feverishly, I scrambled for the boxes, pulling out prints from

Grandma and Grandpa's young married days, in which Mother was a little girl on Grandma's knee. I found alternate shots of the earliest Christmas photo in our family albums, taken when I was five. It was a shock to see that curly-haired boy sitting on Mother's lap beside the little girl who didn't look entirely like me. Other prints showed my parents with a single smiling child between them—a girl whose features added Grandma's nose and Grandpa's twinkling eyes. Standing tall with his hand on Mother's shoulder, Dad still had black hair, his smile proud and tender as he gazed down at his young family. His radiant joy shone pure and true despite the fact that the only child in the picture was me.

As I spread out the photos, I felt calm returning. I was just an image myself; what matter if I had a paper family? That original version of me, long dead, had already joined those I loved in eternity. But the Grandpa I'd called back had been more than a memory or a ghost. Whatever part of me lived now could have Dad again, and everyone I loved.

As Grandma had shown me, I had plenty of cousins I ought to get to know better. They'd probably like having their portraits taken. Grandma would be so happy to know we were all going to stay in touch.

The Cloak of Isis
Sunny Moraine

"Ianthe!"

The call came echoing down the orchard rows, distant but sharp in the crisp evening air. The call of the old woman, Chloe, the housekeeper and the keeper of children—it was the voice that Ianthe had run into the orchard to escape. She tucked a lock of black hair behind her ear and sighed, turning over onto her back in the cool grass. The orange trees hung low over her, secret with evening shadows. She wanted to believe that fairies danced in their branches, gathering the sweet nectar from the blossoms. She wanted to believe that she would not have to go into the great house, arrange her hair for dinner and be fussed about until she was presentable.

"Ianthe!" The voice was closer. Perhaps the old woman had come out onto the steps. Ianthe closed her eyes and pictured her: a plump woman half bent with the ache in her back, her skirts gathered up around her knees. "You come in here this instant or your uncle will be furious!"

It was the invocation of her uncle that did it. She was not afraid of him, not exactly, but he was always cold to her, and she knew that if she exasperated him, it would only mean more exasperation for her. "Coming!" she called, and even then she paused on the cliffs to watch the sun sink down over the western sea, the waves crashing onto the beach far below her, the sighing of the trees at her back and the wind blowing her skirt about her slender legs. There had been a time, when she was a child, when time itself had not placed demands on her. That time was gone now, sometimes distant enough that she wondered whether it had not merely been in a story told to her.

There was a god in the western sea, made of foam and weeds, with a circlet of seahorses for his crown and the whitecaps pulling his chariot. She did not believe this, in gods or in fairies.

She wanted to.

In the great house, Ianthe dressed for dinner, robed in silks worth much gold, and she sat before her polished mirror and pulled a brush through her long hair. She knew that she was beautiful, though something in her was beginning to change, beginning to feel alien deep in the core of her body. The old housekeeper had told her that it was just age taking her and making her body a woman's, but later she had leaned close to her mirror, touched the odd stubbled hair at her chin and wondered.

The old woman had brought foam and a razor and Ianthe had been shaved for the first time. And now it was every morning and every evening, the rasp of the blade cooled with delicately scented creams.

The gods have made you a little strange, child. You'll have to make yourself up to be more womanly. It falls to some of us to be so. But you're lovely and dowered and you'll catch yourself a goodish husband before long.

The gods have just made you a little strange.

But Ianthe did not believe in the gods.

Ianthe was in the forest when she met the boy.

The forest lay past the bounds of the orchard, and though she wasn't supposed to enter its shady depths—not ladylike, not at all—that day she gathered up her skirts and ducked her head under low-hanging branches, and she walked over moss, over deer paths and through dim, sun-dappled groves, until she came to a stream and there she sat down to rest on its banks. The sun slanted into the water and insects danced in its beam. Ianthe watched them and again she thought of fairies. She touched her fingertips to the burbling surface of the water and wished.

She looked up and the boy was there, tall and dark and dressed in hunter's green, bow in hand, standing across the stream and looking back at her.

"Hello," he said, and she nodded mutely.

He was not her own age but some years older, not so much a boy as a young man, and his frame was beginning to take on some of the solidity and strength of a grown man's body. His skin was the color of fresh olives, his eyes were deep and black, and when he smiled at her they twinkled gaily.

"I didn't mean to disturb you, lady," he said, and gave her a gallant bow, and then it came to her to return the smile.

"I'm not disturbed," she said, sitting up a little straighter and smoothing the folds of her dress. "Were you after some game? A deer, or hare?"

"I've had no luck in hunting today, lady," he said, still smiling. "But it may be the gods have granted me some other kind of luck." He looked down and nodded at the water. "May I cross? Again, if I'm troubling you I'll gladly go, but I'd see you closer if I could."

He was very handsome, Ianthe thought as she looked him up and down. A noble lady alone in the forest, approached by a common hunter; the old woman would likely collapse into a fit at this turn of events, but Ianthe felt no fear, and no shame either. So perhaps she wasn't a proper lady—and she didn't care. She lifted a hand and beckoned, and the boy sprang lightly over the stream.

Ianthe laughed. "You're quite the hare yourself."

"It runs in my family," he said, dropping into a crouch beside her and laying his bow and quiver down on the moss. "A great-grandfather, perhaps, or a paternal aunt." He chuckled. "Our secret shame. Tell me, lady, how do you come to be here?"

"Ianthe," said Ianthe. "And before I tell you anything, I'd like to know what I'm to call you, if Lord Hare won't do."

He gave her a bob of his head. "Call me Iphis, lady. It's what everyone does, and it suits me well enough. My family is noble but I love no titles."

"Iphis," she repeated, turning the word over in her mouth, fitting her tongue around the shape of it. A good name, simple and strong.

I'm babbling to myself like a silly girl. I must have taken too much sun, she thought, though she knew it wasn't the sun that had her feeling so flushed. There were other boys, for sure, boys in the town the few times she had been allowed there, and now and then a boy to deliver a side of meat or some cheese to the great house. But those were just boys, all rough and tumble and still growing into their own skins. She had never looked at a boy like this before.

"Lady," Iphis said quietly, and he reached out and touched the back of her hand, soft as the brush of a fern's leaf. "Are you lost? Can I lead you out of the forest?"

"I can find my way back." She looked down at where his fingertips touched her skin, and she felt herself quiver very slightly from the top of her head down to her smallest toes. "Only—I came here to sit in the quiet and to see the trees. I came to get away from the house." She looked up at him. "Do you know what I mean?"

"Maybe I do," he said. He had not taken his hand from her. "Why do you think we hunt, lady?"

"Not to catch game?"

"That," he said, and lifted his gaze to the trees and the dappled sunlight that bathed the forest floor, the cool green ferns and the thick moss, the delicate patches of flowers clustered at the bases of wide trunks. "But not only that. Maybe not even mainly. I hunt often, but it's rare that I catch much. I don't even really try. What I love is the stillness. How secret it all feels."

He lowered his gaze again and smiled at her. "And sometimes the company I chance upon."

She looked away. She could feel that there might be danger here—not the danger of a strange man in a secluded place, but a danger of a deeper and more fearsome sort. A man who attacked her, she thought she might be able to struggle away from, and when she was loose, there were few could outrun her.

She wasn't sure that she could outrun what she felt stirring in her.

"I should go back to the house," she said, unable and mostly unwilling to hide the reluctance in her voice. "They'll miss me."

"Shall I go with you?" Already he was getting to his feet, slinging his quiver and bow over one shoulder and offering a hand. "Just to the edge of the trees, you understand." The corner of his mouth curved upward—not quite a smile but something full of humor and mischief all the same. "There might be beasts about."

Ianthe hesitated a moment, then she took his hand and felt the strength in him as he pulled her easily to her feet. "To the edge of the trees," she agreed. "No further, or I'll take a scolding from my governess if she should catch sight of you."

"Oh, let me guess," said Iphis as he held out an arm for her to take. "It's not proper for a lady to walk alone with a strange man. What will people think?"

"Scandalous things," said Ianthe, covering a smile with her free hand. "Why, they'll say we're madly in love."

"Imagine that." His voice was light but Ianthe thought that something both warm and dark passed behind his eyes. "Is the house very far?"

"Not far. We'll be there long before dark."

They were there before dark, the afternoon sun beginning to slant down through the trees and out across the grass before the orchard, deepening to a richer gold. As they walked they spoke idly of nothing in particular, but there at the edge of the forest they stopped and were silent, Ianthe's hand against Iphis's arm. She looked across the wide stretch of land before the house and felt a reluctance so powerful that it almost made her turn and run.

"Is this the house?" asked Iphis, though she knew by his tone that it was a question he asked merely to break the silence.

"Yes," she said, and sighed. "You should take your leave here." She favored him with half a smile. "Unless you want to see me get a scolding."

"I would want to see no such thing." He stepped away but paused, looking at her, and she felt herself flushing once again under that dark gaze. The sun caught his hair and for a moment she saw strands of deep red threaded into the black, and for that moment she could not pull her eyes away.

"Lady," he said finally, "it would... give me great happiness to see you again. Just to visit, and talk with you when I wish." He reached down and took Ianthe's hand, and she was mildly shocked to discover that his own were shaking. She looked into his face. Nervousness! In one so clearly confident.

"Ianthe," he said, "I... I enjoyed our walk. You're clever, and you must know that you're lovely besides. I suppose that what I'm trying to ask is..."

"Iphis," she murmured, reached up and cupped his cheek and couldn't hold back the strength of her smile. "Are you asking for permission to court me?" That stirring thing jumped within her and it was something like fear, but also nothing like it at all. They would be seen, she was suddenly very sure of it, and she was also sure that she didn't care if they were or not.

And Iphis actually blushed, his skin hot under her palm as he nodded. "I suppose I am, lady."

"By rights you should ask it of my uncle, who is my guardian."

"Ianthe," he said. "The one I care for is you."

"You cannot care for me just yet," she whispered. Somehow they had moved much closer, and she could feel the warmth of his breath on her cheek. "We barely know each other."

"Then I wish to know you better."

"Then you shall." She did not know what made her do it, lying on her bed much later that evening and thinking it over. It was a mad impulse, a desire that she no longer cared to fight, and perhaps that was reason enough. What happened was this: Ianthe leaned up, her hand still cupping Iphis's cheek, and nodded their mouths together in the first kiss she had ever taken that wasn't the light peck of the old woman or the soft kiss of her own long-dead mother. It was deep and sweet, and it deepened further, and Iphis pulled her into his strong arms and kissed her until she shuddered and gasped for breath when they finally parted.

"I'll come tomorrow," Iphis said, grinning. He was still flushed, his dark hair mussed and his lips slightly swollen, and as Ianthe stood there in the grass with one hand over her own heated lips, she thought it was the most handsome he had looked since she had met him. "I'll come and we can walk in the orchard."

"Come," she said, dropping her hand away. "Please, do. I'll wait for you."

Iphis gave her one more look and faded into the trees, shadows and green into shadows and green. Ianthe stood for another moment, watching after him, before she turned and walked toward the long rows of orange trees and the great house beyond. She was trying not to run. She was breathing as though she had.

The gods have made you a little strange, child.

Oh, but we are all such strange creatures. And Ianthe did not believe in the gods.

Except now, perhaps it was just a little bit easier to look out at the wide sea and think of that whitecap chariot, that seahorse crown.

"Ianthe."

The voice was hard and stern and Ianthe looked up from her weaving, trying to keep the alarm out of her face. She hadn't been expecting to be visited, not by a man she only ever saw at breakfast and supper, if then. "Yes, uncle?"

Her uncle stood in the doorway of her sitting room, broad-shouldered and pale, his red cloak slung back over one shoulder as though he had been hurrying. "There's a boy at the gates, and he is asking for you. I thought you might be able to tell me about it."

Iphis. So he had come after all, the very day after, and now she was sure that he should have asked permission first. "That's Iphis, uncle," she said, turning from her loom and trying to keep her voice light, careless. "He's just a boy I met near the forest." For she would not say that she was deep within it, far past the treeline. "He's no one special, but he asked if he could pay me a call some day. He amuses me, so I gave him leave."

"You should have told me that he might be coming," growled her uncle. "Or am I not your guardian? Do not make it difficult for me to guard you, Ianthe."

"I did not think it important enough to mention," she said stiffly, and what she hoped that her uncle would not perceive was that the stiffness was fear. She didn't know why she was so afraid of her uncle; he had never done anything to harm her, never raised a hand against her or punished her in any fashion other than to order her to be shut in her room when she had been naughty as a small child. But she was afraid of him. Something deep in her bones whispered to her that she must be.

Her uncle grunted. Something in his manner seemed to relax and withdraw, if any part of him could ever be said to do either, and Ianthe knew that he was already close to dismissing the matter.

"You may go and speak to him," he said. "And you may visit with him for a few minutes, provided that Chloe is there with you. But in the future, Ianthe, you are to tell me if anyone will be calling for you." He paused, half turned in the doorway, scowling at her. "Or I will be very displeased."

"Yes, uncle," said Ianthe, her head bowed, properly demure, though she felt rebellion rising within her underneath the fear. And more and more, overriding both the rebellion and the fear, she felt a surging excitement.

Iphis. He had spoken the truth, and had not even waited the span of a full day to come to her, for the morning was still early.

When she heard her uncle's footsteps recede down the corridor, she got to her feet, smoothed her skirts, paused by her polished mirror and ran her hands through her hair. She had been shaved not an hour before and her face was smooth, and she smelled of rosewater and cream made from the essence of the orange blossoms. She turned and hurried out to the front gate, the leather of her sandals making a soft clapping sound on the flagstones and echoing into the courtyard.

Iphis was leaning against one of the statues at the entrance, and when he caught sight of her he straightened up, grinning. "Lady. Good day to you."

The silent guard standing to the side gave him a look but otherwise reacted not at all. Ianthe knew, looking at him, that he had been posted there by her uncle to make sure that this ruffian stole no oranges from the orchard or flowers from the rows. Ianthe gave him a nod and he looked away again.

"Iphis," she said. She spread her skirt in a slight curtsy. "You came."

"I said I would, didn't I?"

"And yet I had no reason then to believe you." She held back her smile, but she was sure that he could see it in her eyes. "Now I do. It speaks well of you. Come and walk in the gardens with me." She drew close and took his arm, whispering, "We'll have a chaperone. But she's hard of hearing. We can talk softly together and she'll not hear us."

"And what will we speak of, lady?" he murmured.

In the doorway Chloe was pulling a shawl around herself and frowning at them. Ianthe nodded to her, and the woman stepped down into the courtyard and began to follow them at a distance, muttering to herself. "We'll speak of when I might see you again," Ianthe said quietly. "And how for a night I've been able to think of nothing else."

So they did, and more besides, their voices low under the sound of Chloe's muttering, and when they parted Ianthe had an orange blossom tucked into her dark hair, and though they had not kissed—for Chloe's eyes were far more alert than her ears— Ianthe felt her heart racing just as though they had.

The next morning Chloe came early to her with a rustle of skirts and a worried frown creasing her old brow. Ianthe turned from where she had been seated in front of her mirror, brushing her hair; she had been expecting Chloe to come to shave her, but not this early. "Chloe!" She laid down the brush. "What is the matter?"

"You should have told me you were seeing boys." Chloe carried a bundle of something in her arms.

Ianthe drew herself up, the tension in her shifting from worry to annoyance. "Chloe, I realize that you set high store in my proper behavior, but—b"

"No, no, silly girl." Chloe dropped her bundle onto the bed and its wrappings came undone as she did so, and Ianthe saw what appeared to be small, oddly-shaped pillows trailing with satin ribbons. "We shave you in the morning and in the evening, yes? Well, now, if you're to begin a'courting, we'll have to do more than that." She finished unwrapping the pillows and began to arrange them on the bed. "You don't have much in the way of curves, child. We'll have to fill you out a little. Have no worry, it's commonly done."

"Fill me out?" Ianthe looked down at herself. It was true, she had realized before now, that she was not developing the lovely swells and curves that she knew womenfolk had. But every woman she had ever seen had been different, some with much, some with little. She had assumed... "Do you really think it's necessary?"

"Sure it is." The woman lifted one of the little pillows to Ianthe's chest, and Ianthe saw at once how it was to work. "You like that boy? You want him to like you?"

Ianthe swallowed. "Very much."

"Then this will help you, girl. Here, now, I'll show you what to do."

So Chloe did, showing her each fit of the artificial curves, where to tie the ribbons, how to arrange her dress over them, and when they were done Ianthe turned and looked at herself in her mirror, turned this way and that, and smiled to herself.

The pillows were small, the change slight, and when he saw her next, Iphis only remarked that she looked especially lovely that day, and Ianthe beamed, casting a knowing glance back to where Chloe followed them at a distance. Slowly, bit by bit, they added stuffing to the cushions, a pinch here and a pinch there, so gradually that, Chloe assured her, it would look as though she were simply growing into a woman's body.

"But Chloe," she said on one occasion a week or two later, "will I always need them? Or will I grow into myself someday?"

Chloe shrugged. "Mayhap you'll grow. Some flowers bloom late. But you may always need them a little, to show yourself at your best."

Ianthe frowned as she fingered the pillow in her hands. An unsettling thought had occurred to her days before, and it had refused to leave her. "But Iphis... or anyone else, if I'm to be married... what if my husband should discover it?"

"Pshaw, child." Chloe waved a wrinkled hand. "It's common knowledge that women have tricks for prettifying themselves. They'll not be so surprised, and by then you'll have him—or whoever it's to be—so smitten with your lovely face and sweet nature that he'll not care a whit."

So they went on, and life passed over a series of weeks, a month, two, and Iphis came to her again and again and they walked together, heads bent close, and even Chloe began to frown less when it came to her to guard their propriety. Iphis kissed her again, more than once, but they were almost chaste, nothing like the passionate crushing thing that they had shared that first day by the forest. And though Ianthe missed that kiss, though at night she would lie in her bed and play it over and over in her mind, the taste of his mouth and the strong feel of him and the deep, pleasurable stirring in the core of her, she understood why he did not repeat the act.

In the most roundabout way, there was beginning to be talk of marriage.

Much later, Ianthe would reflect, she should have known that the state of affairs was too perfect to last.

It was late one evening when her uncle came to her. He did not knock as he normally did, but much about him over the past weeks had been other than normal. It was one dark spot in the midst of great brightness, the way he glowered more darkly at her than he had before, the storms in his eyes when Iphis was mentioned, and the looks she caught him sending her way. She did not know just what was in those looks.

But she knew that she did not like it.

"Ianthe," he said, towering in her doorway. She was sitting by her window with a book open in her lap, gowned for bed, and under his gaze she felt uncomfortably exposed. "It's time that we talk about this boy."

"I've been proper," she said, turning on her stool and wondering if she was going to be scolded for some slip of manners. "We've been watched by Chloe all the time, I—"

"I don't mean that," he said and took a step forward, and Ianthe felt a powerful urge to draw back. "I think you wish to marry him, yes? You've become a woman very suddenly, Ianthe. Don't think I haven't noticed it. You wish to marry him and so you may, but as your guardian I have certain rights that gainsay his."

"What rights?" Ianthe was moving now, in spite of herself, inching back on the stool and wondering, though it seemed insane, if she could get past him and out the door. If she could call for Chloe. "Uncle, I don't understand."

"Then let me explain it to you." And all at once he strode forward and laid a hand on her arm, and his grip was painful iron. She yelped and he pulled her to her feet.

"I have rights," he growled, and his free hand closed on the fabric of her gown. "I have the right to see if the girl I may marry off to some foolish lad is still pure."

"Uncle!" It came out as a cry, but a strangled one, not loud enough to be heard by Chloe or anyone else, she was sure, and though she wanted to struggle, something—perhaps terror, perhaps mere shock—held her back. Her uncle was pulling hard at her gown, and as Ianthe finally found her strength and tried to tear herself away, she tumbled backward over her seat and her gown ripped with a sharp sound. And then all was still for a moment, her uncle standing there with a piece of her gown held in one hand, and Ianthe sat in disarray on the floor, nearly naked and too surprised to try to cover herself.

Her uncle's eyes traveled down her body, down her flat chest and belly and lower still until they stopped between her legs, and they widened.

"Impossible!" he breathed.

Ianthe stared up at him. Even naked, she could perhaps still run. She didn't know what was impossible, didn't care. She only knew that she had to get away. But her uncle took a step back, his face now blanched with horror.

"You're a *boy*."

Ianthe shook her head numbly, looking down at herself again. "I'm not..."

"They *lied* to me!" He was still moving back, but the horror was rapidly darkening into a terrible rage. "Your... your mother, and that bitch of a wet nurse. They lied!"

That numbed her again in confusion and fear, for she did not remember her mother and could not imagine what she might have lied about. Or Chloe. But as she looked down at herself and again up at her uncle, as she thought about the shaving and the padding, and Iphis's lithe body and the few times that she had, blushingly, imagined what might be under his clothing...

She did not want to believe it. It made no sense at all.

"*You're* lying!" she cried, lurching to her feet and pounding past her uncle before he had the presence of mind to stop her, pulling the rags and tatters of her gown around her as she ran for the door of the house, her uncle's bellows echoing behind her.

Outside it was raining and she was instantly drenched as she ran into the orchard. There she huddled, though she could see lights moving in the great house. She shivered and shook her head, weeping into the rain. It did not make sense but now she was beginning to see how it was true. She did not even want to touch her own body, for now everything she considered was evidence. She had been a lie all her life, so foolish, so stupid to not see the truth before now, hiding in her own strangeness. It had always been with her, so she had never questioned it, the way one does not question what is deeply familiar and ever-present.

The flatness of her chest. The shaving. The awkward angles of her. Not "her" at all. Never had been.

Ianthe did not want to believe it. But eventually she did.

❧

"Ianthe?" The call was low and familiar. Ianthe sat up, still shivering, though the rain had stopped an hour or so before.

It was Chloe.

"Here," she called, keeping her voice low, and against the weird glow of the low-set clouds she saw the hunched shape of the woman turn toward her and approach. Chloe bent and a cloak was laid about Ianthe's shoulders, and she snuggled into it, grateful in spite of herself.

"Ay, child," moaned Chloe, sinking down into the grass at Ianthe's side. "If I could have saved you from that... I tried, for so many years. But time and that wicked man were both against me."

"Is it true?" Ianthe's voice was cold. "Am I...?"

Chloe hesitated, but at last she moaned again and wrung her hands together. "It's true. When you were born... you see, your uncle wanted no male heirs. Your father was dead and there was no one to protect his wife. He would have killed you. But we were told that we could save you... if we made you a girl."

"Who told you?"

"A lady." The misery in Chloe's voice was fading, replaced with something else. Something like confused wonder. "She came to the gate... she said that she knew of our plight. She told us what to do." Chloe paused. "She said you'd have her protection."

"Protection," Ianthe spat bitterly. The entire story was bizarre, dreamlike, but that word was simply preposterous now that she was ripped away from herself and huddled brokenly in the wet grass. "That's a relief. Look what good it's done me." She looked up toward the house. "What will happen to me if I go back?"

Chloe was silent, and her silence was her answer.

"Very well." Ianthe shoved herself up to her feet. Her muscles felt like lead. Her body felt like a prison, one she couldn't break away from or outrun. No longer her own but something that had been thrust on her without her consent, even before her birth. *I am no boy.* "I'll go."

"Ianthe!" Chloe reached up and clutched at her, but she pulled the cloak away and began to walk, her bare feet chilly in the wet grass. "Where will you go?"

Ianthe did not know. So she did not answer.

In the end she went where she knew she would go. Iphis had told her where he lived, not in any great detail, but when she came to the place in the road that he had mentioned, the bend and the great old tree, there was nowhere else that he could possibly mean. The house was enormous, dwarfing even hers and glowing in the rainy dark, and she stood at the gate and stared up at it, feeling like a ragged beggar at a palace door.

Worse than a beggar. A living lie.

At last she called out, and presently a guard shuffled out to her, clearly displeased at having been called into the rain. But she pleaded, smiled in what little light there was, and at last he shuffled away again, grumbling and ordering her to wait.

She waited for what seemed like a very long time, pulling her sodden cloak tighter about herself and wondering what she could possibly be hoping. If she thought that, on learning the truth, he would merely sweep her into his arms again and kiss her. If she believed that he might ever marry her now.

And he was going to learn the truth. She was beginning to discover something horrible: that she truly loved him, and that, in loving him, she was unable to let a lie stand between them.

At last the guard returned to her, opened the gate and beckoned her silently into the courtyard. There were steps leading up to the huge front door, and when the guard opened it and she stepped inside, she felt very small indeed, small and foolish and extremely wet.

She was ushered through a large front hall lit with flickering lamps and into corridors lined with elaborate tapestries, more than the equal of anything she had in her own house, and finally into a small room furnished only with two chairs and a low table where she was once again told to wait. This time the wait seemed to last barely minutes before Iphis entered, his brow furrowed with worry and his breath coming as though he had been running to her.

"Ianthe." He stepped forward and took her by the shoulders. "You're... have you been out in the rain? Where are your shoes? What's happened?"

She looked miserably up at him, flinching away when he reached up to push a lock of wet hair out of her face. His eyes darkened and for a moment she was sure that she would merely turn and run without a word.

Then she sobbed, once, and shook her head, her hair falling into her eyes. "I can't go home. My uncle..."

Iphis drew her nearer to him, bending close as he slid a finger under her chin and tilted her face up. "What of your uncle? Tell me, Ianthe."

She sobbed again and pulled away from him; the lamplight was dim and she almost felt that she might hide from him—but no, there was no more hiding. She flung the robe from her shoulders and pulled the rags of her gown aside, and her body stood bare in the flickering light, revealed and true.

For a moment Iphis simply stared at her, incomprehension plain on his face. Then, like the sunlight moving slowly across a chamber floor, understanding dawned, and his jaw went slack.

"You can't be," he murmured. "Ianthe..."

She could see the horror in his eyes. She was sure of it. Just as plain as it had been on her uncle's face, to look at her body and see something that should not be there. She looked down at herself and felt a surge of hatred. There was a dagger at Iphis's side and for an instant she thought of seizing it, driving the point of it into her own flesh, carving herself like a wooden statue until her body was as it should be, for now it was a horror that did not belong to her, that never should have been hers, and it would be the undoing of all her bright future. It had made her uncle hate her. It was making Iphis hate her. She should punish it for being so *wrong*.

Instead she pushed past him, pulling her cloak back around herself again. "I'm sorry," she whispered, and passed through the door, and in the corridor she began to run. It had not been a mistake, coming here. At least now he knew, and he could be with someone who wasn't a farce and a sham. She ran, her bare feet pounding, her cloak flying and spattering the floor with stray drops of rain, and so loud was the beat of her footfalls and the rushing of the breath in her ears that she did not hear Iphis calling behind her.

"Ianthe! Ianthe, wait! Please, I didn't—It doesn't matter!"

And in truth, if she had heard him, she would not have stopped.

She made her way to the town and wandered the backstreets until the rain stopped, and started, and stopped again, and the lights in the windows of the little houses dimmed and went out. She leaned against a wall and threw her head back, water running from her hair into her mouth. Her beautiful hair, her pride... boys did not have hair like this. Perhaps she should cut it off. She curled its damp strands into her fist and pulled until she whimpered with pain.

She would have to go somewhere. She would have to do something. A boy on a ship, perhaps, or a farmhand. Somewhere where she would be asked few questions about who she was, questions she would not even know how to begin to answer. She knew nothing about either of those kinds of work, or indeed many others, but perhaps she could learn.

But she would live as a lie, yet again. She would live with her soul crying for release all the while, crying to be who she knew she should have been. There was no escape from it, no matter what she did.

Perhaps... perhaps she would not have to go anywhere or do anything. There was a river running through the center of the town, and at the point where the bridge crossed it, it ran fast and deep. With that water, and the rising chill in the air, perhaps it would be quick and relatively painless. It would be clean. Perhaps the water would simply carry her away, out to the mouth of the river and into the vastness of the western sea, lost forever in the kingdom of the sea god.

Ianthe did not believe in the gods. "Protection," she whispered, and laughed until she was crying again.

In the end she stumbled forward once more, heading vaguely in the direction of the river and the bridge. She had made no decision but was simply moving for the sake of itself. Her mind was hazy with pain, and she might have kept going until she reached the bridge and plunged headfirst into the icy water, had a tall shape not stepped out of the shadows and into her path. By the time she noticed, it was too late. She collided with the shape with a grunt and pulled back, sure that it was her uncle, ready to run her through with his sword.

But the shape pulled back the hood of its long cloak and it was a woman. Long and slender, dark in hair, in skin, and in eyes, and even in the dim light of the few burning lamps, Ianthe could see that she was very beautiful.

"You should watch how you go, child," murmured the woman. Her wrists were thick with bracelets that jangled a low music when she moved, bracelets of a strangely glowing metal that matched the large amulet that hung between her breasts.

"I beg your pardon," Ianthe mumbled. She must look enough like a filthy urchin; perhaps this lady would merely pass her by. But the woman put out a hand and smoothed Ianthe's hair back from her face, and such was the softness and warmth in that touch that Ianthe simply leaned into it as though caressed by her own mother. And indeed, it felt that way. Instantly comforting, as though now there was nothing more to worry over or to be afraid of.

"No pardon to beg, girl," said the woman, and Ianthe didn't

think to correct her. "No pardon needed. What's a little thing like you doing out so late on a cold night?" The woman's eyes moved up and down Ianthe's form and Ianthe was sure that despite the dark, the woman could see her plainly. She lowered her eyes, feeling her cheeks flush.

"I'm on an errand for my uncle, I—"

The woman clucked her tongue gently. "Girl, don't lie to me. You're not very good at it. Haven't had much practice, have you?"

Ianthe swallowed. She was still not afraid of this woman, but she was sure that this was not someone to lie to.

"I ran," she said miserably. "I ran from my uncle's house because I fear for my life." So there it was, out in the open and no taking it back.

But the woman merely nodded. "There. Not so hard, was it? And now, that's a shame. But come and give me your hand, child. Let me feel your lines."

Though the warm comfort still lingered around her, Ianthe thought briefly of running. There were things here, moving behind the darkness and the shadows, and she didn't understand them. But perhaps they meant her no harm. She lifted her hand and the woman took it in hers and closed her eyes.

"Yes. Yes, you've been safe until just tonight. There's been long years of safety... and love, not long before now." The woman smiled. "And now... fear and pain. And you no longer know who you are."

The woman's eyes opened in a flash, and Ianthe would have almost sworn that she saw light. "I thought I might find you here, Ianthe. You should have stayed with that boy of yours, you know. His love for you surpasses the trivialities of the body."

Ianthe froze. "How did you...?"

"Before I made you, I knew you," said the woman, and grinned. Her teeth were very white. "Not my words, not in my book, but they're nice enough. The crone told you: You have my protection. Should I not watch what I've sworn to keep safe?"

Slowly, Ianthe shook her head. She was not disagreeing. When she had been small she had believed in the god of the sea and the fairies of the orange blossoms, and she had believed that a sorceress queen kept watch over her and all the house, though by her magics she was invisible and only as solid as the air.

But it had been a very long time since Ianthe had believed those things.

"But my uncle," she stammered, and the woman raised a hand and silenced her.

"Your uncle," she said, and let out a scornful laugh. "I should have foreseen that I couldn't trust him to behave himself. Know this, girl-child: when the bastard Seth scattered the pieces of my husband, I made him whole again. I breathed life into him, and from him I took a son. If you think your troubles are a match for me, you should think otherwise."

"I'm not a girl-child." Ianthe said it in a shivering whisper, instantly hoping that the woman might not hear. But the woman only laughed again, slid her warm hands in to cup Ianthe's cheeks, tilted her face up and kissed her brow.

"Of course you are," said the woman. "You have been from your birth. Didn't you know?"

Ianthe stared at her, uncomprehending, and then the change began.

At first she barely noticed it, a warmth seeding in her belly and spreading slowly outward. The woman was still touching her, and warmth also issued from that touch, beyond that put out by a living body. Warmth became heat, and Ianthe gasped with a strange mixing of pleasure and pain as her very bones seemed to be glowing within her like coals. She was shuddering, vibrating from the inside outward, and in that vibration she felt herself begin to swell. Except that, too, was not quite the right word. She closed her eyes and she saw the orange blossoms, small white buds that grew and unfurled themselves into a riot of delicate splendor.

The gods have made you a little strange, child.

Ianthe let the cloak fall back from her shoulders, reached down and ran her hands from the swells of her hips over the soft inward curve of her waist, up to the pleasant weights of her breasts, and she laughed and laughed. And as the woman placed a final, departing kiss on Ianthe's brow, her grin was bright in the darkness.

Her gown was still in tatters beneath her sodden cloak and her feet were still bare and filthy, but she practically floated back up the road, away from the town and back to the tree and the great glowing house beyond. It was late now, perhaps not many hours until dawn, but Ianthe was not tired. When she reached the gate, she called for the guard and at length he came to her, slouching and glaring sleepily at her until the light of his lantern caught her face, and then his glare faded.

"Lady," he said, bewildered. "You look... did something happen to you?"

"Yes," said Ianthe. She felt an authority come into her voice that had never been there before.

She knew herself now.

"Never mind what it was," she went on. "Let me in. I must see the son of your master."

"Mayhap he's asleep, lady," the guard said doubtfully, but he opened the gate for her and stood aside.

"If he's asleep, I'll wake him," said Ianthe, and in her rags and bare feet she walked up to the enormous door with all the confidence of a queen and knocked until she was let in.

After explaining her purpose to a drowsy servant, she was not ushered into the same little waiting room as before, but was instead led down a broader hallway and let into a large, dimly lit room with a fire burning before a broad hearth and two high-backed chairs facing its flames. The walls of the room were lined with shelves that were filled with books, and Ianthe knew immediately where she was. Her uncle had a library, though she had never been allowed to see it. But once as child she had crept into it while he was away, and had stood in open-mouthed wonder before so much accumulated knowledge.

Now she did not stand in wonder of any kind, but she bowed her head respectfully when, out of one of the chairs before the hearth, an old man with a white beard and dark eyes rose and beckoned her closer. For an instant she was freshly ashamed of her appearance, so ragged and dirty and wet, but then out of the other chair rose Iphis. His face was pale and troubled, but the trouble melted into relief when he saw her. He pushed past the chair and went to her, taking her cold hands in his warm ones, and for a moment she could barely breathe.

"Ianthe," he began, his voice quick and low, "I don't care, you must know that I don't care. I don't understand it... but whatever's happened, I've been talking to my father. He knows how I love you, and I want to say—"

She shook her head, her vision blurring and eyes prickling, and she pulled one hand free and wiped at them with the back of it like a tired child. "No, it's all right now," she said. "Don't—" And as Iphis looked at her his eyes widened, and she knew she would not have to pull back her cloak to show him the difference in her.

"Iphis?" The old man was peering at her with interest, and when she looked at him again, Ianthe saw that his face was wrinkled with smiling and his eyes were kind, though puzzled. "Would you be so kind...?"

"Father," said Iphis, turning, Ianthe's hand still held in his. "This is the girl who has so completely captured me. I still don't understand the trouble that she's in, but I want to make it clear now that I intend—"

"Yes, yes," said the old man, waving Iphis to silence. "You intend to marry her, I know. You think I didn't know it weeks ago, with the way you talk about her? That doesn't matter now. You say this lady is in trouble?" He looked Ianthe over, and though his eyes were keen, she felt no judgment in them. "You certainly *appear* to have been visited by some adventure, my dear, if you don't mind me saying."

Ianthe smiled faintly. "I have," she said. "But now it's over, and

I'm well." But just then a wave of cold and weariness swept through her and the old man took her gently by the arm.

"Come and warm yourself by the fire," he said. "And I'll have dry clothes brought for you. One of the maids is about your size, I think, if you do not mind wearing a maid's gown."

Ianthe did not mind, and as she sat by the hearth she told them some of her story, her uncle and his violence, her fear in returning home, her desperate run into the night. As she spoke, the faces of both Iphis and his father darkened, and once Ianthe was dried and freshly clothed with a cup of hot wine in her hands, Iphis's father rose from his chair and paced the floor before the fire.

"Shameful," he muttered. "Absolutely shameful. No man of any nobility..." He trailed off and looked at the two of them as if suddenly reminded of something. "Ianthe, child, do you wish to marry my son?"

Ianthe nodded. "I do, my lord," she murmured, and took Iphis's hand in hers. "With all my heart, I do." And she half expected to be told that it was impossible. Her uncle could deny her a dowry, and now he likely would. He could deny her everything, make her landless and without anything to her name, a poor prospect for a noble marriage.

But the old man smiled.

"Then I can't say anything for your scoundrel of an uncle," he said. "But as for me, you both have my blessing."

The sun was beginning to sink down into later afternoon when Iphis and Ianthe returned to the house by the sea, the orange blossoms like white clouds in the orchard. They had slept a little and talked much, though Ianthe had not told him of the woman in the town, the sorceress queen.

"But you must tell me how it came about," Iphis had protested, eyes moving over the curves under her gown, still too astonished to be particularly desiring. "It's simply fantastic. Like something out of an old story."

Ianthe had only nodded, leaned in and kissed him softly. Because that was exactly what it was like.

Now they had returned to Ianthe's house with an escort of guards. Thinking it over in the quiet of her mind, Ianthe had decided that while she would have been happy enough to never see the place again, there was still the woman who had raised her, who had loved her, and who might now be imagining that any number of horrible fates had befallen her charge. She deserved to have her mind set at ease.

And Ianthe wanted to see her. Just once more.

Ianthe stepped up to the gate and let out a sharp call. The guard who answered it looked merely annoyed at being disturbed from what Ianthe was sure had been an afternoon nap—until his gaze fell upon her, dressed as she was in a gown of rich blue silk, her dark hair combed back and secured with pearled clasps, and she heard him gasp.

"My lady—!" he stammered. "We had thought you lost... your uncle, you must know—"

"I don't care anything for my uncle," Ianthe said coldly. "You will bring Chloe here to me. I would speak with her."

The guard hesitated, as though there was more he wanted to say, but he looked once more at her and scurried away.

"You already have the appearance of a queen, love," murmured Iphis, standing with a hand at the small of her back. "Now you begin to behave as one."

Ianthe tipped her head back to look at him, trying to hide her smile. "And does it not suit me?"

"No, love." He reached up and touched one of the clasps, tugging a few strands of black hair free. "It suits you very well."

"Ianthe!" The word was pushed out between gasps and Ianthe turned again; Chloe was coming toward them at a quick waddle, her face red and her eyes wide with shock. "Oh, my darling girl... I was so sure we should never see you again. And to see you like this!" She stopped in front of Ianthe, eyes moving over her. "Why, you look like an empress from over the sea! With guards at your side, and your lad! And you—" She stopped, her mouth moving soundlessly, and Ianthe knew what she had seen. Curves that had not been there before, curves that were not the product of the little pillows with the satin ribbons. And more than that, for more than that had changed.

"Ianthe," Chloe murmured. "How...?"

"It doesn't matter, Chloe," said Ianthe, her face breaking into a smile as she forward to embrace her. For a few moments they simply stood together, and when they stepped away again Chloe was wiping tears from her face and Ianthe was passing her fingertips over the corners of her eyes.

"I'm to be married, Chloe," said Ianthe. "I wanted to come to tell you. You see, it's all come right again." Her brow furrowed, not quite a frown. "And if you want to be away from my uncle, I'm sure you could—"

"Oh, child," Chloe exclaimed, clasping her hands to her breast. "I must tell you, it's the strangest thing: he's gone. Dead, we suppose. It happened very suddenly last night, in fact, not long after you left."

Ianthe stared. Her uncle, the force of nature, always there all through the years of her life. A god in his way, with the power to give and to take, to govern the very rhythms of her life if he so chose, though for most of that time he had not. She had somehow always assumed he would never die, but would always be here in the house beside the sea, perhaps here even as the house crumbled around him. And now...

"Dead?"

Chloe nodded, and Ianthe noticed that she did not look particularly grief-stricken. "He was in a rage after... after you ran away. He was pacing the house, striking the walls with his fists and raving. He went out into the gardens, close to the cliffs. I was not there, but Aeson says he saw a woman appear, cloaked and very tall. He says she grappled with him, and in short order he was flung over the edge of the cliff." She shook her head, her face solemn. "We searched the rocks for his body, but found nothing. Perhaps the sea took him."

Ianthe thought of the sea god, and the whitecaps that pulled his chariot.

"If my uncle is dead," she said, "everything he owned passes to me and to my husband. Does it not?"

Slowly, as if realizing it for the first time, Chloe smiled.

So Iphis and Ianthe were married on the cliffs by the sea, and their way was scattered with orange blossoms. Far off among the rows of trees, there might or might not have been a tall, dark woman standing and watching them, melting away into the shadows when it was over. Iphis and Ianthe were married and they lived in the great house and they were happy. On warm afternoons and cool evenings, they would walk in the orchard together and gather the ripe oranges, and sometimes Ianthe would look off toward the western sea. She could not see gods there, nor anywhere else, nor fairies in the orange blossoms.

But now, she could almost believe.

How To Dance While Drowning
Shanna Germain

JoJo wants a mermaid's face. He tells me this while I've got one hand inside his dress, feeling around for his fake boob. I have to bend down to reach him—I'm a tall woman, nearly six foot, with shoulders broader than two JoJos put together. The dressing room is full of men shorter than me, sitting at mirrors, their mouths gaped open as they work to make their lips disappear or to double the size of their eyes.

"One of the Silkahorns," JoJo says. "They have the most beautiful cheekbones."

"You," I say, as I fish the lost blob of silicone out of his bra and press it between my hands to warm it back into its proper shape, "have the most beautiful cheekbones. I just spent an hour sculpting them."

He reaches a hand up, touches his face gingerly, as he does every time I sculpt his face for him. With his face on and his long, green-dyed hair threaded and curled, he really is exquisite. Naturally tiny lips, coated in a pale gloss to minimize them further, big, high cheekbones that rise up to nearly meet his bone-blue eyes. "I know, Sweetie," he says. "But can you imagine having real ones? And their skin. I would get the hair too. That blue-blonde color, the rare one, so it would match my eyes."

Nobody's listening to us talk. Actually, they probably are, but they don't really care one way or another. Dreams fill this place so big you can barely breathe in here some days. Everybody's got one or six or none. It's nothing new, not even anything interesting. Broken dreams? They eat those up like scavengers, cawing their grief over you while they pluck out your eyeball and swallow it whole.

I lower my voice some anyway, lean in, my hands still cupped around his boob. "JoJo, who are you kidding? You couldn't even afford a Mayna. Not on this salary."

He makes a face, twisting his nearly absent lips sideways, a gesture that I'm glad for. Too late I realize I've thrown a little too much reality into this conversation, which had a foundation of uplifting each other through vanilla-flavored lies and small kindnesses. There are days when a response like that might have induced a four-hour crying jag.

"Who wants a Mayna anyway?" he says. The confidence in his desire makes my hands sweat around the material, multiplying the scent of the dressing room, which always reminds me of fucking—condoms and sweat and expired air. "Pure waste of money."

It's true. Once Mayna mermaids were all the rage, with their flat faces, like fishy Pomeranians. They were discovered by a fisherman off the coast of Scotland, and for a long time, no one knew what to do with them. You couldn't eat them—they tasted bad, like licking the inside of a tuna can. They died in aquariums and Sea Worlds and bathtubs, and they refused to be trainable. No one knew what they ate for sure, so there was no incentive, and they weren't social like dolphins. Their parts became expensive objects d'art: people used their tails like flags in the front yard, turned their scales into jewelry, their faces into masks. Eventually someone—I think it was at a burn center—figured out that the faces of the recently dead mermaids were transplantable, just like human's. There was little rejection in the Maynas and their faces brought top-dollar at the surgery clinics, so much so that they were nearly made extinct by poachers and the black market.

But then scientists discovered the other species: Karrans, McClintics, Putternoses, seven in all. Some say that's just the beginning, that there are many more out there, just waiting to be found. Silkahorns are the most recent, and considered the most beautiful. Only four feet tall, with pearly skin, cheekbones that nearly block out their eyes and thick, silky hair that always looks wet, they're the least human-like. One in every three face transplants is rejected. No take backs on that one.

JoJo takes the warm boob back from me and stuffs it into his bra all cockeyed, which is how it keeps getting lost in the first place.

I let it go and double-check his face. He needs his eyelash implants heated again. The cheap ones never stay curled.

"Fine, no Maynas, then," I say as I dig up the eyelash heater. "And you're going to get the money from where again?"

"I'll get a Richie," he says.

I don't say anything while I dig in my makeup kit for the eyelash curler, anything truly, avoiding his eyes for real and in the mirror. We both know he can't get a Richie. Richies are the men who go to the clubs, scouting for a pretty plaything. Sometimes women too, but mostly men. Richies don't come to this club, though—we're second-rate and our patrons aren't quite Richies. They're either on their way up or their way down, or they're nobodies burning out the last of their small funds in an effort to make themselves seem like Richies. The real Richies are elsewhere—the highest end clubs or their own exclusive gigs, paying top dollar for gorgeous tiny boys with exquisite faces.

"Up," I say, and he tilts his head up obediently, lets me have at his lashes with the heated curler.

We're silent for a moment. The energy of the dancers is getting frenzied, sharks before the kill, as each man evaluates, picks apart and then chooses one last to-do, the final fix that will make them beautiful, perfect, just before the curtain opens.

"I could make Front Tier with that face, Dal. I know it. I've got the body for it, the eyes. I've got you."

I switch eyes, turn the curler inside JoJo's lash, let him talk. Up until last week, JoJo was a Second Tier dancer. For three years, he's danced behind the most beautiful seven, always on the cusp of breaking forward. He deserved it, lithe and lean, only five foot five. If he got into First Tier, he could get noticed, become some almost-Richie's good catch.

But a few weeks ago, Gianna came to Under the Sea. Petite, blonde Gianna with the angel's face. A Silkahorn's face, his cheekbones like alabaster hills, invisible lips. His tiny frame with its swell of hip and breast. And now JoJo's dancing in Third Tier, framed on one side by Shanta, a five-foot-five man with a bad wig, and on the other by a former go-go dancer whose knees give out every other show.

JoJo takes a breath, talks without fluttering his captured eyelashes. "I could have my legs done. I bet they could get me down to five three, maybe even five two."

I know why JoJo's obsessing. Once a year, the Richies—not just the wanna-bes, but the real Richies—come to Under the Sea. It's a special night, when you can take home the Fin Dancer of your choice for the right fee. The proceeds go to the Mermaid Coalition, which pumps research into trying to save them from extinction through a breeding program. The men don't get any money, not a cent, but of course they hope that their Richie will find them irresistible, invite them to stay.

Next month the Richies will come. JoJo wants, he needs, to be in the First Tier.

"I'll make you a better face," I say. "A perfect face."

He tightens his pale lips into a pucker. "Not good enough," he says. "You're good, but you're not that good, Dal. Nobody's that good."

"Dal, don't you ever just want to be beautiful?" he asks.

His question makes my hand shake. I touch the top of his eyelid with the curler. I don't mean to, and it's a contact so brief that I'm already pulling away before it connects. The lid welts instantly, an angry red that's going to look like a sty in about an hour if I don't dig up some ice.

"Mother of fuck, Dal." JoJo hasn't moved—the faith he has in me is blind stupid, but he's blinking hard, tearing up. His mascara's lacquered on, so it's not going to run. His cheekbones, however, will. The putty can stand up to water, but not to salt. We don't have time to start over.

"Hold on," I say. "Hold on hold on. Just hold it JoJo."

I fumble around on the dressing counter until I find the can of compressed air. "Eyes closed," and before he actually gets them shut, I hit the button. Cold air fills the room, and I get a hit of that taste—fresh out of a can, which is always something my brain has a hard time processing. I aim the nozzle at the bump on his eye, cooling that side of his face.

JoJo is still muttering, "Shitfuckshitfuck," under his breath, but he's sitting still and his face is intact. A few of the other dancers turned at his initial outburst, but no one stops putting on their face, no one offers to help. Around here, it's sink or swim, may the best man drown so I can take his place. A ship's horn blows, signaling that it's almost show-time, and men start standing up, patting their long green dresses down over barely-there hips and thighs, adjusting boobs and wigs.

"Okay, open," I say.

He does, and I'm a little shocked as always when he aims his bright blue gaze at my face. The skin under his eyes is turning waxy and dark, despite all the cover-up. "When was the last time you ate, JoJo?"

He shrugs. The movement brings his bony shoulders up toward his ears, like a coat hanger hung with skin.

I hand him an apple out of my bag, which he picks apart with his pointed fingernails but doesn't put in his mouth.

As I always do, I watch the dancers from behind the wings. My job at Under the Sea isn't really to do JoJo's face and hair—that just happened, when he found out I was good at it. And I don't mind. I like making him beautiful. Sometimes I help out the other men too, the Fifth Tier crew. Fifth Tier are men on their way out, retiring or their bodies falling apart from age and overuse. They need all the help they can get.

My real job, the one they pay me this pittance for, is to clean up after the dancers go. I sweep the sequins and false eyelashes from the stage, wipe the sculpting putty off the dressing tables, repair the broken heels and the popped breasts for tomorrow's show.

My view is from the side, which is somehow disconcerting,

because the sculpted and transplanted faces aren't as beautiful from the side as they are from the front. You see the flaws in them, the not-smoothed ridges, the edges of the hairline where transplant scars are visible. From the front, the men in their shimmery green dresses flow and swim like weightless underwater beauties. From the side, it looks like they're lined up against the edge of something unseeable, bumping and grinding again and again against invisible glass.

JoJo's face looks perfect under the dim blue lights.

I touch my own face with my putty-covered hands, feel the broad-jawed, flat plain of it. Of course I want to be beautiful. Who doesn't?

"Beautiful is overrated," I say beneath the music. It's something my nana used to say. I didn't know for that longest time that she was talking about me.

The dancers shift and from this angle, I can see Gianna, gyrating in the front row and beyond that, the men at the tables, holding rapt, money and drinks and cigars in their hands. He is perfection, or something close to it. Perfection except for the long pink lines that run down the sides of his face transplant. They're too dark, nearing the kind of red that comes not from recovering scars but from growing infection, an angry red. Gianna's body is already rejecting his new face. I wonder if he knows.

JoJo doesn't mention his new face again in the next few weeks. But there's something in his gestures, in the way that his eyes study Gianna's face, that tells me he's thinking about it, devising a plan. I want to ask him what it is.

Instead, I make his face as perfect as I can. My nana is a putty-shaper, creating one-of-a-kind mermaid masks and toys. She's the one who taught me to shape faces, and she has a new putty, something finer, that holds better to the skin. It's so dry that it burns my hands, cracks them open to near bleeding each time I use it, but it turns JoJo's cheekbones into mountains, rising peaks that frame his face. But he doesn't say anything about them.

Two weeks until Auction Night, and the dancers are abuzz with news: The city's richest will be here this year. Cardona's taking a day off to get his new face. There's some new surgery for eyes that opens them up wider. One of the dancers, a Latino boy named Braum, has his lips taken off by a black-market surgeon and his mouth is a red scar for a week. No one really cares—he's a Fifth Tier anyway, so it doesn't open a new slot for anyone. And he's healing fine.

When I go home nights, I chip the dried putty from my hands with my nana's putty knife. Nana coats my hands in sea salt and Vaseline, makes me wear her gloves to bed to keep my hands coated.

"Comes off easier that way," she says, although she gave up on her hands years ago.

Even with nana's help, there's no way to get it all off. My skin is lined with the dust and dirt of the material, my nails constantly caked with the pale remainders of JoJo's face.

"Dal?" It feels odd to hear JoJo's nickname for me come out of a mouth that sounds nothing like his. Gianna's voice is pitched, not squeaky, but nearing it.

I'm sitting in the dressing room, holding pins between my lips—JoJo's lost more weight in the last week, his dress is too big in the waist. The material between my hands is thick with dirt and grime from the dance floor, my hands are sticky with things I don't want to think about.

I turn to see Gianna standing in the half-shadow of the dressing room. I open my mouth and let the pins drop to the floor, ping-ping-ping.

"Dalilah," I correct. I don't mean to be unkind, but I have too many familiar wrongs in my life. I'd like this one to remain unfamiliar if I can.

Gianna doesn't say anything. Even in the half-dark, even from the front, I can see the edges of his face. They look like they're beginning to peel away from his real skin, to flake off. Around his ears, the skin is layered like gills.

"Dalilah," he says. And this time I can hear his audible swallow in the middle of my name. "I don't know what to do." Pain tightens his vocal cords, makes him sound high and squeaky in the dim space.

The fabric of JoJo's dress is wavering inside my grip, the needle grows sweaty between my fingers.

I hate the thing I see in Gianna's eyes, but I can't help him. I owe whatever loyalty I have to JoJo, whatever hopes I have for beauty are placed in him.

"Talk to JoJo," I say. "You talk to JoJo and you tell him what a bad idea this is, every bit of it. You say all of that to him, and I'll do your face tomorrow night. I'll give you one last night of beauty before..." Even I cannot say that, even I am not that cruel.

He nods and he backs out without turning around, his eyes big and empty inside the falling off space of his face.

❧

There's an odd buzz in the air that hits me like foam as soon as I walk into the dressing room the night of the big show. No one's talking, but they move in a whirled frenzy of activity. At first I think it's the performance, tonight's grand finale, but there's something else, something darker. I'm early—the plan is to do Gianna's face before I do JoJo's, but neither are here yet, so I spend the time prepping my workstation and helping a few of the Four- and Five-Tier guys with small dress fixes.

One of the men I help is Shanta, who has a new, better wig, dark blonde, made from real hair. I help him position it properly, use a couple of pins to keep it on.

I'm leaning over him, a hand stuck in his hair, when he shifts suddenly, bursts the words out in a whisper, as though he's been holding his breath too long and can't bear it anymore. "Gianna has COLORS."

I have to breathe very carefully in order to not stab him with the hair pin. So that's what the buzz is all about—it's everyone trying to pretend they're not glad for it.

"What? Jesus," I say. "Jesus. How? When? Jesus."

"Black market. His face came off the black market."

My fingers shake as I put the final pin on and go to JoJo's station to get setup. COLORS. Christ. So few diseases are passable from mermaids to man, but this is one of them. Blood borne, makes the skin pass blue then green then gold and then, well, then nothing. Death is a color too, I suppose, but I don't know which one.

And yet a part of me knows that Gianna's down. He's done for. And what reason then would he have to pass my plea along?

"Where's JoJo?" I ask, but no one answers me. Their mirrored reflections, their lipless mouths moving, these are the only things they can hear.

Now that I don't do JoJo's face, I come in late. Usually just in time to watch the last dance from behind the wings.

First Tier, smack dead center. A gorgeous blue-blonde with a face that's so perfect it cannot be man-made. His lips all but disappearing in the overhead light, round eyes carrying the blues of the ocean. Hips shimmy and shimmer. The green dress tugs around his waist like a perfect pair of hands.

You would have to know that dancer really well, you would have to be the kind of girl who used to create his face and sew his dress, the kind of girl who tucked his boobs in next to his heart, you'd have to know him that well in order to catch the other glimmer of green, that thin line like seaweed that tangles along his jawline. You'd have to know him that well in order to see the tiny glint of pain already sharpening his steps as he dances.

The Richies don't know him at all. They lean forward in their seats, money in their hands, hunger in their eyes.

My hips move but my feet stay still. I close my eyes against the colors that swim in front of me, push my fingers into my mouth. My skin tastes of sea salt. My hands are too clean.

Treasure And Maidens
Sarah Rees Brennan

Emma knew she was doing something stupid. She wasn't sure whether this made her less stupid because at least she knew, or more stupid because she knew and she was still doing it, but she felt she had no choice. The heating was out again, and it was the middle of the night. By the time dawn came, Emma would be a tragically human-shaped popsicle.

When she'd complained about her unreliable heating to her landlord, he'd given her a patient look. A look that said, essentially, that this was a down-market New York apartment, and Emma could count herself lucky if she wasn't eaten by rampaging alligators.

The place was pretty old: a five story building on Flushing, crumbling in a way that only new bread or old brick did, which must once have been a nice home where children played and which had now been sliced up into twenty different apartments where New Yorkers could freeze. Her landlord had run a hardware store on the ground floor for twenty years. If there were alligators around, he would've had time to train them to attack.

Emma had backed down, but now she was thinking bring on the alligators. It'd be a quick death.

The tiny disused fireplace in Emma's bedroom was her only hope. She'd made a frantic search for matches and lighters, but Lilli was gone and all her smoking paraphernalia with her. Emma was pretty sure that she'd had a lighter once, but Lilli had obviously taken that too. Some girlfriend.

It was entirely Lilli's fault that Emma was now, after several attempts to create fire by striking two clay statuettes together, bending over her toaster and trying to light the edge of a newspaper. She looked down at the red-hot bars inside the toaster and felt she was seeing her own death. She was going to set the floor on fire, die in an inferno, and then her mom would be proved right about Emma not being able to take care of herself.

On the other hand, she'd be warm.

"I hold with those who favor fire," Emma informed her toaster, and applied the newspaper to the glowing bars.

The edge immediately crumbled into black ash and disappeared into the depths of the toaster. Emma, gripped by the sudden conviction that this would make her toaster explode, picked it up and tried to shake the ash out.

It was then that she looked up, caught by a vivid yellow light coming through her window. At first she thought it was the moon, but it was too large and too close.

It wasn't the moon.

Catching the light in a gleaming, living way that no moon could have was a great yellow eye. The pupil was slit, like a cat's eye. Around the eye, and filling her window from edge to edge, were black scales.

It could have been one of those rampaging alligators coming for her at last, but it wasn't. Emma knew that it was a dragon. She didn't know how she knew, but she did. The great, mysterious certainty that this was a dragon and nothing else seemed to fill the room, pushing out the cold air, pushing out everything Emma had ever known about the world and replacing it with that one word: *Dragon*.

Emma dropped the toaster on her foot.

The pain was a shock that brought her back to awareness of her body and especially her throbbing foot; she yelped, cursed and hopped around. Then the dragon spoke.

It came as an even greater shock that she could, even for a moment, have forgotten about the dragon outside her window because her foot hurt.

Emma stood and stared and thought that she must have a defective brain.

"Hello," said the dragon, in a deep, soft voice Emma thought—but was not quite sure—was female. "Will you invite me in?"

"I don't think you could squeeze in," said Emma.

Emma had a sudden surreal vision of the dragon in her three-room apartment, snout jammed in Emma's mildewed shower, a scaly haunch squashed against Emma's threadbare sofa and a long tail wrapped around the ancient, creaky fridge. She suppressed a hysterical laugh and had the wild thought that if the dragon thought she'd fit into a Brooklyn apartment, she was obviously new to New York.

"It won't be a problem," the dragon assured her, "as long as you'll invite me."

"Isn't that how it works with vampires?" Emma asked suspiciously, and demanded: "Are you a vampire dragon?"

Emma cringed once she realized how ridiculous that sounded. The dragon laughed, a low rich sound that wasn't unpleasant in itself, but did sort of put Emma's life into perspective. Emma McLaughlin, ladies and gentlemen: Secretary. Sagittarius. Laughed at by flying reptiles.

"Invitations are necessary for most of our kind."

"Well," Emma said, trying to reclaim her dignity, "Are the—the rules the same? Once you're invited in, you can do anything you like?"

"That's the spell," the dragon said. "Those are the rules."

"It's not a spell, it's an invitation," Emma said. "It's just words."

"The right words. That's what a spell is. It's in all the stories, Emma. Let me in."

The dragon's slit pupil reflected Emma, captured in a mirror of jet and surrounded by a circle of light. She stared at her own fascinated face and realized that she wanted to obey that deep sweet voice.

She couldn't. It would be madness.

"Um," Emma said. "Sorry if it's impolite to ask, but—is there any chance that once you're in, you'd like to eat me up and crunch my bones?"

"I only want one thing from you," said the dragon. "And it only counts if it's given willingly. I won't hurt you unless you ask me to."

"Ahaha," said Emma. "Don't hold your breath waiting for me to ask."

"Can I come in?" persisted the dragon, patient in a way that seemed effortless and eternal, like a mountain.

It was like putting the newspaper in the toaster on a larger scale. Emma knew she was shocked silly, acting like a lunatic, and yet she couldn't quite help herself. She didn't want the dragon to give up and fly away.

She opened the window and said: "Yes. You can come in."

The dragon turned into smoke.

From a staring eye and scales to smoke, a thick coil of darkness like a small tornado that spun into Emma's kitchen and shaped itself into something new. Emma felt a sudden strange urge to be a proper hostess—she'd invited a dragon into her apartment and there were toasters all over the floor! She bent down, scooped up the toaster and put it in a pleasingly symmetrical position on the counter.

When she'd fussed around with the toaster long enough for her hands to stop shaking, she turned and looked at the dragon.

The dragon was tall, about the same height as Emma, but noticeably unlike Emma she was a long lean sweep of muscle from long legs in high boots, strong thighs in leather trousers, and a waistcoat showing slim but powerful-looking shoulders with enough white, curving flesh revealed that Emma could be quite sure the dragon wasn't wearing a bra.

The dragon smiled when she saw Emma looking, her lips curling upward to reveal a mouth full of pointed teeth. The smile made her eyes, still yellow and still slit, narrow lazily over her high cheekbones. Her hair was short, black and spiky, and if she hadn't looked so incontrovertibly dragon-like Emma would have thought she was trying to look like a biker pixie from hell.

Emma felt more scared than she had been by the flying reptile. This was the kind of glamour that caught you by the throat, cornered you in some dark alleyway of your brain and robbed you of all common sense.

She was seized by the sudden pressing urge to say something cool.

"Hi," she squeaked, and her voice had the all the alluring

resonance of a mouse being squashed by a door.

"Hi," murmured the dragon. Now she was no longer a huge flying reptile, Emma could admit her low voice might also be described as husky.

It made all kinds of thoughts stir in Emma's mind. A creature from myth had turned up at her window and asked to be let in, and then transformed into someone supernaturally gorgeous. Emma had a vague idea, fluttering inside her head like an over-excited budgie, of what should happen next.

"So," Emma said feebly. "Would you—would you like some tea?"

The dragon shrugged fluidly. "Sure."

"Maybe some suh-cereal," Emma continued, and wondered whether it was her mom's training that made the word 'sex' come out as 'cereal.'

"Love some," said the dragon.

Had Emma ever imagined a rendezvous with a supernatural hussy, she would not have pictured Cheerios featuring largely.

On second glance, the leather the dragon was wearing was black and faintly patterned with scales, as if she'd killed her former self and was wearing the skin.

Emma tried not to take a third glance right away. Instead she put the kettle on and as she dropped teabags into mugs with shaking hands, she said: "Er—may I ask your name?"

"I'm a dragon," the dragon said blankly.

"Okay, Dragon," said Emma, and Dragon smiled.

Emma picked up a mug and held it as a tiny useless shield between herself and that smile.

"Names are human things. Like spells."

"Oh yes," said Emma, in an unconvinced tone. "Well—Dragon. What are your interests and hobbies?"

Wonderful, Emma, she congratulated herself. *Conduct a job interview with the dragon.*

Dragon raised her eyebrows, which were dark and strongly marked, going up at the ends as if they were poised to take flight. "The usual dragon interests. Treasure and maidens."

Emma spilled tea on herself and screamed.

"Sorry! Treasure, you say? And—and maidens. Fascinating."

"All dragons like maidens," Dragon told her. "That's in the stories."

"Mm," Emma said. "It's just that I don't recall any, uh, girl dragons in the stories."

"Would you prefer me to become a man?" Dragon asked.

Which was the million-dollar question.

"Uh," said Emma.

"I was under the impression this form would be most acceptable to you."

"Yes it's very nice!" Emma said, and formed a desperate plan to distract the dragon with conversation. "Um—so, do you have any current plans to devastate New York with fire?"

Dragon waved a dismissive hand. "Of course not. People have bombs and fighter planes now. Anyway, it was never more than an encouraging gesture so the city would hurry up with its best maiden."

"Oh," Emma said.

"I like your hair," Dragon added, apropos of nothing very much.

"Oh," Emma said again, brilliantly. After a moment of guilt, she added: "It isn't real."

It had seemed like a good idea at the time. Having long, frizzy brown hair meant having hair nobody noticed, and a simple bottle of color gave her something that was technically a Red-Haired Mane, which she'd thought would be the ticket to a more exciting life.

It seemed she'd been absolutely right.

"I know," Dragon told her, and at Emma's confused expression, she explained, "Well, you don't think that I would come for a maiden before I'd checked her out thoroughly, do you?"

Emma stared. Dragon laughed and continued to eat her Cheerios.

When Dragon was done eating, Emma washed up. Her hands

were already numb, so the cold water didn't affect her. She just watched her skin go egg-shell blue and wondered what the hell she should do.

She turned from the sink and found Dragon was rising from her seat.

"I should be going."

"Oh," said Emma. "Well, uh, thank you for coming, it's been—"

"I will come back," said Dragon, "if you permit it."

The dragon's gaze caught and held Emma as it had from outside her window, until all she could see was a dark opening into light and all she could say was yes.

"All right," she whispered.

Dragon's yellow eyes traveled over her, slowly, in the way fire seems slow sometimes before you realize how much damage it has done.

"I'll come for seven days," she said. "That's part of the spell."

"What spell? Whose spell?"

"Yours," Dragon said, with such a smile. "Only at night, of course. Dream lovers only come at night."

"Aren't the rules different for dream Cheerio eaters?" Emma asked faintly.

Dragon's smile did not waver. "Seven days. And at the end of seven days, you tell me if I can have what I want."

"What do you want?"

"Your heart," said Dragon. "You aren't using it, are you?"

She didn't wait for Emma's answer before she threw herself out the window.

Emma made a strangled sound and rushed forward. For a moment she saw the terrible sight she'd expected to see—a small human figure in free fall towards a catastrophic landing. Before Emma could open her mouth to scream she saw wings billow out like a parachute, trailing a long dragon's tail, and with one vast surge of those wings the dragon was suddenly aloft, her body skimming over the skyscrapers.

The dragon moved fast enough to chase the dawn and as Emma

stared her dark shape dwindled into the distance, until all any early riser would have seen was a swallow over Brooklyn Bridge.

చ్చు

Emma was viciously tired at work the next day. Luckily data entry required no actual input from her brain.

It couldn't have happened. She was a secretary in a firm of accountants. The only reason she lived in New York was because she'd thought that moving to the big city, like dyeing her hair, would make her exciting. She wasn't exciting. She didn't even think she was exciting enough to be a *lesbian*.

She'd never thought about it in her small school in her small town back home. She'd gone out with boys without being particularly enthused about them, and she'd had sex with a lot of them, mostly because they seemed to like her and it would be embarrassing to say no. Her mom had said she was too soft-hearted. Her friends had said she was kind of slutty.

Then she'd moved to New York and made friends with Jon who lived downstairs and was gay, and she'd congratulated herself on being daring enough to be a fag hag. And then Jon's friend Lilli had pounced and she'd wanted to be exciting and, just like with all those boys, she'd been too embarrassed to say no.

Sex with Lilli was a whole lot better than with those boys. It was that, and the fact that she was dizzy with how daring she was being, how *different*, which made her ignore the fact she didn't know if she actually liked Lilli.

Lilli had purple hair and tattoos. She was a proper lesbian, the kind people whispered about back home. Emma didn't know if she was cut out for it. She'd dyed a strand of her hair blue once at a slumber party, and woken up in the night panicking about what her mom would say and chopped it off. She'd never sat around at school and thought, oh yeah, love the ladies. She didn't even like the right music. She really hadn't liked it when Lilli had cheated on her. Emma had cried and dumped her and Lilli had said she was boring and conventional.

She did like sleeping with girls, but with Lilli gone she'd had less than no idea what to do about it. She had thought about going back to boys, who were so much easier to find and who wouldn't upset her mother, and then worried that having that thought made her a terrible self-hating homophobe. And she'd thought that maybe if she met the right guy, the sex might be awesome and the problem would be solved. Not that being gay was a problem!

It was all so complicated.

She'd been contemplating a lifetime of secretarial celibacy when a dragon had flown in her window.

Emma knew it hadn't been a dream. She also knew things like that couldn't happen to anyone, and especially couldn't happen to her.

She remembered Dragon's smile as she'd said 'dream lovers.'

Then she remembered Dragon's teeth, and hastily crossed her legs.

She didn't have a decision to make, because things like that were impossible and Dragon certainly wouldn't be there tonight. She didn't have to think about it at all.

She thought about it all day, during work, during a call from Jon arranging to have a drink that night, during a call from her mom when her mom asked how she was doing and she remembered Dragon's little comment about checking her out thoroughly and almost answered: "Lesbian dragons are spying on me in the shower. How about you, Mom? Are you well?"

Emma suppressed this insane urge, and later went out for the drink with Jon. She sat sipping her screwdriver in a bar full of leather queens while Jon looked around with acquisitive eagerness; when Jon found more exciting company, she went home.

Before Jon went to check out more leathery pastures, he said: "You seem kind of nervous. Met someone you like?"

Emma's laugh crackled uneasily from her throat, almost hurting her as it came. "No," she said. "How could I?"

She got out at Union Square and bought groceries from Whole Foods on her way home because she knew nothing was going to happen. She climbed the five flights of creaking stairs and saw no light under her door, and of course she wasn't disappointed, because she hadn't expected anyone to be there.

She pushed open the door and for a moment thought she had been right. There was no great yellow eye at her window filling the room with its light. Emma closed the door and leaned against it, taking a calming breath. Then in the familiar darkness of her flat she saw a faint gleam of yellow, like light striking off a knife edge. The bag of groceries fell out of her hands as she fumbled for the light.

Dragon was sitting on the sofa. She rose as Emma stood there and gaped.

"I thought," Emma said, and her voice sounded young and stupid, scared and thrilled. "I thought you wouldn't come."

Dragon stalked toward her, narrowed eyes intent, and reached out a hand. Her long, strong fingers curled around Emma's hair, her fingertips holding Emma's jaw in place.

"I never lie," whispered Dragon, too close, full lips and sharp teeth a rich confusion in Emma's dazed eyes. Then Dragon kissed her.

As it turned out, Dragon was very careful with her teeth.

"Would it be really inappropriate at this point to make a joke about silver tongues?" Emma asked some time later, collapsed back against the pillow.

Dragon slid up along her body, sleek and sure, and laughed into Emma's face. She licked her lips, ran her tongue along those glittering teeth, and Emma saw that her tongue was gleaming like silver in the shadows.

"Who's joking?" said Dragon.

"Oh, no way," breathed Emma, and she rested careful hands on Dragon's back, which didn't feel like a human back; it had too many muscles bunched in preparation to be wings.

Dragon scraped Emma's throat with those teeth, and Emma shuddered and laughed and wrapped her legs around her.

It wasn't just the sex. Emma could have withstood just sex: her mom had prepared many wise words to get her through that sort of thing.

Her mom had never said anything about your chest constricting because you put on some music and discovered your dragon liked indie rock. On the third night, Emma took Dragon out clubbing because she wanted to see Dragon dance.

Of course, the only club Emma knew was one Lilli had taken her to, a club in a small dark street off a neon-bright road where the bouncer wore eyeliner and a nose ring and the boys usually had longer hair than the girls. It was one of those places where Emma felt she never knew the secret Real Lesbian password.

And of course Emma met Lilli at the bar. Emma clutched her drink and wondered whether dragons brought bad luck.

"Hi," Lilli said, her nose stud sparkling in the light.

"And a big hey to you too," Emma said in a manically cheerful voice. She'd left Dragon somewhere out there in that sea of people and multicolored lights, hips moving lazily and head tipped back, throat exposed and shining with sweat.

"You here with anyone?" Lilli asked. Her lip curled as she anticipated the answer that Emma was here with Jon.

"Yes," growled Dragon, low and cold, her arm suddenly around Emma's shoulders, pulling her back against the strong curve of Dragon's body.

Lilli looked dazzled and amazed and Emma, pressed against Dragon with Dragon's cheek laid against her neck, felt powerful and desirable suddenly, not belonging here but no longer caring, raised above Lilli. Flying.

"Excuse us," she said. "We have to go—"

She would've said 'dance' but Dragon cut her off with a kiss, mouth hot and demanding, and Emma was left staring helplessly into those heavy-lidded yellow eyes.

"Or we could go do that," she said.

When she thought to look around for Lilli, Lilli was long gone.

Walking back home through the cold streets, hand in hand with Dragon, Emma said: "So, seven days."

"Yes."

"And from then on, I mean, what were you planning on doing? Would you—were you thinking of—going through my circle of acquaintances?" Emma's intestines felt like knotted string someone was pulling on.

"You mean Lilli," Dragon said, in a blessedly unimpressed tone, and then spat on the sidewalk. Emma watched her spit sizzle when it hit the cement. "What would I want with that one?" Dragon asked. "Her heart would be like a dried apricot."

Emma's personal heart almost stopped.

"So when you said you wanted my heart," she said, speaking carefully. "Did you, in fact, mean the sort of having my heart that would leave me extremely dead?"

"No," Dragon said, in an almost wounded tone. "No. It wouldn't kill you. Oh, Emma. I wouldn't kill you. I don't want you dead."

"Th-thank you," Emma stammered, and then because that seemed such a pathetic thing to say she tried to smile. "That's just what every girl longs to hear."

She kept trying to smile. It was all a joke.

She couldn't be sleeping with someone she thought might hurt her. She just couldn't.

Dragon was suddenly standing in front of her, running her hands up Emma's body.

"I want your heart," Dragon whispered, her breath frighteningly hot. "I don't want to move on. Give me your heart, and I can stay with you: I want to be with you until I die."

Emma leaned in, her lip caught between Dragon's lips, her tongue touching Dragon's silver tongue. Her insides felt like they were melting under a blast of fire, even while her mom shrieked in her head and pointed out that a girl dragon was touching her daughter's breasts in public.

"You have to be the one who decides," Dragon said. "You're the only one who can cast the spell."

"I can't do spells," Emma whispered.

"Human words are spells," Dragon murmured, a tooth grazing the edge of Emma's mouth. "Haven't you noticed how often what a human says becomes true? Look at Lilli. When she cheated on you she told that other girl she didn't have a girlfriend and it came true. Amazing."

Emma hadn't thought it was terribly amazing at the time, but almost anything seemed amazing right now, with Dragon's sharp nails tracing under her short dress, up her thigh.

"Dykes," some punk kid muttered, shoving past them, and Emma drew back a little.

She found Dragon looking at her, head tilted. She couldn't quite read her expression.

"That bothers you?"

"A little," Emma said. "It's not nice to hear strangers hating you for no reason. And it's none of their business."

Dragon nodded. For a moment Emma just thought Dragon's face was very serious, her jaw set, and then she realized her jaw was actually becoming stronger before Emma's eyes, cheekbones angling differently until it was not her face anymore, but his. Dragon made a gesture that reminded Emma of spread wings in the night, and his shoulders spread outward a little.

He stood before Emma, the boyfriend she'd secretly wanted, the one she could take home to her mother and who would be a girl behind closed doors.

Dragon offered her his hand. She could walk down the street holding his hand, or kiss him, and nobody would ever look twice.

"I'm glad you can do this," Emma said. "It's making everything very clear for me. Could you—do you mind changing back?"

A ripple spread across Dragon's face, like touching a pool of water and seeing a reflection blur and change, and she stood before Emma smiling.

When the next person offered a sneering comment Dragon snarled at him, teeth showing and eyes flashing like the headlights of a car, and he ran like hell.

"I'm finding this whole experience very empowering," Emma said.

Of course, it occurred to Emma that Dragon could be lying. She only had Dragon's word that Dragon didn't lie, and that thought chased around in her head like a squirrel chasing its own tail.

One thing Emma did not doubt was that Dragon wanted her. Emma had never been what you'd describe as overwhelmingly confident, but she was certain of that much: every time Dragon was near Emma could feel her burning restless need, her hot eyes resting on Emma and trying to drag a response out of her.

"I find you beautiful," Dragon murmured on the fifth night, Emma's breasts crushed against Dragon's. She traced the curls of Emma's hair against the pillow, as if trying to find her way on a treasure map. "I would burn cities and rain destruction on the fields and abandon gold, just to have you."

"You say the sweetest things," Emma said, shaken between laughter and a fierce desire to believe her, believe anything she said.

The sheets shifted, and a draught filtered in and made Emma shiver and press herself closer to Dragon. Dragon laughed and fire circled out of her mouth, a bright snake that flowed through the air towards Emma's fireplace, and then rested there.

The fire burned all night long.

ॐ

On the sixth night Emma's rescuer arrived, and she sent him away.

"Hey, Em, you've been so weird all week, I came up to check on you," said Jon, twirling the spare set of keys on his finger and dressed for clubbing, his shirt gleaming like tinsel.

Or like armor, Emma thought. Dragon believed in stories. Dragon had frozen as soon as the shining knight came in.

Emma reached out to Dragon, seized her hand, to protect her or to keep her, and said ridiculously: "She's invited."

Jon looked from Emma to Dragon, and started to grin. "Oh right," he said. "Well, good on you, Em. I'll just be going."

With the cheerful slam of the door ringing in their ears, Dragon said: "Thank you."

Dragon said human words were powerful. Emma tried to think

about that, to realize what she'd really said: that she did not want to be saved.

It was her second-to-last night with Dragon.

She held tight onto Dragon's hand, pressed her against the kitchen counter and whispered, her throat aching: "You have my heart."

Dragon kissed Emma's aching throat. Her lips were so warm.

"Not yet," Dragon whispered back. "You have to say I can take it."

On the seventh day, half an hour or so before the sun slipped behind the skyscrapers and made it the seventh night, Emma called her Mom from a phone box and found herself crying, out there in the streets.

"I like girls. I've—I've met someone," she said, words tumbling out as they never had when she'd had a real relationship, a human girlfriend, as she'd never felt they needed to until now when she spoke and knew why she had to speak. "I love her."

"Emma, Em, my darling," said her Mom, voice crackling over the miles. "Do you think I care who you like? I love *you*."

"I love you back, Mom," Emma said, and bawled with busy Manhattanites flicking her mildly intrigued glances as they went by. A tramp kindly tried to distract her by stopping by the phone booth and exposing himself.

"Don't bother," Emma said wearily as she stepped out. "I'm a lesbian."

When she came home to Dragon in the dark, she started crying. Dragon put her hand under Emma's chin and started licking Emma's tears away with her hungry silver tongue. Emma stood and shook and even laughed a little, wondering if Dragon's tongue would leave silver trails in the moonlight, as if a snail had got lost on Emma's face.

She knew it should end there, that this should become a bittersweet and magical memory, a lesson she had learned. She remembered Dragon's face changing into the face of the perfect boyfriend, and knew that there should always be a limit to how much you would change yourself for a lover.

She knew all that and still, later that night, quiet in moonlight and crumpled sheets, Emma reached out to Dragon and touched her hand.

She heard her own voice come out, low and trembling and unlike itself.

"Don't leave me," she said. "I love you. You can have my heart."

"Oh," breathed Dragon, soft and overcome as if she'd just seen a miracle.

"What do you usually do now?"

"Usually?" Dragon laughed. "This has never happened before. You're my first. My first and last."

She laughed again and kissed Emma, and Emma felt happy and relieved: this was nothing more than the words Dragon said were spells and now they would be together, she had all she wanted, and Dragon traced reverent fingers along the crest of Emma's left breast.

Then she ripped her heart out.

Emma did nothing. She didn't even scream, mind shocked by the betrayal and body shocked by the incredible amount of pain, nothing but prey already caught and pinned under the dragon. Dragon's sharp nails burrowed their way in, and then Dragon bent her dear black head and her sharp teeth gnawed and carved a larger hole in Emma's flesh. She lifted her head once and smiled at Emma with gory shreds hanging from her lips.

Dragon reached inside with one blood-red hand and clutched Emma's heart in her fist. Emma felt it beat one last time, trying to escape the prison of Dragon's fingers. Then it was gone. She saw Dragon's face, ecstatic and triumphant, as she pressed the heart to her lips and swallowed it whole.

It was all over then. Dragon stretched out on the blood-soaked sheets and lay down beside Emma, her breast against the red ruin of Emma's chest, content as a lion curling against a half-devoured deer, and sank into sleep.

꩜

Emma woke with a gasp and found her sheets clean, and Dragon sleeping beside her in the dawn light with her black head pillowed on her white arm.

Emma was surprised to feel nothing but mildly startled. She had the sense that she should be feeling something else, memory clawing at the edges of her mind, and then she dismissed the feeling as the lingering shadow of a bad dream. Where else would Dragon be? She belonged here.

Emma felt a little sick. She padded, trying not to disturb Dragon, into the bathroom. She splashed cold water onto her face, leaned her face down towards the cold porcelain. There were dark dreams in the back of her mind and she thought she was starting a fever, she felt thirsty and hungry and hot and cold at once.

She looked up and saw her eyes flash yellow in the darkness.

She told herself that it was just Dragon behind her, that all she had to do was turn around and find herself reflected in the dragon's eyes. She told herself that but there was a cold void in her chest that said otherwise: that said she was already seeing her reflection.

Her hand shot out almost of its own volition to the light switch. The light came on and she still looked like Emma, nothing as certain and dangerous as Dragon, but when she opened her mouth her teeth were a little too sharp, her tongue was touched with silver, and her chest was a vast, terrible emptiness.

She knew what dragons wanted. Treasure and maidens, Dragon had said it on the first night. Emma had never thought to ask how dragons were born.

She stared into the mirror.

This is how dragons are born.

She screamed and the sound made Dragon come running.

"Emma. Emma, darling—"

Emma turned on her, flew at her with her hands clawed, ready to tear, and she beat her hands on Dragon's chest and felt her heart beating in there, desperately knocking, as if it was trying to get out.

"Give it back," she hissed, a dry reptilian noise, and then repeated it louder, frantic, begging, "give it back!"

"Oh Emma," Dragon said, her face so sad. "That's not how the spell works. Have you ever heard a story where a heart could be taken back? When you give your heart, it's forever."

"No," said Emma. "No!"

She should have been crying, but it was Dragon who was crying, and when Emma sank to the cold bathroom floor Dragon sank with her and clung to her. Dragon's face was full of human pain and love.

Emma thought of her mother and felt nothing. She knew suddenly that her mother would never again be anything to her but a distant memory of warmth. No feeling seemed real, except for her screaming, arid desire. She wanted her heart back, oh, she wanted it back, and she gathered Dragon to her close so she could feel her heart near her.

"Emma, darling," Dragon crooned. "I love you so much. I'll stay with you until I die."

Humans should be more careful about what they say, Emma thought. Their words are spells. They come true.

She had Dragon, loving her with all of Emma's soft heart, and she would stay with Dragon, nobody else would ever do, because nobody else had Emma's heart. She would stay with Dragon until Dragon died, the way humans did. Then Emma would spread her wings and launch herself out into the night, into a long cold quest for a maiden who would trust and love her enough to betray her own heart.

"Emma," Dragon whispered. "Do you hear me? I'll love you until I die."

Emma gathered her close, but not close enough.

"Yes, my darling, my heart," she whispered, voice a hot thread of smoke down her lover's neck. "But what then?"

Lady Marmalade's Special Place In Hell
(A Picaresque Burlesque of the Nether Realms)
David Sklar

For starters, honey, I don't believe in Hell—that's just some old man's way of telling me reasons why I can't be me. Like "biology is destiny" means I have to be a boy. But *somebody* believed in Hell—believed in it loud enough that I wound up there—with tortured screams, blistering flames, and all that sulfur stinking up my hair. But hey, as Jean-Paul Sourpuss liked to say, "*L'Inferne, c'est les autres*"—and I just *adore* les autres. So I went out to make some friends.

I walked out on an outcropping over lava as red as bordello curtains. This yellow-ocher guy with a big potbelly was whipping a line of anorexic-looking people, some of them so far gone you could see their innards. "And what are you trying to do?" I asked the yellow guy with the whip.

He glared at me. "You dare address me thus?" He had hooves with a split down the middle and big curly goat horns with ridges like a rumble strip.

"I'll address you however I want to, sugar," I said, my voice all sweetness on top but no nonsense underneath.

That big jaw moved unbelievingly, with the pointy teeth too far apart. "But you—" he stammered, "—you should be in unspeakable agony!"

"Agony? Bitch please. Don't talk to me about agony until you've walked a mile in my shoes. And by shoes I mean those black pumps I picked up last week in the French Quarter. Half a block should do it, really. *Then* I'll talk agony with you."

"Why—" he said and started to raise the whip.

"Don't you crack that whip at me," I said, and I showed him what a glare is really like.

He backed down.

"Give me that," I said, and I took the whip from his hand. "See, you never give a straight boy a whip—they just want to prove their manly strength." I bent it partway down the lash and examined the weave. It was very well made, and supple, and finer than I would expect in a place like this. But then, a lot of places spend extra on the equipment they use a lot.

"A little finesse," I said, running my fingers along the lash, "and you can achieve outstanding results with a gentle touch." I looked over the crowd and picked out the guy who really wanted it. There's always one. Cowering theatrically, with his face low to the ground, but with anticipation in his eyes, sticking out in that sea of terror like...well, you know what sticks out if you don't strap it down.

I snapped the whip right at him so the tip barely kissed his flesh, in a tender place right over the shoulder blade—stung him so gently that the real torment was that I didn't do it harder.

He gasped.

"I want to see you *beg*," I said, and I cracked the whip again, just over his head.

"Please," he whimpered, with a shudder in his voice.

"Please, what?"

"Please, *mistress*." And the quiver of his shoulders showed he knew I was in charge.

I didn't know his safe word, so I had to take it slow, but honey, speed wasn't as important as reducing him to tears. So I built it gradually, bit by bit, until his moans filled the caverns of Hell, and by the end he was trembling, curled in a ball, letting soft little sobs shudder out of his quivering mouth. And everyone else on the outcropping was cowering with fear.

And ugly yellow goat-foot boy was standing there all stunned. So I coiled the whip back up with a fluid motion of my wrist, and I proffered him back the tool of his trade. But he did not move to take it back from me. I put my other hand on my hip and waited, holding that fine looped whip there in the empty air between us, a long and drawn out moment until finally, slack-jawed goat-boy found his tongue. "D'y'wanna job?"

"Depends," I said. "Do I have to grow horns?"

I won't bore you with the negotiations, but eventually I came out of the deal with little red horns that just poked out of my bouffant, and faux-distressed bat wings with holes in the skin like preworn jeans. They gave me a black leather corset that fit around the wings, and knee-length boots with stiletto heels. I don't want to think about what the leather was made of. Most important, I got the run of the place, so I could go where I chose—or as far as I could make it in those boots.

I didn't use that freedom right away. My first months in Hell I spent building a clientele, a few key submissives who could appreciate my skills, whose moans of delight sounded like real pain, and who would rather be tormented by me than by anyone else on staff. But after a couple months I was tired of beating the same old men every day, and I decided the time had come for me to look for Princess Buttercup.

Princess Buttercup had rented a room from me when she first moved down from Tulsa. Her parents disapproved of her lifestyle, and she really took it hard. I mean, nobody's parents really approve, but it seemed to matter to her in a way that most people wouldn't care.

This one time, I was putting my eyelashes on, and then Princess Buttercup was there in my mirror, standing in the door to my room, saying "Doesn't it bother you?"

"Doesn't what?"

Now, Princess Buttercup was a very beautiful girl, with hair the color of butter and languid eyes, but she was even prettier as a boy, with pouty chiseled features and short black curls, and he was standing in my doorway in plain gray sweat pants and a white T-shirt with the sleeves and neck cut out. I could forgive him a lot of self-pity if he would just stand there and let me look at him. "What we are, Marm," he said. "What we do. Doesn't it... hurt?"

I smiled. "If it doesn't hurt, you're not doing it right," I said, brushing a touch of Midnight Blue across each eyelid.

"No," he said, pursing his lips in luscious frustration, "I mean—doesn't it bother you, what we do? Doesn't it feel wrong?"

I smoothed my eyeshadow out to a gentle fade going up the eyelid. "Honey, if it felt wrong I wouldn't do it."

"My father talks about a special place in Hell for people like us."

Now, a chance to look at that beautiful boy buys a fair amount of patience. But everything has its limits. "Well, your father is a fool."

"But the Bible says—"

"I don't care what the Bible says."

Now I think it's important that I said that then. Because, if Hell was real, then having said that in the past should have made things really rough for me when I got there. But instead I got promoted to middle management. On my first day. I mean, it's not like I put demon on my list of career objectives, but here I was whipping people into shape. And I'd never had any kind of management job before.

I put down the sponge and turned to face Buttercup. "Sweetie, the Bible says lots of things—some about love, some about how to treat your slaves. If you get hung up about just one thing, you're going to mess yourself up."

"But—"

"I know. My parents made me read it too. But I cheated: I read the whole thing—not just the parts they told me to."

"But—"

"You're OK." And I stood up and spread my arms, and he came to me from the doorway, and I folded him into my arms, and he held on tight. And let me tell you, he had such firm, slender shoulders to hold that I wished he wasn't my roommate, because I wanted so badly to open up my robe and fold him inside of there with me. Inside of me. His hands explored my back, gently. A loving touch. A touch that wanted more. I imagined myself a woman, and Buttercup still a man, imagined him taking me face to face, the way straight couples do. But surgery wasn't something I could afford, even if I wanted it. And if I really were a woman, would Buttercup even want me?

I pulled away.

Two weeks later I found Buttercup in her bed naked, with the pills spilled out on the floor. I called the ambulance, but she was already cold, and when she didn't wake up to CPR, I finally just clung to her and cried my tears over her and kissed her vacant face.

I covered her boy parts up before the paramedics arrived; she didn't need them to remember her that way. And I didn't know—nobody knew—if she meant to do it or just took too much.

Either way, it seemed much too likely she would end up where I was, and she didn't have the balls to get by there on her own. So I cashed in on the privilege of my station and set off to find Princess Buttercup in Hell.

It was a lot of walking. In spike heels on uneven ground. Those wings were too tattered for flying, but they sometimes helped me balance, and they were good for cooling off when I got too hot.

Of course I had to whip someone everywhere I went. If I didn't, then...well...I don't want to talk about it.

Usually I could find someone who wanted it—and if I couldn't, well, they knew where they were and what they were in for. It was better than what would've happened to me if I got caught showing mercy. Plus, there was no way I would find Buttercup if I lost my job. And after a while it seemed like I wouldn't find her anyway. Which was good news. Maybe. Or really bad. Because it could mean that she wasn't there, or it could mean that she was there all alone and I just couldn't find her.

But I didn't find her in the river where the stones insult you. And I didn't find her in the kitchen where they make everything with sand. Or in the room full of mirrors that chatter about your extra ten pounds. I was tempted to smash those mirrors myself— I really was. But as expensive as a mirror like that might be when you're alive, I knew I couldn't afford what it cost in Hell.

I had pictures of Princess Buttercup, as a girl and as a boy, that I developed from my memories. When there were no other tormentors around, I showed these pictures to the people I met in

Hell, but mostly I had to rely on my own eyes. I visited bearers of false witness and bearers of false coin; dealers of drugs, dealers of blackjack, and people who could not deal with themselves. And at last I came to the place in Hell for those who cast out their own children, where a middle-aged man with an angry face looked at Buttercup's picture and said, "That freak? You won't find him here."

"So you know her?"

"Not as well as I thought." I swear, I was afraid that scowl would cut the laces on my corset.

"No," I answered wistfully—and more honestly than I should have—"Me neither, now that I think of it."

"Were you one of Jonah's fruity friends?" There was a scathing accusation in his voice, and I realized suddenly who I was talking to.

"Yeah," I deadpanned back at him. "I'm a regular piña colada. But it seems to me, if you're in Hell and she isn't, you might want to rethink your attitude."

"I don't know how that faggot cheated the Devil," he snapped.

Then I snapped too.

Now understand: when I made my way across Hell, I had to whip some people who didn't really want it. I was where I was and I did what I had to do. But Princess Buttercup's father was the first person I truly *delighted* in torturing.

I took that bitch *slow*—let him think he could hold his own as I stripped the flesh from his back. Only when his smile told me he *thought* I'd failed to break him—only *then* did I make him scream like he had never heard of pain.

And that's how it went. I gave him line, let him believe he might outlast me, only to strip that hope away in a single, vicious moment. Over. And. Over. Again. And slowly, relentlessly, I took his dignity and his strength, until I left him a whimpering pulp curled on the floor, begging for relief, with deep scars on his back and thighs, no skin at all on his belly and neck, and his spine severed in seven places by my stiletto heel.

And I leaned in close to him—so close he could feel the secret beneath my skirt. I pressed it gently against his backside—let it press between his cheeks as I whispered in his ear: "Hell has a special place for a man like you. Perhaps I will come back tomorrow and show you the way."

And oh! How I relished the fear in his shoulders and back. I arose with newfound clarity. If the halls of Hell were filled with men like Princess Buttercup's dad, then torturing them would be no dilemma for me. An old man stared in terror as I strode across the rock, and I slashed him across the throat with the tip of the lash, cold comfort for whatever child he had failed to love. A young Latina gasped and I rebuked her across her face. And in all those around I saw terror, and I saw also their delicate places, exactly where I could hurt them most. And the rage of vengeance burned in me, for all who had been wronged, and one by one I took it out on everyone I saw—on eyes, on thighs, on backs, on butts. As their screams shook the cavern walls I felt the fiery blossoming deep in me of what I could become.

But as my inner demon rose to claim its place, I heard across the screams of torment, through the seething of blood in my ears, my mother's timid whisper, asking, "Roger?"

Oh, this will be good, I thought, and I turned to face her. My father stood beside her and just behind. Here, now, in this perfect moment, I saw the foundation of the rage I had just unleashed, the source of the fury I had not known I carried all these years. My black wings stretched out to their fullness as I began to raise the whip.

And my mother said, "Roger, can you ever forgive us?"

"*What?*" My eyes were fixed on them, but somebody told me later that every soul around me cowered, more frightened by my voice than by the lash.

"Can you forgive us?"

I snapped the whip inches from her face. "*Here?* You ask me that *here?* After all these years you have the nerve to beg my forgiveness *here?*"

"It's just—it's just—"

"This is gonna be good." I put my hand on my hip and waited.

"It's just—Roger, you don't belong here."

The whip kind of wobbled in my hand.

"...and if anything we said or did turned you into this, we're sorry. We're sorry we didn't see the beauty in who you were when we were alive."

I looked at my father, slightly stunned that he hadn't interrupted already. He nodded agreement. I stood there a moment, felt the abyss within my heart.

"Can you forgive us?" my mother asked again.

And standing there in Hell, I realized, finally, I could. The rage that had taken me faded, and I held my arms out to them. My mother ran immediately into my embrace. My father stood on the ridge. "Dad?" I asked.

He stood where he was. "I'm sorry, son. I..."

"Dad?"

"I love you, son, and there's lots I wish I hadn't said... but I still can't hug you dressed like that. I'm sorry."

And I'm told the souls around me cowered in terror once again.

"It's OK, Dad," I said. And he gave me a thumbs-up.

And honey, they say you should never let them catch you crying in Hell, but I couldn't help myself. Dripping tears all over the outcropping, watering flowers that weren't there a moment before.

જે૭

The next few days were all about contrition. I apologized in person to everyone I'd whipped in my rage. I knew the risks, but flipping out like I did, that wasn't cool. I had a face-to-face with each of them, about what they were in for, how long they'd been damned, and what they hoped to accomplish while in Hell. Most hadn't thought about that. Not that I blame them. But it gave them something to focus on, and as we discussed it, their whip-scars faded away.

All except Buttercup's father, still flayed and segmented from what I had done to him the day before. Even ripped apart like he was, he had the anger left in him to crane his broken neck up and spit in my face. I tried to coax some mercy out of him, but I found none. So in the end I handed him the whip and sent him away. He ambled off with hate in his eye, and his disassembled spine making his shoulders and arms hang over like a broken marionette.

Once he was gone, the rest of us set to work for real. Piece by piece we built a house in West Gehenna, with a view of the Lake of Fire. From the outside it looked like a fortress, with spikes on the walls and skulls on the ramparts, but on the inside it had tab curtains and granite counters, and the flowers that sprung from the ground where my tears had fallen.

It was crowded there, with all those people inside, but we continued the work we'd started after my rampage, and people helped each other work through their damnation. There was occasional stuff with the thumbscrews, just to appease the higher-ups, but it was done on a rotating basis, with everyone taking turns.

And one by one, the damned souls in my care worked through their issues and set off on their own across Hell to make right the crimes of their life, to apologize to the people they had wronged. I wished I could go with them and keep them safe. But there are some things you just have to do on your own. So I gave them corsets and bony protuberances, to make it look like they worked for me, and I let them go.

And, after years of group therapy, when there was nobody left in the house but Mom, Dad, and me, my father sat down on the sofa beside me and said, "Son, you done good."

"Thanks, Dad," I said. I wanted to hug him, but... we still hadn't gotten there.

My mother set a plate of fresh-baked spider cookies on the table and wrung her hands. "So..." she asked me, "what's next?"

I looked at my boots. "I don't know. I can't run another group therapy session—they'd yank my franchise. Going back to the dominatrix thing feels like a step backwards. I don't know."

My mother looked me over nervously. "Honey...it's none of my business...but...do you still have... it?"

"I beg your pardon?"

"Do you still have... it? I mean, are you still a boy underneath?"

"I know what you meant, it's just... why are you asking me now?"

I could tell this was not easy for her. "Well... because... because that's how your friend Jonah got away."

I stared at her, stunned. "Princess Buttercup was *here?*"

"Well... yes. But he left."

"Wha—how?"

"Well... Roger... he came in as a boy. He was totally naked. And he left as a girl."

"You mean..."

"I don't know if it was sleight of hand or a glitch in the filing system, but once he changed his clothes he was free to leave."

"So all I have to do is..."

"Be Roger again, long enough to get out the door."

For the first time in my afterlife, I was speechless.

"I'm sorry, honey—I'm not asking this for me. But if it can help..."

I smiled.

"I wanted to tell you sooner," she added. "But I didn't know *how* to tell you *this.*"

"And the work you were doing here," my dad added. "That mattered."

I laughed and jumped up out of my chair. "You're apologizing for getting me out of Hell? Get over here!"

And my parents came over and hugged me—*both* my parents—and I wrapped them in my wings.

৵৹

The next morning we all awoke early, and I dressed myself as a man. I gave my father my horns so he could have some freedom in Hell. I kept the wings. My father gave me his jacket, and I tucked my wings underneath. And the three of us walked together from our beautiful house in Hell to the gate where Princess Buttercup made her escape. I wished I could take them with me, but some things you just have to do on your own.

The gate was ominous and iron, with jagged rusty curls and a pair of masks for the handles—one weeping in despair, the other twisted in cruel laughter. "Take care of each other," I said.

"You take care of yourself," Dad answered.

"Give Jonah our love if you find him—her." Mom added.

"I will."

As I was about to step through the gate, my mother wept.

"You'll be OK," I told her. "You have the house."

"It's so much space," she said. But the look on her face had nothing to do with the drafty guest room.

"What's wrong, Mom?"

"Oh, Roger—honey—I've waited...I've waited so long to see you like this again, but it's... it's not *you* any more, is it?"

"It never was."

"And now..." she started sobbing. "...now your wig and your stockings and all that stuff... it's back at the house. You won't have any of that where you're going..."

I hugged her. "It's OK."

My mother kissed my cheek. "My baby girl."

"Careful," my father told her. "You could get him stuck here."

I pushed the gate open, trying hard to think manly thoughts, and I took my first step through. It slammed like a mousetrap on my foot. And suddenly my French-Quarter pumps were no longer the height of pain. The smiling mask cackled.

That was the first time, since I arrived, that I truly understood what Hell was about.

"Oh, Roger, you can do it," my mother coaxed.

"You can do it," my dad repeated.

"Dream on," said the comedy mask.

I pushed on the bars, but they would not part. "Help me," I said.

My parents pushed with me, and we got the bars open enough that I could pull my foot clear. I fell down on my derrière to weep.

"Oh, poor little prissy queen," moaned the mask that wept.

"You had to talk about him as a girl," Dad snapped at Mom.

"Well, I can't help it if I love my child and want him to be happy. If you had stopped once in a while to think about—"

"Oh, now this is *my* fault?"

"Isn't it?" taunted the laughing mask.

Mom huffed. "I'm just saying, if you had—"

"Nothing changes," said the weeping mask. "Not here."

In my time in Hell, hearing my parents bicker about me again was the first time I truly felt damned. "Stop it!" I insisted. "I can... this can work. If I can give you horns with the strength of my will, then I can certainly think my way through this door."

"Oh," my mom said.

"Sorry, son," said Dad.

"Good luck with that," said the laughing mask.

I imagined my way through to the other side. Imagined sunlight on my face, fields of tall grass and wildflowers, swaying in a light breeze. And clothed in thoughts of beauty, I pushed the gate again. And once again it slammed shut on my foot.

"You think we're that easy?" asked the frowning mask.

"Perhaps you've mistaken us for you," the smiling mask jabbed.

"You'll be stuck here forever," said the mask that frowned.

I pulled my foot painfully out of the gate and sat down on a rock. My pants were torn. "They're right," I said. "I'll be here forever. Dad—I need my horns back."

Dad sat down on another rock beside me. "Hold on a minute."

"Dad, I *need* my horns." I could barely—no, I *couldn't* keep it together.

The smiling mask cackled.

Dad looked at the gate. "Maybe you're not going about this right."

I glared at him. "Ya *think*?"

"You never do anything right," said the weeping mask. "Not if you ask him."

"Until you're standing over him with a whip," the laughing mask added.

"No." Dad paused. "I mean... you said it was about your will, right? About *shaping* things with your will, like when you gave me these?" He touched his horns. My horns, on his head.

"Those used to be yours," said the Comedy mask.

"Now you'll *never* have them back," added Tragedy.

"I *tried* that already," I said to Dad, doing my best to ignore the masks.

"You could *take* them," Comedy suggested.

"If you're strong enough," Tragedy added.

"*Your* will, Roger. Yours." Dad looked at me like he was saying something important.

I eyed the seams where the horns joined his skull. My fingernails grew long and sharp.

And then I understood.

"Honey?" my mother asked.

I stood up. But instead of imagining sunlight around me, I put the sun within. And I felt the warm white sunlight fill me up, and I let it grow two pomegranates where they had to be.

They weren't big, but they weren't small either, and they were firm and round like they were new. I mean, they *were* new, and there they were. I opened the second button on my shirt, to give them room.

"Nice tits, pansy," said the smiling mask.

And then I turned my attention below. I spread my hips wider to make room, and I grew a tree within me, the seat of life, with a special place inside it where a new life might begin. Once that was there, inverting the boy parts was easy, like turning a sock inside out. I didn't subsume the boy parts, but kept them reversible, like a jacket, because—what can I say? I do like a little variety now and then.

And I was me. I was finally, *finally* me.

"Hey baby," said the smiling mask. "Come a little closer."

"Why can't I find a girl like you?" wailed the frown.

With a light touch, I called forth marabou tufts from the metal faces. "I'm outta here," I said. "Get used to it." I pushed those masks aside and slid through the gate.

I guess that's what my life is like, even in Hell. Like I thought the gate would open if I pretended to be someone else, when the trick was going through the gate as me.

"I love you," I said on the other side, but I don't think my parents heard. And then I was falling through a vast expanse of nothing, on my way—I don't know where.

I took the jacket off and unfolded my wings. They may not be for flying, but they're fine for slowing your fall. And when you glide across the abyss, I found, it also glides across you, and it feels kind of tingly on your skin.

I don't know what's next. If Heaven exists, what will I look like there? If I get to live again, who will I be? I hope I find Princess Buttercup, but if I can't then I hope she's OK.

And drifting through the darkness, the torn places in my wings begin to heal. And I wonder. I flap them once, and I slowly rise. I am woman, feel me soar. But the sound of them is different, and something tickles my back. I look over my shoulder, and—will you look at that? Just yesterday these babies were tattered skin. Now look at them, decked out in rainbow feathers. And... well... damn. I'm glad I left my clothes behind at the house—because now I'm going to have to rethink my whole wardrobe.

Contributors

Alma Alexander is a Pacific Northwest novelist who writes for both grown-up audiences (*The Hidden Queen, Changer of Days, The Secrets of Jin Shei, Midnight at Spanish Gardens*) and YA audiences (the Worldweavers trilogy: *Gift of the Unmage, Spellspam* and *Cybermage*); she is also a short story writer whose work has appeared in a number of anthologies and magazines, and is also an anthology editor in her own right (*River*, from Dark Quest Books). Her work has been translated into fourteen languages worldwide, including Hebrew, Turkish, and Catalan. She is currently at work on a new series of alternate history novels with roots in Eastern Europe. She lives in Bellingham, WA, with her husband, two cats, and assorted visiting wildlife. Visit her website at www.AlmaAlexander.com, or her LiveJournal blog at http://anghara.livejournal.com

C.S. MacCath's poetry has been nominated for the 2011 and 2012 Rhysling Awards, and her fiction has received honorable mention in *The Year's Best Science Fiction: Twenty-Sixth Annual Collection*. Her work has appeared in *Strange Horizons, Clockwork Phoenix: Tales of Beauty and Strangeness, Murky Depths, Mythic Delirium, Goblin Fruit* and others. At present, she's working on the first trilogy of a nine-novel science fiction series entitled *Petals of the Twenty Thousand Blossom* and a collection of short stories tentatively entitled *Spirit Boat*. When she isn't writing, she owns and manages the Triskele Media web development company, studies the Gàidhlig language and plays traditional Celtic and West African folk drums. She lives in Nova Scotia, the most beautiful province of them all.

Paolo Chikiamco has placed in the Palanca Awards, and his short stories have been published in *Steampunk Revolution, A Time for Dragons*, and the *Philippine Speculative Fiction* series. He is the writer of several comic books, including *High Society*, a steampunk alternative history. He is the editor of *Ruin and Resolve*, the *Usok* webzine, and most recently, *Alternative Alamat*. He is also the founder and editor of RocketKapre.com, a creative imprint and blog dedicated to publishing and promoting speculative fiction by Filipino authors.

Tiffany Trent writes in the Blue Ridge Mountains of Virginia. She is the author of the *Hallowmere* series, and her short stories have appeared in *Magic in the Mirrorstone*, *Corsets and Clockwork*, and *Subterranean Magazine*. Her newest book, *The Unnaturalists*, a YA steampunk adventure, is just out from Simon & Schuster. Visit her at www.tiffanytrent.com.

Melissa Mead lives in Upstate NY. Her stories have recently appeared in *Bull Spec*, *Daily Science Fiction*, and *IGMS*. She will also be appearing in the forthcoming *Sword & Sorceress 27*. She's a member of Codex and the Carpe Libris Writers Group, and has a Web page here: http://carpelibris.wordpress.com/

Tanith Lee was born in London, England in 1947. Being slightly dyslexic she didn't learn to read until almost 8, then started to write at age 9. After various schooling and sundry jobs she was able to become fully professional in 1975, when DAW Books USA published her first 3 adult novels. Since then she has published over 90 books—Fantasy, SF, Historical, Horror, Detective, Childrens', YA, and Contemporary. She's also responsible for well over 300 short stories, and has also written for radio and TV. Lee lives in East Sussex with her husband of 20 years, (writer/artist John Kaiine) and 2 beautiful tyrants generally reckoned to be cats.

Aliette de Bodard lives in Paris, in a flat with more computers than warm bodies. She has a day job as a Computer Engineer; and writes speculative fiction in her spare time, indulging in her love of mythology and history: her trilogy of Aztec noir fantasies, *Obsidian and Blood*, is published by Angry Robot, and her short fiction has appeared in venues such as *Asimov's* and *Interzone*, garnering her nominations for the Hugo and Nebula Awards.

Lyn C. A. Gardner's first poetry collection, *Dreaming of Days in Astophel*, came out from Sam's Dot Publishing in 2011. Once upon a time, Lyn loved being editor for The Mariners' Museum and projectionist for AMC Theatres. She's currently building a TARDIS in her hallway closet. Lyn is also literary executor for her father, Delbert R. Gardner. Stories and poems by either or both have appeared in *Strange Horizons*, *Daily Science Fiction*, *Legends of the Pendragon*, *The Doom of Camelot*, *Challenging Destiny*, *Sybil's Garage*, *The Leading Edge*, and more. Lyn is an active member of SFWA and a graduate of the Clarion West Writers Workshop. Learn more at www.gardnercastle.com.

Sunny Moraine is a humanoid creature of average height. They're also a PhD student in sociology and a writer who has published short stories in *Strange Horizons*, *Jabberwocky*, and *Shimmer*, among lots of other places. Their days are spent in balancing teaching, research, writing, and healthy doses of nothing whatsoever. Their life is a trick of light, so don't blink.

Shanna Germain changes her face every seven years. Last time, she became a merman. This time she plans to become a dark creature of the depths. Her stories about lust, love and leviathans have appeared in places like *Absinthe Literary Review*, *Best American Erotica*, *Best Gay Romance*, *Best Lesbian Erotica*, *Blood Fruit: Queer Horror*, *Crossed Genres*, *Wired Hard 4.0* and more. Visit her online at www.shannagermain.com

Sarah Rees Brennan is the sort of person you want to make up stories about, just to see her reaction. In short, she's awesome. She is the author of the *Demon's Lexicon* trilogy, co-authored *Team Human* with Justine Larbalestier, and her next book, *Unspoken*, is due out from Random House any day now. Visit her at www.sarahreesbrennan.com.

David Sklar grew up in Michigan, where the Michipeshu nibbled his toes on the days when Lake Superior felt frisky. His publications include fiction in journals such as *Strange Horizons* and *Space and Time*, poetry in journals such as *Paterson Literary Review* and *Bull Spec*, and the novella *Shadow of the Antlered Bird* from the wonderful but short-lived Drollerie Press. David lives in New Jersey with his wife, kids, and cat, and he works as a freelance writer and editor. For more about David and his work, please visit http://davidwriting.com

Thanks and Acknowledgments

They say it takes a village to raise a child. Well, in this case it took a community to finance an anthology. My thanks go out to everyone who helped to make this a reality, whether they spread the word, kept me sane throughout the process, or contributed in other ways. However, I definitely have to show my appreciation, on behalf of everyone involved with Scheherazade's Façade, to all of the many wonderful people who contributed to the Kickstarter campaign. So in no particular order, here goes:

Paul Olson, Cecilia Tan, Sharyna Tran, S. Bartoo, Duffi McDermott, Laura J. Pinson, Jan Sparenberg, Shawna Jacques, J. Nilsson, Martha C. Smith, Jaakko Kangasharju, C. Corey Fisk, Jess Haley, Nathalie Boisard-Beudin, Maggie Sheer, Angelika Holz, Jon Stern aka Wee Heavy, Christopher Mangum, Alan Yee, Morva Bowman, Emily M. Siskin, Claire Z., Brian Y., Heathyr Fields, Zoe Wadsworth, Rhel ná DecVandé, Nicci Mechler, Sarah A., Syd McGinley, A. Birchall, Jason Cohen, Peter Aronson, Liralen Li, Carl Rigney, Rebecca Harbison, Amanda K. Dawson, Misha Dainiak, Brian M. Oldham, Mary Spila, Twila Oxley Price, Shelly Mohnkern, Stephanie Franklin, Ciaran Campfield, Lisa Padol, Rebecca Rahne, Xap Esler, Molly KB Hunt, Gwen, Kirrell, El Wes, Kirsty Connor, J. Aronson, Sean Davies, B. Kitchell, Dan Campbell, Bill Pearson, Dianne Connell, Barb Moermond, Catherine Lundoff, Julie Andrews, Emily Veinglory, Kate Linnea Walsh, Connie Wilkins, Kathy Daniels, PJ Deyo, Mia Nutick, Kendra Tornheim, Regina Davan, Ana Steuart, Danielle Bell, Andrew Blythe, fae townsend, Donna Hutt Stapfer Bell, Jonathan K. Stephens, Megan Sohar, Nathan Blumenfeld, Jaime M. Garmendia III, Dee Morgan, Jenna Adler, Laura Watkins, Luke Egan, Robert E. Stutts, Bryn A. McDonald, Jim Lai, Talia Levy, Matt Besterman, Jasmine Stairs, Jeremy Reppy, Aylee E., Cameron Harris, Wolf SilverOak, Nayad Monroe, Lauren M. Roy, Julia Rios, Terry Baucom of B&D Comics, David Lovely, Cheryl Dowling, Mary Agner, Angela Korra'ti, Lizzie S., Kelly Myers, Diana Peterfreund, Stephanie King, Fred C. Moulton, Serena McMurray, Mojca Rupnik, Rowan Teasdale, Kevin Tibbs, Amanda Halperin, Ann Walker, Joseph Hoopman, flowerysong, H. Cykana, Poppy Arakelian, Lola McCrary, steve, CathiBea Stevenson, James Beal, Priscilla Spencer, Lauren Schulz, Emily January, Lauren E. Mitchell, Greg McElhatton, Natisha L-D, Renee LeBeau, Jasra, LKL Studios, Sandra Ulbrich Almazan, Vae, Samantha Rohaus, Claire, Yileen Liu, Stella Harris, Sabrina Marie Chase, "Friend Mark," Rrain Prior, Paige Phillips, Ttamson, Miquela Sierra, naath, Ferrett Steinmetz, Cathy Mullican, Fatima, Greer Woodward, Tralen, Lawrence Evalyn, Dahlia Horner, sharon wood, Sarah Page, Shira Lipkin, Lianne, Rose Fox, Rebecca Tushnet, Sean M., Elizabeth Parmeter, Angela N. Hunt, Violetta Vane, Clare K.R. Miller, Nadia Cerezo, Elizabeth Rivera, Linda Frankel, Estara Swanberg, Alex Turner, Ty Barbary, Betty Widerski, Selkie, Rebecca Newman, Kris Marchu, Ashkai, Mo McFarlane, Daniel Franklin, Michael Feldhusen, chamekke, Jane Patterson, Ann Lemay, Carolyn VanEseltine, Johannes B., Paul S. Enns, BD Wilson, Heather Towers, Michelle Muenzler, Emily Goodman, Brian Williams, Evenstar Deane, Friend, Alicia Cole, Merchimerch, B MacLeod, Chris, David Eggerschwiler, Patricia Engel, Allen Salyer (Detroit), Gregory R. Gunter, Shannon Parker, Tina Bounds, Charlie L., Fabio Fernandes, Janni Lee Simner, MW, MO, Judith Tarr, John Creamer, Michelle Augello-Page, anon genderqueer, several other anonymous donors, everyone who didn't want to be individually thanked, those who didn't get their names in on time but who deserve to be thanked anyway, my "Very Supportive Old Man" (AKA The Colonel), and of course my adoring and long-suffering wife, Mary. Did I miss anyone? Yes, I'm thanking you as well. You rock.

Michael M. Jones (July, 2012)

other titles you may enjoy from Circlet Press!

Up For Grabs edited by Lauren P. Burka
$5.99   ISBN: 978-1-885865-66-3

An anthology of erotic stories where gender is up for grabs. Thousands of people spend time on the Internet identified with a gender other than the one they were born with, for erotic gratification or to stretch their imaginations. But we asked our writers what if you got a tax break for changing your gender? What if you could choose to be no gender at all until you went on a date? What are the implications, both sexual and social, of gender possibilities beyond the choices and ideas our society currently holds.

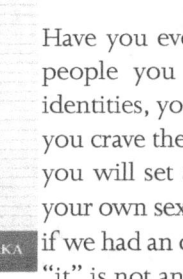

Up For Grabs 2 edited by Lauren P. Burka
$5.99   ISBN: 978-1-61390-001-7

Have you ever dreamed of being so close to the people you loved that you could share your identities, your emotions, and your pleasures? Do you crave the touch of intersex flesh so much that you will set aside everything you believed about your own sexuality? What would the future be like if we had an option beyond male or female, where "it" is not an insult?

Like A Cunning Plan edited by Michael M. Jones
$5.99   ISBN: 978-1-61390-054-3

From Coyote to Loki, Anansi to the kitsune, tricksters are a staple of mythology, folklore, and pop culture. Some might call them selfish, but we all know the truth: they're just focused on the next big score or clever trick. Armed with a sly smile and quick wit, they act as agents of change, leaving chaos and confused victims in their wake. Of course, tricksters also make great lovers: unpredictable, creative, adventurous, and experienced in all the right ways.